SPEC[illegible]ADERS

THE ULVERSCROFT FOUNDATION
(registered UK charity number 264873)
was established in 1972 to provide funds for research, diagnosis and treatment of eye diseases. Examples of major projects funded by the Ulverscroft Foundation are:-

- The Children's Eye Unit at Moorfields Eye Hospital, London
- The Ulverscroft Children's Eye Unit at Great Ormond Street Hospital for Sick Children
- Funding research into eye diseases and treatment at the Department of Ophthalmology, University of Leicester
- The Ulverscroft Vision Research Group, Institute of Child Health
- Twin operating theatres at the Western Ophthalmic Hospital, London
- The Chair of Ophthalmology at the Royal Australian College of Ophthalmologists

You can help further the work of the Foundation by making a donation or leaving a legacy. Every contribution is gratefully received. If you would like to help support the Foundation or require further information, please contact:

THE ULVERSCROFT FOUNDATION
The Green, Bradgate Road, Anstey
Leicester LE7 7FU, England
Tel: (0116) 236 4325

website: www.ulverscroft-foundation.org.uk

GRAHAM NORTON

HOME STRETCH

Complete and Unabridged

CHARNWOOD
Leicester

First published in Great Britain in 2020 by
Coronet
an imprint of Hodder & Stoughton
an Hachette UK company
London

First Charnwood Edition
published 2021
by arrangement with
Hodder & Stoughton
an Hachette UK company
London

All characters in this publication are fictitious and any resemblance to real persons, living or dead, is purely coincidental.

A catalogue record for this book is available from the British Library.

ISBN 978–1–4448–4689–8

Published by
Ulverscroft Limited
Anstey, Leicestershire

Set by Words & Graphics Ltd.
Anstey, Leicestershire
Printed and bound in Great Britain by
TJ Books Ltd., Padstow, Cornwall

This book is printed on acid-free paper

For Paula and Terry

1987

I.

It was Bill Lawlor who found them first.

No rain had fallen for four days but he knew it couldn't last. He decided to take no chances and was working late at the garden centre. A pallet of peat moss sacks that had been delivered in the afternoon needed to be moved into the long store. By rights, young Dunphy should have been doing it, but he had looked so desperate when he came running into the shop asking if he could go early. His hair freshly flattened with water from the tap in the yard, his shirt tucked into his jeans.

'Get away out of it. I'll see you in the morning.'

The young lad beamed and in his haste to leave he tripped over his own feet.

'Thanks! Thanks, Mr Lawlor.'

Bill wondered if there was a girl waiting. Was young Dunphy going to walk his lady friend along the river to the weir and then lure her under the railway bridge for a kiss or maybe more? He chuckled as he made his way down the yard. Hadn't he done it himself?

The plastic sacks safely stored under cover, Bill threw the padlock around the gate and got into his car ready for the short drive home. Afterwards he tried to remember how he knew something was wrong. Had he heard the crash? He didn't think so. All he could recall was that everything seemed unnaturally still as he approached Barry's roundabout. There were no other cars and the early evening light gave everything a flat, washed-out air. Without deciding to, he found that he had slowed down. On the far side of the roundabout by the turn-off to the coast road, he saw two men, more like boys really. One was kneeling on the overgrown verge, his black and purple rugby shirt like a bruise against the green of the grass. The other was tall and thin, standing over him, gesturing with his long pale arms. Had they had a fight? Then he saw the thin threads of smoke rising up into the marmalade sky of dusk, and to the right of them the broken bank of shrubbery.

Everything suddenly accelerated. Bill was out of his car, running towards the boys.

'Is everything all right? Is anyone . . . ' But before he could form the question, the answer became obvious.

A navy estate car was lodged in the drainage ditch that ran along the bottom of the bank below the roundabout. Judging from the battered roof, it had rolled at least once, maybe more. From the back window protruded an arm, porcelain white, with a crack of red creeping from the armpit towards the wrist. The limb was still. Through the broken windscreen he could see long brown hair fanned out across the dashboard and from beneath it, a dark viscous pool was spreading towards the steering wheel on the other side of the car.

'Is help coming? How many are there?'

The two figures just stared at Bill as if he had interrupted a private conversation.

'Has someone called an ambulance?' Bill asked with a growing sense of panic and dread.

The boy in the rugby shirt looked up.

'Four. There are four of them.' His face, covered with a summer crop of freckles, looked almost childlike.

'Six.' The other young man spoke, his voice more certain, almost calm. 'Six altogether. The two of us and four in the car. You're the first. Nobody has called an ambulance.'

'Right. Don't move!' Bill shouted as he began to run back towards the petrol station. His legs felt heavy and there was something about the thin slapping of his feet against the road that sounded hopeless.

* * *

Maureen Bradley had just been put under the dryer so she didn't hear the sirens.

She licked her fingers to turn the pages of the *Family Circle* little Yvonne had given her to pass the time. She wasn't really reading the magazine, just relishing the solitude. There was no peace to be had at home with everyone pestering her with questions. She hated having other people in her kitchen, especially her mother-in-law, but at least after tomorrow it would all be over. Her daughter Bernie would be a married woman and the house would probably be so quiet that Maureen would wish they could have the wedding all over again.

Yvonne would come up to the house in the morning to do Bernie and the bridesmaids, but she'd asked if she could get a literal head start on Maureen tonight. She was the only one who needed her roots done so it was easier in the salon with all the brushes, foil strips, bottles and toners needed.

Everyone politely referred to Yvonne's' as 'the salon', when it was clearly nothing more than a converted garage on the side of the house. In fairness, she had done a lovely job. Fully tiled throughout and it was only on the worst days of winter that you might need one of the travel rugs she had on hand to offer her clients.

With her ample frame wedged into the chair, and her magazine resting on the soft shelf of her bosom, Maureen didn't see the young woman running up the hill. And the noise of the dryer meant she didn't hear the door to the salon being thrown open. It was only when a grim-faced Yvonne tapped her on the shoulder that she looked up to see her younger daughter, Connie, standing in front of her, all flushed in the face, tears streaming down her cheeks. She was saying something but Maureen couldn't hear her. She wriggled free of the dryer with the help of an apologetic Yvonne.

Connie's voice was a mixture of sobs and swallowed words that made no sense.

Maureen struggled to her feet.

'What is it? What's wrong?'

Just managing to control her heaving gasps, Connie said, 'Daddy says you're to come home.

Oh Mammy, the guards were at the house.' She tried to say more but her mouth was overtaken by threads of snot and spit. She collapsed into her mother's arms, her tears soaking into the pale pink towel that was still draped across Maureen's shoulders.

* * *

Less than a mile away, over the bridge and in a small terraced cottage down the entry beside the hotel, Dee Hegarty laid five buttonholes in a line on the kitchen table.

Each was a single red rosebud framed by a white shock of baby's breath. Dee was carefully wrapping them in damp tissue paper before they were to be stored in the salad drawer of the fridge overnight. As she worked she couldn't stop smiling at the sight of her own hands. They looked like they belonged to a stranger. Her nails pink and shiny like the inside of a shell. She couldn't remember the last time she had worn nail varnish, but it was a special occasion and she didn't want David to think she wasn't excited about his big day. The buttonholes were placed head to tail like floral sardines in a shallow cardboard box. Dee had to admit that they had turned out very well. Red and white were the Cork colours. It was about the only detail of the wedding plans that David had been involved in. He insisted on everything being in his team's colours. Bernie and her mother had finally agreed, since he had allowed them to decide on everything else.

Dee was trying not to worry, but despite herself she stole a glance at the clock above the cooker. Gone half seven. She hoped he hadn't been dragged to the pub. With all the excitement and the lovely evening, it was no surprise if that was where he had ended up. The last thing he needed tomorrow was a hangover. He might be a clever lad, a kind one, but even his own mother had to admit he seemed to lack any common sense. Not for the first time, Dee questioned the wisdom of her son walking down the aisle. He was just twenty-three, still a boy. What was the rush? Himself and Bernie swore blind that no shotgun was involved and her family seemed thrilled, but why wouldn't they? In a few years he'd be a fully qualified dentist. Dee liked Bernie and the Bradleys well enough but a doubt about this marriage still nagged at her. Could David do better? As a girlfriend, Bernie was fine, but was she really a fitting wife and mother? She was just so loud. If she hadn't been her son's girlfriend, Dee might have described her as coarse. She hated herself for having these disloyal thoughts, especially after Maureen and Frank Bradley had been so generous. Of course, it was tradition for the bride's family to pay but people didn't really hold with that any more. Nowadays everyone chipped in but, without ever embarrassing her, they had made it clear that she wouldn't be expected to contribute. After David's father died things hadn't been easy, but she had managed. Dr Coulter took her on as a receptionist and the little cottage she had bought after she sold the big house, the family home, out on the New

Road, suited her and David fine. Her son had waved away her objections. 'They can well afford it and look what they're getting — me!' He flashed that big grin of his and flexed his muscles. Dee couldn't help but laugh as she chased him out of the room with her tea towel. Her big, silly, baby boy.

The evening glow had begun to fade and Dee had just stood up to put on the kitchen light when a loud firm knock came at the front door.

* * *

Washing and drying his hands for the final time of the day was Michael Coulter's favourite ritual.

Job done. He stared at his face while he did it. The nose hairs needed a bit of a trim and there were a few reddish veins on his cheeks, but other than that he couldn't really complain about what he saw. Yes, there was grey creeping around the sides of his head, and the wrinkles on his forehead remained now no matter how hard he tried to smooth his brow, but he was, and he didn't consider it vain to think this, a handsome man. It was just a simple fact. He hadn't allowed himself to go to fat like so many of the boys from his year at school. Never trust a fat doctor, was a mantra Professor Lyons had drummed into his students and Dr Michael Coulter had never forgotten it.

He folded the hand towel and placed it carefully on the rail beside the sink in the corner of his office. The desk lamp was switched off, the door to the street double locked and then he made his way down the hall towards the house. He could smell fish frying. Despite the surgery being attached to the family home, Michael was very firm about keeping them separate. The worst scoldings his son ever received when young were when he and his friends had dared to bring their games or high-pitched chases into the corridor that ran from his office down to the door of the house. At night he made a point of locking the door.

He was just turning the key when he heard the surgery phone begin to ring. He sighed. These out of hours calls were invariably time-wasters or hypochondriacs, but he could never forgive himself if it turned out to be a genuine emergency. He reopened the dark wood door and almost ran back to the tall narrow desk in the reception area.

'Hello, Dr Coulter speaking.'

'Doctor, it's Sergeant Doyle. Sorry to ring so late.'

'That's all right. What can I do for you?' He never liked getting a call from the police.

'There's been an accident down at Barry's roundabout. One ambulance is there and another is on its way but I'd say they could do with any help.'

'Of course. I'll come now. Very bad is it?'

'Oh, a fierce mess. A clatter of young ones in an estate car rolled over into the dyke. At least a couple dead anyway. Thank God there were no other cars involved.'

Dr Coulter's mouth was suddenly very dry.

'Was it . . . was it a Cortina?'

'It was.'

'Blue.' The two men spoke in unison.

* * *

Caroline O'Connell hadn't wanted to go to Cork the day before the wedding.

The point was that she didn't have a choice. Why Declan couldn't comprehend this simple fact was beyond her. The face on him. The huffing and puffing as he went out to the car.

'You've nothing else you could wear?' he asked incredulously.

'No.' This was not a discussion she was willing to have. There was no way she could wear the dress with the large red and white flowers if those were going to be the colours at the reception. She didn't want people thinking that she considered herself a part of the top table or the wedding party just because one of her daughters was a bridesmaid.

This wedding had been nothing but aggravation and Caroline normally enjoyed weddings. Her niece was getting married next spring and she was looking forward to that, especially now she knew she could wear the red and white flowers. Declan seemed very unimpressed by this particular silver lining as they sat at the lights by Wilton shopping centre. He peered over the steering wheel looking even shorter than he was, his breathing suggesting he might be about to have one of his rare outbursts. Damn Bernie Bradley and her red and white wedding reception. Why Carmel couldn't have mentioned the colour scheme before this morning, she didn't know; well, except she did . . .

All mentions of the wedding had been more or less forbidden since Bernie had decided to ask Carmel to be a bridesmaid but not Caroline's other daughter Linda. She couldn't understand it. The three of them had always been inseparable. If you were having three bridesmaids, would four be so difficult? She didn't want to get involved but Caroline could see why Linda was so put out.

She had been happy to hear that morning that the three of them were spending the day at Trabinn, by the seaside. It was the first time in weeks that she had heard her daughters laughing together. Good. Nobody wanted bad blood on the big day.

At the back of Dunnes, Caroline finally found an acceptable dress in pale blue that came with a matching coat that had a pretty shoelace tie at the neck. Pleased with her purchase she felt a sudden surge of affection and sympathy for Declan, who sat slumped on a chair by the changing rooms reading an *Evening Echo*.

'What do you say we head into town and treat ourselves to a mixed grill in Moores Hotel?'

Declan's head jerked up. 'If that's what you fancy yourself,' he said, willing her not to change her mind.

'It is. It's just what I fancy and it'll save cooking when we get home.'

She slipped her hand into his and the odd couple, statuesque woman with diminutive man, walked out towards the car park.

* * *

No one was at home to answer the knock at the door when it came. The house stood in darkness, waiting. Later that night when Caroline and Declan returned, bags in hand, flushed and easily amused after the couple of drinks they had had with their meal, it was Declan who nearly stepped on the postcard that was resting lightly on the hall mat asking them to call the Garda barracks at their earliest convenience.

* * *

Ellen Hayes paused on the brow of the hill to savour the moment.

That feeling of finishing work for the week — but before she returned home to her mother's nagging and her brother's sly digs. She took a deep breath. From this vantage point, Mullinmore looked its best. The whole town had a sepia glow as dusk faded to night and the amber street lights spluttered into life. Through the centre of the town her eyes followed the smudge of green where trees traced the route of the river. On the hill opposite, the chapel with its empty sloping car park marked the western edge of the town, while the red brick of the convent school dominated the eastern side. Even after two months Ellen still found it hard to believe that she would never have to go back to that building.

At the bottom of the hill the narrow street opened out into the main market square where her family had their pub. She noticed that the large Guinness sign above the door wasn't illuminated. Odd. Maybe the bulb had gone.

Walking as slowly as she dared without dawdling so much that people would notice and think there was something wrong with her, she reluctantly made her way down into the town. One of their regulars, old Mr Hurley, was standing outside the pub leaning on his stick. She gave him a half-smile and a nod before pushing the door. It was locked and behind the frosted glass was darkness. Mr Hurley gave a cough and said, 'You'd better get inside.' Ellen just stared at him. She didn't like this. Her imagination immediately homed in on the worst possibilities. She remembered her mother had complained about having a headache. What if it was a brain tumour? Had she gone blind? She rooted through her bag to find the rarely used key to the street door that led straight up the stairs. Taking two steps at a time she ran up calling, 'It's me! What's wrong? What's after happening?'

Her mother was sitting on the sofa. She looked up when Ellen came into the room. Her face was streaked with tears. Ellen's father was standing at the other end of the room by the door into the kitchen.

'Ellen, sit down love.' His voice was soft and gentle. It didn't sound like him. Ellen could feel her bottom lip beginning to quiver and a pressure building behind her nose.

'Oh Daddy,' she whispered as she sat beside her mother, who reached across and took her hand.

‘Connor was out with Martin Coulter and a few others.’

That made no sense. Connor wasn’t friends with Martin.

Her father continued, ‘There was a crash and at least three of them are . . . ’ His voice faltered. ‘They were killed.’

Ellen raised her hand to stifle a scream. ‘Oh no. Oh Connor!’

Her mother squeezed her hand. ‘Your brother is fine, love. He isn’t hurt.’

Ellen looked at her parents, confused.

Her father bit his lip and looked away.

‘Connor was the driver of the car.’

II.

A sign in the window of the pub would have been too strange — after all, the Hayes family hadn't suffered a bereavement — but at the same time Dan and Chrissie knew they couldn't open the doors. It would have been disrespectful.

The police had come and gone. Afterwards Dan and Chrissie had conducted their own interrogation of their son. Why was Connor driving? Had he been drinking? Why was he with the Coulter boy and his friends? Connor had sat with his hands clenched between his knees.

'I said I'd drive. I was the only one who hadn't been drinking. They asked me to go. It was sunny. The beach. I wanted to go to the beach.' When all the questions had been answered he was allowed to fade away, back to his room.

The pub stayed shut until the Tuesday. Then Dan just went downstairs and turned the lights on without speaking to any of the family. He sat on a stool behind the bar playing solitaire on the counter with an old pack of cards he kept over the till. About nine o'clock a foreign couple, German, maybe Dutch, came in looking for food. Dan sent them over to the hotel. He waited until eleven o'clock came and then relocked the doors and extinguished the lights.

The next night when he walked towards the

stairs, Chrissie looked up from her book. 'Are you going to bother?'

Dan sighed. 'I am, I think.'

'Is there any point, love? You could sit up here and stare at a clock.'

'I know, I know. I just think we ought to open. Show people that we aren't ashamed. We've done nothing wrong.'

Chrissie leaned forward and hissed at her husband, 'Aren't you ashamed? I know I'm ashamed.'

Dan turned away and with weary steps slowly headed down to the bar.

That night Tadgh Hurley came in and sat nursing his usual pint of Murphy's for an hour. The old man was there most nights and never spoke much, but tonight his silence seemed to fill the pub. He couldn't even look Dan in the eye as he said goodnight and did his soft-shoe shuffle towards the door. About half past nine Dr Coulter walked in. Dan stood up and braced himself against the bar. The doctor's face suggested it wasn't a drink he was after.

'Dan.'

'Doctor.'

'A terrible business.'

'Very sad.'

A silence. Dr Coulter cleared his throat.

'I'm here on an awkward mission, if I'm being honest.'

'Are you?' Dan took the lone empty pint glass off the bar.

'Yes. It's Maureen Bradley.'

Dan kept his eyes on the doctor. Was he

supposed to know what this was about? Should he ask a question?

'Right.'

'Well, Dan, she came into the surgery today and well, she'd prefer not to see Connor at the funeral.'

The doctor paused and tried to gauge how this news had gone down. In truth Dan was almost relieved. He wasn't sure what they had been going to do, so this, at least, made their decision for them.

'I understand.'

'She didn't say that she had spoken to the others but the impression she gave was that they feel the same way.'

'I understand,' Dan repeated.

'You and the family are of course very welcome to attend.'

Dan must have looked confused because the doctor then added for clarity, 'It's just Connor.'

'Thank you. Thanks for letting us know.' They both nodded to acknowledge that they were two men who understood each other.

'Will you have a drink?'

'I won't. No. Thanks all the same, Dan. I'd better get back.'

'Right.'

At the door Dr Coulter turned. 'How is Connor?'

Dan thought about his son upstairs locked in his room for four days. He wasn't even sure if he'd eaten or drunk anything.

'Hard to know. He's a quiet lad. Very upset obviously.'

'Well, tell him Martin was asking after him.'
'I will, Doctor. Thank you.'
The door swung shut.

III.

Grief is not a competitive sport, but if it were, the whole town agreed that Dee Hegarty would be the holder of the unwanted trophy. True, Maureen and Frank had lost Bernie the day before she was to be a bride, but they still had each other and Connie and Kieran, their remaining children, to keep them going. The bridesmaid Carmel had been killed, but Caroline and Declan O'Connell could still pray that her sister Linda might recover or at least live. They had hope. But David's mother Dee had nothing, just another grave to visit.

Such a reserved little woman, none of them really knew her. Perhaps that's why it was such a shock to witness her at the funeral. Her thin frame draped in a shapeless black coat, she picked her way up the aisle all alone, her feet in black high heels that appeared to be a couple of sizes too big and were probably borrowed. She walked like she was navigating her way through a series of puddles. As people dutifully filed past her, muttering their few chosen words of sympathy, her swollen red eyes seemed not to register anyone's existence. Shaking her hand was like taking a dog's paw. Then at the end of the service when she staggered forward to kiss the coffin, loud howls broke free from deep within her. When she fell to her knees, people weren't sure what to do. This was grief you'd see in a film. It was too much, too raw, and there was no one to support her, to urge her to pull herself together. She lay like a pile of broken twigs on the floor. Eventually it was Dr Coulter who went and led her back into her pew. People wondered how he must feel. It had been his car but he still had his son Martin with hardly a scratch on him sitting beside him, and his wife, while poor Dee Hegarty's heart was breaking in front of the whole town.

Maureen had suggested that David and Bernie be buried together but Father Deasy had felt that was a little unseemly. Dee was happy to concur with the priest. Maureen had rolled her eyes and later complained to her husband Frank. 'It's not as if they'd be living in sin! They wanted to be together, we all know that, and now they'll be spending eternity apart, all because of a few vows not taken. My poor lonely girl.' Frank had never seen his wife this defeated by anything. He tried to stay strong for her but at the funeral his own grief had overwhelmed him. Where had the tears come from? Hankie after hankie soaked through.

Maureen had insisted on wearing her wedding outfit, though Frank had talked her out of the hat. It was pale blue with a matching coat that had a pretty shoelace tie at the neck. Caroline O'Connell, through her tears, stared at Maureen aghast, thinking of the dress hanging at home that she had never worn. Was this what was meant by small mercies?

Father Deasy had reluctantly agreed that Maureen could use the wedding flowers at the funeral, so large red and white arrangements sat before each window and on either side of the altar. Nellie Kehoe, who had attended every funeral that had taken place in Mullinmore for the last fifty-five years, wasn't impressed. 'Will she be feeding us wedding cake at the afters?' she sniffed. People pretended not to hear. Undeterred, she continued, 'And those young ones. Very disrespectful. A yellow and blue anorak at a funeral. Shameful.'

'Will you wisht, Nellie?' her friend Peg hissed at her. 'Aren't they hardly more than children themselves? What need do they have for funeral clothes? It breaks my heart. Awful, just awful to see pews of young people sat at a funeral.' Chastened, Nellie retrieved a linen hankie from her handbag and dabbed at the tip of her nose.

The last funeral held was for Carmel O'Connell. They had waited because her sister Linda had suffered such serious injuries the doctors hadn't been confident she would live. Eventually Linda was transferred up to Dublin where she remained in a coma.

Her mother Caroline swapped Linda's bedside for Carmel's graveside. How had this become her life? She had seen tragedy visit others but somehow, she had always assumed that if misfortune was heading for her family, there would be some sort of warning, a sign at least. This was like falling through a trapdoor and still not knowing if she had hit the ground.

Caroline had watched Dee Hegarty and knew

that she wasn't going to behave like that. She would stay strong for Declan and for Linda. She would happily have admitted to anyone who asked that it was only vodka that had got her through that awful day. Nothing could take away the pain, but just a few shots of Smirnoff stopped it pinning her to the floor. Declan had been her hero at the funeral. He never took his arm from around her waist, his self-consciousness about his wife's height forgotten. He made sure he spoke to everyone, thanking them for their kind words. With him standing beside her, she wouldn't fall.

After the funeral people had come back to the house. They hadn't stayed long. It was too much for everyone. They were exhausted by all the mourning. The Coulters had laid on a spread in their house for David. Dee had been the doctor's receptionist for many years, and no one could have expected her to squeeze people into her cottage, especially pummelled by loss as she was.

Maureen and Frank had hired the function room in the hotel. That was when people had gone to the bar and washed away their sorrows for a few hours. They couldn't be drowned.

At the O'Connells', neighbours had arrived with trays of sandwiches and only a few accepted the whiskey that Declan offered around. Mrs O'Mahony from across the road quietly took Caroline up to bed when she found her swaying a little unsteadily in the hall. When everyone was gone, Declan made his way around the house turning off lights and locking doors before he climbed the stairs and lay fully dressed on top of the covers along the length of his sleeping wife. He wrapped his arms around her. The heat of her, her steady breathing. He held tight as if trying to contain the life inside her, for fear it too might vanish.

IV.

Bernie, David and Carmel were gone. Linda remained in intensive care. Martin returned to university to follow in his father's footsteps as a doctor. From the tangled wreck only Connor was still in Mullinmore.

He locked himself away in his room above the pub, crying, pretending to read and thinking about his future. School had finished two years ago. Since then he had given remarkably little thought to what he might do with his life. He had had a vague plan in his head that he might go to Cork and try to get bar work there. The city wasn't so far away but it felt like being with strangers would allow Connor to start again, or at least try to see who he was when he wasn't the boy who worked behind the bar in Hayes.

He cursed himself for not paying more attention in school. All those dreary lectures about the importance of your leaving cert results had turned out to be true. His friends had either gone off to college with their As and Bs or started work in family businesses that had far better prospects than a small pub in Mullinmore.

Now even pulling pints seemed beyond what life had to offer him. He was going to appear in court. He'd have a criminal record. That day, that horrible day. He just wanted to reach back in time and rip it out like an unwanted page in history. He thought about his dull life before Barry's roundabout, and it seemed like a blue-skied idyll full of possibility and promise. What future could there be for Connor Hayes now?

His father and the solicitor had just talked about him as if he hadn't been in the room when Connor and Dan had gone to consult someone about his defence. His mother had not come with them, seeming to be of the opinion that legal matters were best left to the men of the family. Connor had found it difficult to concentrate on anything his father and the solicitor had been saying. He grunted his answers while an impatient Dan filled in any details that were needed. The meeting had gone on for over an hour but all Connor could really recall was the way the leather chair he had sat in squeaked if he moved, the sheen on the solicitor's fingernails, and an unlikely speck of toothpaste in one corner of the fastidious man's mouth. Connor's interest had only been piqued when his father had asked about prison. 'Unlikely' was the word the man on the other side of the heavy desk had used. That was very different from a firm 'no'. It meant the possibility of him having to go to jail was still real. How would he cope if that happened? Could he survive? The fear came and pressed on his chest as he lay in the darkness, waiting for sleep.

During his days Connor sometimes stood at his window looking out over the rooftops of the town, swirls of smoke drifting up to meet the sky. Clearly life was carrying on. He pressed his face against the chill of the window glass and surrendered to self-pity. He thought about the others, the ones who were gone, and a part of him envied them. He lay on his bed listening to his *Joshua Tree* cassette on headphones until the tape became stretched and Bono's voice transformed into a baritone slurring its way through 'I Still Haven't Found What I'm Looking For'. He wept again. The task of untangling the mess of secrets that he had created seemed so impossible. He could not see how this life could continue. Of course, he considered ending everything. It made perfect sense. Erasing himself from the face of the earth was the best solution for many people. His very existence was an insult to the families who had lost so much. If he disappeared, then his parents would be free of their shame. People might even find some sympathy for them or him, if he did the honourable thing. And yet, and yet . . . The problem was the unknown. To take the leap into that dark mystery with no hope of second chances or return was just too frightening.

He studied his room with the curtains drawn against the world. Everything looked so childish and innocent. His Madonna posters, the pile of glossy annuals and comics. The Connor who had lived in this room already seemed like a distant memory. He could scarcely recall how it had felt to have no real worries. The only comfort he could find was that as horrible as his situation was, at least he understood it. Everyone hated him and he would have to live with that fact. There would be no dressing-gown cords fashioned into a noose, or pills stolen from the bathroom cabinet, just this huge weight of shame and regret crushing him forever.

There was a firm knock on his bedroom door and before Connor could respond, it burst open and his mother came in. Chrissie Hayes was a woman who had had enough.

'So, have you given up working for a living?'

'I can't go down there, Mammy. I can't serve people.' His voice was a child's not wanting to go to school.

'There's more to running a pub than pulling pints. I'm not having you festering in here.'

Eventually his mother forced him out of his room. He couldn't work behind the bar, but he could still be useful. The cleaning of the pub became his responsibility and restocking the shelves or changing barrels before his father opened up were also part of his new duties. At night he would retreat back to his room. He had tried sitting with his mother to watch television but it was filled with reminders: funerals, road safety films, car chases. Without comment his mother would change the channel but before long there would be a weeping actress or an actual news report. Alone in his bedroom was easier.

It was so quiet. The hush of fabric as someone passed his room, the careful creaks on the stairs. Nobody knew what to say so they simply chose not to speak. Connor and his sister Ellen, with their two-year age difference, as well as attending different schools, had never been especially close. Anything that might have passed for conversation between them tended to be just harmless teasing or petty squabbles, but this was different. Ellen hadn't said a solitary word to him since the day of the accident and he understood why. She was now the sister of the boy who had killed three people, so her life was also on hold. Something else for him to feel guilty about.

V.

Ellen walked through the empty pub when she came home from work and wondered how long it would be before Hayes Bar shut its doors for good. Seeing her mother and father pretending not to worry broke her heart. At work over the hill to the south of town in the large farm supplies outlet, she found she had been removed without comment from standing behind the counter and now spent her days in the back office going through invoices or sorting boxes of nails and screws into bags. The other girls weren't rude or hostile, but they did stop conversations abruptly whenever she appeared. Ellen knew that she would have behaved in exactly the same way in their position, but that didn't make it any easier. One night on the walk down the hill she spotted Mrs Bradley walking towards her. She froze with an unfamiliar mix of fear and embarrassment, but when the older woman noticed her, she immediately crossed the street and ensured that no eye contact was made. Ellen began to walk faster and was practically running by the time she reached the pub, but still not fast enough to avoid people seeing her crying in the street. She cursed herself for deciding to work for a year before going to college. How could she survive twelve months of this?

Ellen's best and really only friend was Catriona, Trinny for short. She worked part time at the farm centre at weekends, so if they could, she and Ellen would take their lunch break together. Usually they just sat hunched on chairs by the staff lockers but if it was fine, they could be found outside perched on the wall opposite the loading bay, Trinny banging her heels against the bricks so she seemed even younger than she was.

'The thing is, Ellen, at the end of the day, you didn't kill anyone. No one is upset at you. It's just in your head.' Trinny took a firm bite out of her sandwich to emphasise her point.

'You don't know what it's like. They look at me, but they see him. Mam and Dad can't exactly disown him so it's like we're all on his side, like we don't care or something.'

Trinny chewed thoughtfully before swallowing. 'For now. These things blow over. People will forget soon enough.'

Ellen stared at her friend.

'Blow over? Trinny, people are dead! Families are in mourning. Is there anyone in Mullinmore whose heart doesn't break when they see little Mrs Hegarty shuffling up the town all alone in the world?'

'God forgive me, but I'd say that one is half cracked. I wouldn't be worrying about her.'

'Trinny!' Ellen exclaimed, genuinely shocked. Her friend looked a little sheepish.

'Well, you know what I mean. That carry-on at the funeral. Pure mental.' She bent down to her sandwich and ripped out another bite. Ellen gazed across the yard at a seagull as it marched up and down a rusty oil tank. Trinny tugged at her sleeve to regain her attention.

'Here, do you know who's after getting engaged?'

It seemed the conversation had moved on.

No one understood. How could they? Even Ellen struggled with it. She knew that this drama wasn't about her and yet she could feel her life slipping away, all her assumptions about who she was and what people thought of her upended through no fault of her own. She accepted she had no right to ask for sympathy. She had been at the funerals and seen what real grief looked like, but just because others had lost more than her didn't mean that she had not lost anything, either. At school she had sometimes bristled at the injustice of her status, constantly outshone by girls who were prettier, smarter, or better at sports than her, but the harsh spotlight that the crash had shone on her and her family was much, much worse. The attention made her feel almost physically sick as she walked around the town. After work she had taken to hiding at the back of the town library leafing through the big photography books, taking solace in images of people with lives that looked harder than her own.

In the past she would probably have confided in her mother, but her parents were dealing with their own problems. Connor's court date was looming. He had been charged with dangerous driving causing death. Ellen wasn't sure how serious that was, but she assumed it meant that he could go to jail. She wanted to ask somebody but there never seemed to be the right person or opportunity. A dark thought formed at the back of her mind like hair caught in a plughole. Maybe he should go to jail. It might help. Perhaps people could forgive her family if Connor was seen to suffer. But then she thought of her parents and how they would feel if their son went to prison. No, she couldn't wish for that. It was too awful. She had to accept that there were no solutions, only different ways for her life to be worse.

VI.

The weather had changed to match the mood of the town. The long warm evenings of late summer had vanished, and now, without pausing for autumn, the heavy grey skies of winter had rolled in. If it wasn't actually raining, then it promised to do so very soon. The roofs and roads wore the constant dark sheen of damp.

On the day of the court case Ellen got back from work to find the pub unopened and no lights in the windows above it. She sat in the kitchen still wearing her coat, waiting for the others to return. She hadn't turned on any of the lights so that the room was lit only by reflections from the street. Long shadows moved across the wall opposite while she waited for the sound of a key in the lock. Something must have gone wrong. They weren't meant to be this late. She chewed anxiously at a clump of her hair.

She couldn't imagine how she had managed to fall asleep and yet she must have, for the next thing Ellen was aware of was sitting up with a jolt, the neon strip above her flooding the kitchen with light. Connor was standing in front of her, dressed, she imagined, how he might have been at any of the funerals: one of his father's ties, grey school trousers, and a jacket that their mother had bought especially for the occasion.

'Well?' she asked.

'Two years suspended.' He didn't seem pleased or upset.

'A big fine?' she asked, trying to get more of a sense of his mood.

'No. No fine,' her brother told the linoleum. Just then their father came into the room and placed his arm around Connor's hunched shoulders.

'Your brother is a very lucky boy. No actual jail time.' He patted the boy on the back and smiled at Ellen.

'That's great!' she replied, but even as she said it she wondered if it was. How could you be driving a car when three people died and then just walk away? It might be the law, but she found it hard to believe that anyone in Mullinmore would think justice had been served.

'Very lucky,' her father continued. 'Young Martin Coulter gave evidence and spoke very well. Described him as a responsible man. The judge seemed to believe him and of course he wasn't over the limit, so.' Dan stopped speaking as if he had reached a conclusion. Ellen struggled to understand what might be considered good news or what was bad.

Chrissie walked in dabbing at her eyes. Clearly, she had been crying.

'Are you OK, Mammy?'

'You've not heard?'

'Two years suspended sentence?'

Her mother waved her hankie dismissively. 'No prison time, it's true. But Connor has other news, haven't you?' The two women looked at him but his gaze didn't leave the floor. Instead it was Dan who cleared his throat.

'Connor is going to be leaving us. The Brennans have a cousin who runs a couple of building sites over in Liverpool, and a fresh start is what this man needs.' He punctuated the end of his little speech by patting Connor's shoulder twice. Chrissie pushed her hankie against her mouth and rushed back out of the room.

For years afterwards Ellen would try to forgive herself for her first thought at hearing the news. She was glad. Elated to hear that her brother was leaving and the rest of them might have a chance of getting on with their lives. Perhaps now the blight would be lifted.

VII.

It wasn't as bad as Connor had expected. He had thought the work would defeat him, but it appeared he was stronger than he believed, or perhaps it was that the barrows of blocks or hods of cement weren't as heavy as he'd feared. Half the time it was just guttering or pipes for plumbing and they were plastic. He enjoyed being told what to do, liked to be given a time and a place to be. Going to bed tired and having dreamless sleep was a welcome change from the previous few weeks in Mullinmore.

Leaving, however, had been worse than he'd anticipated. The sight of his mother huddled inside the door at the bottom of the stairs so people on the street couldn't see the state of her. The crying. One arm raised against the wall to support herself. He thought of Carmel, Bernie, David and their parents. Their children were gone forever, never to be seen or heard again. He was just going to Liverpool and yet he didn't see how his mother was going to cope. His father had driven him up to Cork and dropped him at the bus station. Dan couldn't find anywhere to park, so his farewell to his son was an awkward hug across the gear stick before pressing an envelope with an English tenner and four five-pound notes into his hands. Cars behind had started to sound their horns. Dan didn't even get to wave goodbye, just drove on, hoping that Connor hadn't seen his face crumple into tears.

As he travelled through the night, the journey had seemed endless, though now he found he could scarcely remember any of it. A small girl running up and down the aisle of the bus singing the few lines she knew of 'Molly Malone'. The man with the flat cap sitting in front of him in a fog of stale piss. The loud clanking echoes that rang out across the port in Dublin. The big arc lights that made it look like a movie set. Looking down at the dark thick rolls of water between the ferry and the wall of the dock he imagined how cold it must be. On board he moved from seat to seat out of boredom. The occasional yell from a small group of drinkers at the bar. Feeling drunk himself as he tried to make his way to the gents' toilet, staggering from wall to wall with the swell of the ocean. A Spanish-looking man on the windswept deck — a lorry driver from the continent, Connor imagined — smiled at him and held out a packet of cigarettes. Was he just being friendly, or was it something more? Connor had panicked and rushed back inside, the wind snatching the door from his hand.

The lights of Liverpool had seemed exotic and full of promise when they first threaded themselves along the horizon but by dawn when they actually docked, everything took on a strangely familiar air that made Connor feel even more exhausted than he was. This didn't look so very different from the place he had left. A light drizzle washed his face as he and his fellow foot passengers made their way down the long gangway. Young, old, families or alone, he wondered what awaited these people. What had brought them here? Some struggled with heavy cases, while others, like Connor, walked with a stuffed backpack towering above their heads.

Once inside the terminal building, a youngish man with dark hair flecked with premature grey approached him and immediately Connor felt flustered and nervous.

'Connor Hayes?' The man had a strong Dublin accent.

'Yes.' A handshake. Connor was struck by how rough and cold the man's hand seemed. He assumed his own would feel that way before too long.

'Ciaran. I have the van outside. Is that you?' he asked, indicating Connor's backpack.

'Yes. That's me. Nothing else.'

'Grand.'

Ciaran turned and walked away.

The van looked like it was intended for deliveries but inside it had been fitted out with rows of seats like a minibus. Connor sat up front with Ciaran. Everything was covered in dust or smeared with bits of mud. A *Daily Mirror* was rolled up and shoved between the dashboard and the windscreen.

'Did you sleep?'

'Not really, no.' Connor pulled at the sleeves of his jacket. He knew he didn't look right. Ciaran was just so comfortable and correct somehow. He looked like he had always been meant to be wearing his old denim jacket over a brown wool jumper and driving this van. Connor in his school duffle coat and a pair of pristine Doc Marten boots felt it must be obvious to Ciaran that this newcomer had been hopelessly miscast.

'Too bad. I'm just bringing you in to Huskisson Street to drop your stuff and then straight out to the site. The first day is always brutal.'

Huskisson Street. Connor remembered that was the address he had been given for where he would be living. The Brennans' cousin shipped Irish lads over and not only gave them work but also collected rent by providing them with somewhere to live. He was operating a full economy.

As the van slowed to a stop, Connor looked around. This wasn't what he had been expecting. A terrace of large redbrick buildings with fanlights perched above wide front doors. It reminded him of the Georgian terraces he had seen when he had gone to Dublin for the weekend. As if reading his mind Ciaran clarified, 'It's not as fancy as it looks. At least our gaff isn't!'

He was right. The once-splendid front door had peeling red paint and the railings on either side of the stone steps were splattered with patches of rust.

'I'll get you your own key later today,' Ciaran said as he opened the door. The entrance hall was wide, with a couple of bikes piled against one wall while the opposite one contained a long narrow table covered with piles of unopened mail, free newspapers and glossy takeaway menus. Ciaran headed to the back of the hall and disappeared down some stairs. Unsure of what to do, Connor followed him.

The basement kitchen was enormous and filled with a gloom that even the brightest midday sun wouldn't reach. A large table covered in a red and white checked oilcloth dominated the centre of the room. It was littered with debris, pizza boxes, crushed lager cans, mountainous ashtrays. The smell reminded Connor of coming down to clean the bar in the morning. Mullinmore. They'd be having breakfast now. The sound of his mother scraping butter across hot toast. Ellen trying to put together her packed lunch. The tinny chatter from the radio. The weight of his backpack suddenly seemed immense.

'You've time for a tea if you want one.'

Connor hesitated. 'Are you having one?'

'If you're making it I will.' Ciaran smiled and his friendly face caught Connor by surprise. He felt himself blushing. He turned away to hide his face and simultaneously unburdened himself of his luggage, letting it slip to the ground.

'I will so,' he said and risked a small smile in return.

'Good man yourself.' Ciaran sat down and took a packet of cigarettes out of his jacket. 'Smoke?'

Connor shook his head. 'No thanks.'

He took the kettle from the gas cooker that looked far too small for the room. The sink was so full of used plates and mugs Connor had to remove some just to get the kettle under the tap.

A rumble of footsteps on the stairs announced the arrival of a tall young man with long loose limbs. He looked even weaker than Connor felt, which reassured him about the day's work ahead.

'Gents!'

'Knacker!' Ciaran replied. 'This is the new fella. Connor was it?'

He nodded.

'Do you want tea, Knacker?'

'I will.'

'Rinse another mug there like a good man.'

'Welcome, Connor! My name is actually Brian.'

'But everyone calls him Knacker.'

'Knacker?' Connor asked.

'He let slip one night that his parents have a caravan in Courtown and the lads have been ripping the piss ever since.'

Connor smiled and lifted his chin to indicate he got the joke.

'Really really funny. Bunch of wankers,' Brian said, taking one of Ciaran's cigarettes. 'And tell me this, Connor, were you working on the buildings back home?'

'I wasn't, no. Pub work, mostly.' He hoped that might be the end of questions.

'And what's the story? You know old Brennan is it?'

'No,' Connor replied quickly, knowing that he should distance himself from any personal connection to the boss. 'My father knows his cousins or something.'

'Father!' Brian said, mimicking Connor's accent. 'Aren't you a fancy whore for a big freckly fucker.'

Ciaran laughed. 'He is mad freckly all right.' He turned to Connor. 'In fairness you are.'

'It was a good summer back home. They start to fade now thank God.'

He put mugs of tea in front of his new workmates.

'There should be milk in the fridge over there.'

Connor turned obediently.

Another figure appeared at the door.

'My head!' A northern Irish accent. He seemed older than the others, with a high forehead and dark bags under his eyes.

'Late one was it?' Ciaran enquired.

'Robbo got out the cards and you know what he's like.'

'Connor, this is Frank.'

Frank greeted him with a half-hearted salute.

'Jesus but you're freckly!'

'I just said the very same thing!' Brian crowed and the two men high-fived each other.

Connor tried to smile. All this attention was making him feel nervous.

Soon the kitchen was full of young men, eight or nine, all moving around the room slurping up bowls of cereal or tearing at jam-covered slices of bread. Ciaran had stopped introducing them to Connor, who was warming his hands on his mug of tea while trying not to look too awkward standing to the side of the sink. As if there had been a secret signal, Ciaran suddenly stood, adding another cigarette butt to the ashy mountain, and clapped his hands.

'Let's hit the road, lads!'

Various groans and sighs greeted this announcement, but mugs were put down and everyone shuffled back up the stairs.

The packed van now smelled of men and sweat of various vintages. Connor was reminded of the changing rooms at school and that familiar feeling of awkwardness. An alien trying to pass as human. Connor was squeezed in beside a stocky young man who he guessed was in his mid-twenties. He was unshaven and his dark hair sliced his forehead with a severe fringe. He showed no interest in Connor. They rode in silence past unassuming streets and small arcades of shops until they reached stretches of hedgerows and trees. Beside him he could hear his travelling companion breathing heavily through his nose. Their silence had begun to feel awkward, so Connor put out his hand and introduced himself. 'Robbo,' was the reply and then he shook Connor's hand as if he was doing him a favour.

'You were playing cards last night.'

'I was. What's it to you?'

Connor immediately regretted his attempt at familiarity. 'One of the guys was just saying . . . ' His voice trailed away and he gave a vague indication with his left hand towards where he thought the man from Northern Ireland was sitting. Robbo just stared at him, his dark brows pressed low. Had the gesture been too girly? His wrist swivelled too much?

'Prick,' Robbo muttered and turned his attention to the window.

Connor's face felt hot and he knew that he was close to tears but that couldn't happen. That would be the end of everything. He thought again of being in the car going around Barry's roundabout. One moment, one random moment, just a wheel hitting the kerb at the wrong angle. If things had just been fractionally different then he wouldn't be sitting here heading to work on a building site with these strangers he didn't want to know. But there was no going back, no changing what had happened, and so his whole life was ruined. He bit down hard on the inside of his cheek.

The van came to a halt and everyone stepped out onto a wide muddy strip that one day would be a street leading to the houses that littered the horizon half built.

VIII.

A Christmas card had arrived with an English stamp on it. Ellen recognised the writing and sighed as she picked it up. She dreaded seeing how her mother was going to react.

'To everyone back home, love Connor.'

Chrissie could hardly get the words out before clutching the card to her breast and emitting a low moan. Dan got up and went around the kitchen table to hug her shoulders. He kissed the top of his wife's head. Ellen looked away, embarrassed by this highly unusual display of physical affection.

'Don't be upsetting yourself. He's a big lad. He'll be doing grand.'

'Could he not . . . ' Chrissie wiped her tears away with the sleeve of her dressing gown. 'Could he not have told us something? A little note?'

'Ah Chrissie love, that's boys for you.'

'I suppose,' she replied, trying to calm herself.

'Did you put a letter in with our card?'

She looked up, as if reprimanded. 'I did of course.' Her voice was indignant.

'Well then, I'm sure he'll reply to that and we'll get all his news. If anything bad had happened we'd know. No news, as they say. Isn't that right, love?'

'I suppose.'

'Now are you ready for your second cup?'

'It's in the pot.' She stroked the Christmas card on the table as if it was the hand of a loved one.

Ellen did her best to pretend that everything was back to normal but clearly things weren't. The regulars had returned to the bar slowly over the past few weeks, like wandering cats returning home to be fed, but Hayes Bar was rarely what anyone would call 'busy' any more. Ellen would never have dared ask her parents about money, but she wondered if the sparse population of rogues and pensioners was enough to make ends meet.

'Fierce quiet for the lead-up to Christmas' was the most she had heard her father say about the state of the business.

Up at the farm centre things continued as they had before the accident, though somehow Ellen found she enjoyed the whole idea of working less and less. She wasn't sure if that was to do with Connor or if it was simply that the thrill she had felt at earning her own money had begun to fade. Folding plastic sacks, using the wide yard brush to sweep up the stores, or stamping 'Overdue' on invoices before sending them out for the second or third time, all just made her dream of college. Seeing Connor's undistinguished departure from school two years earlier, leaving him without options, had spurred her on. She had forced herself to study and her exam results had been a pleasant surprise to everyone, including herself. The glossy prospectus for the

Cork College of Commerce was permanently propped up by her bedside lamp. With the encouragement of her mother and the slightly less enthusiastic careers advice counsellor at the convent, Ellen had applied and been accepted for a legal secretary course, but what she really wanted to do was walk around the city with a gang of girls who knew nothing about her, laughing and smoking cigarettes. Increasingly, she firmly believed that if she could just stop being Connor Hayes' sister, then everything would be all right. Her life could start again.

It was the week before Christmas and the three other girls were moaning to each other about how busy it was going to be. As a rule, Ellen never initiated conversation but she found herself compelled to ask, 'People buy presents in here?' She looked around incredulously at the sacks of chemical fertiliser and displays of power tools.

The eldest girl, Deirdre, gave Ellen a look that suggested she almost pitied her for being so stupid. 'No. But every job they've been meaning to do all year suddenly has to get done for Christmas. I mean, what's so special about Christmas?' The others rolled their eyes in agreement as they buttoned up the green nylon housecoats that served as their uniform. It struck Ellen as sad that they found no joy or festive cheer. She had always loved this time of year, the pub busy every night, her parents tipsy and cheerful, the excitement of the parcels under the tree. It was a multi-coloured oasis in the grey wastes of a Mullinmore winter. Of course, it would be different now. It wasn't that she missed Connor exactly, but she hated things not being normal at home. She had never looked forward to a Christmas Day less.

She was in the back office on her hands and knees trying to untangle spools of electrical cable when Deirdre stuck her head around the door.

'There's someone out front to see you.' Her face floated out of view.

Ellen immediately felt nervous. This was a time for bad news, so surely this would just be more of it. Had Connor done something stupid over in England? Perhaps it was her parents.

The last person she expected to see waiting at the counter was the doctor's son, Martin Coulter, but there he was, taller than she remembered, with a long navy Crombie overcoat hanging loosely over his jeans and white sneakers. It gave him a slightly artistic air, bohemian even. His dark hair fell over his eyes as he pretended to be interested in a pile of leaflets about a sponsored Christmas Day swim. She hesitated. This was bound to have something to do with Connor. Unsure of how to address him — she couldn't remember ever speaking to Martin Coulter before — she simply said, 'You wanted to see me.'

His head sprang up. 'Ellen. Hi. Yes, I did.' He was smiling at her in a way that relaxed her. This couldn't be terrible news.

'You're well?'

'Yes thanks.' Ellen was surprised her voice emerged quite even and calm. 'Yourself?' This was what conversations between adults sounded like.

'Great, yeah. I'm just back from uni for the holidays.'

'Right.' They smiled at each other. Ellen hoped he would speak again because she was struggling to think of another question.

'Any word from Connor?'

'We had a Christmas card there, so he must be doing grand.'

'Great.'

Another smile-filled pause. Ellen considered offering him assistance finding what he was looking for in the shop, because, well, that was the only reason she could think of for his visit. Martin cleared his throat.

'Well, Ellen, the thing is, I have a couple of tickets for the Rugby Club dinner dance on Thursday.'

Ellen wondered what this could have to do with her. He wouldn't need a babysitter. What might it be? Her head tilted to the side like a dog trying to interpret what its master was saying.

He pushed his hair off his face and continued, 'So I just wondered if you'd like to come with me?'

His invitation was so unexpected that Ellen thought she might have misunderstood the question.

'Oh. I see.'

Martin quickly filled the silence: 'It might be awful but it might be fun too. But look, if you're busy or whatever, no big deal. Don't worry about it.'

Did Martin Coulter actually believe for one second that she wouldn't want to go on a date with him?

'No. Sorry. No.' Why was she flailing her arms? She put her hands on the counter to keep them still. 'That sounds great. Thanks.'

Martin looked relieved. 'Great. I'll pick you up around seven thirty? From the bar?'

'Yes. That would be grand.'

'Brilliant. See you Thursday night then.' And before she had a chance to say anything else his coat was flapping its way down the wide aisle away from her. He was slim but his shoulders were nice and square. She liked the way he walked, full of purpose and confidence.

All at once she was very aware of her shapeless uniform and her unkempt hair that wasn't exactly blond nor light brown. What had just happened? She felt a little thrill of excitement and maybe, no definitely, desire. Deirdre appeared at her side.

'What did the doctor's son want?' Her breath smelled of soup.

'Well, he asked me to the rugby dance.' Ellen felt her face flush. This information seemed very personal, intimate in some way. Not the sort of thing she would normally have shared with the girls at work.

'Awwww, isn't that sweet of him. That's a nice thing for him to do.' She patted Ellen's arm and walked off, doubtless in search of the others to share the news that Martin Coulter had taken pity on Connor Hayes' sister.

Ellen felt like such a fool. Of course, that's

what this was. A well-brought-up young man doing something nice for the girl who had lost her brother. He didn't fancy her, he just felt sorry for her. This version of events made total sense, and yet she couldn't help remembering the way he had looked at her. His smile. Ellen knew she wasn't a great beauty like Sarah Mooney or Katherine Begley. She wished her hair was finer or blonder, and when she stood on the edge of the bath to see herself in the mirror, she did wonder if her legs were a bit short for her body and her hips a little wide but there was nothing weird about her either. She didn't have a nose like Beaky or terrible heavy eyebrows like Liz Phelan. She liked her lips and while her eyes weren't vivid blue, they were still pretty. Would Martin Coulter really date someone out of politeness? Maybe his parents had forced him to invite her, but he had seemed so sincere, keen even, or at least not someone being coerced into doing something. Deirdre was just a jealous bitch.

A rapid clicking of heels on concrete announced the arrival of Trinny. Her uniform was so big for her she looked like a child playing dress-up.

'What's wrong?' she asked, touching her friend's arm.

'Martin Coulter is after asking me to the rugby dance.'

Trinny's face beamed with delight.

'That's wonderful news. Why are you upset?'

Ellen bent forward and whispered so as not to be overheard by the other girls. 'He's just doing it to be nice. He doesn't fancy me.'

'Of course he does. You're gorgeous, you just don't know it.'

Ellen pushed her hair off her face self-consciously.

'Well if that's the case, why did he never pay me a blind bit of notice up to this?'

Trinny put her index finger up to the corner of her mouth, like a drawing of somebody thinking. Then a smile. She'd got it.

'Your brother! Maybe when Connor killed those people driving his car, Martin spotted the sister and saw how beautiful you are. I told you something good would come from all of this mess, didn't I?' She reached up to give her friend a hug that Ellen wasn't sure she wanted. Could that possibly be true?

* * *

If only her mother hadn't hesitated. If only she had managed to arrange her features without the momentary flicker that betrayed her true feelings. The 'Oh, isn't that lovely!' and wide, warm smile meant nothing, because Ellen had already seen the doubt. Her own mother didn't think she was good enough for the doctor's son. Head lowered to avoid revealing her tears, she turned and retreated as fast as she could down the corridor to her room. 'Ellen, what is it?' her mother had called after her. A door slam was the only reply. Ellen felt sick. She lay face down on her bed hugging her pillow for comfort. Her own mother! Clearly no one could believe that

Martin Coulter would ever want to date her unless it was an act of charity.

She would cancel. An illness would be invented or perhaps some family emergency. What did it matter? It wasn't as if Martin would care; he'd probably be relieved. He could assure his parents that he had done the gallant thing, but the pitiable little girl from the pub didn't want to go to the dance. He'd be off the hook and she'd be spared the public humiliation of dancing with Martin Coulter while he made faces at his friends over her shoulder. A pang of guilt pierced her worst-case scenario. Maybe he wasn't that sort of boy, but the alternative was just as bad; people looking at the doctor's handsome son as if he was some sort of saint while she was nothing more than an object of pity.

Later when she heard her mother head downstairs to the pub, Ellen crept out and retrieved the phone book from the hall table. She quickly found the number for the surgery, along with the out of hours line which she assumed would be their house phone. Her mouth was dry. She should ring now, this very evening, because the longer she waited, the more difficult the call would be, but like a mist of delusion rolling in, she had begun to accept that she wasn't going to pick up the receiver and dial the number. An internal counter-argument had begun. A side of herself that she knew was not her friend, a strange, as yet unexplored part of her personality refused to give up all hope. A tentative confidence whispered to her that everyone might be wrong. They couldn't know for certain and maybe Martin Coulter was special. A man with the imagination to see beyond her nylon tabard and mousey hair. Surely men like that existed? Ones who were attracted by deeper, intangible qualities. The odds might be hopelessly against her, but that night, lying in her childhood bedroom, Ellen Hayes decided to take a gamble on herself.

IX.

The weekends were the worst. Monday to Friday, when he was working or spending the evenings sitting in Huskisson Street while the lads bantered and bitched, it wasn't much worse than school. Connor had long ago learned how to blend into the background. Not so much that people thought you were weird or a loner but just enough so that people weren't that aware of you. Laugh at jokes but never try to crack one. Offer to make tea but don't ask questions. Only his freckles failed him and drew attention but being referred to as Dot instead of Connor didn't seem so bad when he thought of some of the names they might have called him.

On Saturdays and Sundays he felt he couldn't just hang around the house. The others drifted off in noisy packs to find pubs that showed the GAA matches from back home, or places where they could observe groups of uninterested women. Connor didn't want them to come home and find him sitting alone watching the small portable television or, even worse, reading a book. On a couple of occasions Connor had gone out with a few of the other lads. The first time hadn't been too bad, apart from the hangover, but the second time they had all ended up in a pub with strippers. Well, Connor assumed they were strippers, though they appeared to have dispensed with the performance element and just wandered around the pub wearing nothing but panties, getting punters to put money in a pint glass in return for being allowed to paw at them. Connor hadn't just found the whole experience horribly uncomfortable; it had cost him a fortune.

Now, at the weekend, he tended to sneak out of the house before lunch while most of the others were still asleep. Hands deep in his duffle coat pockets, he would walk down the hill into town and look around the shops for an hour or so. He'd sip a coffee and read his book in one of the little cafés that lined the lanes leading off Victoria Street. In the late afternoon he slipped into the cinema muttering, 'One, please,' as if someone might challenge him for this suspicious behaviour. He would slump in his seat before the lights went down in case anyone saw him, and then surrender himself to the blessed distraction of the darkness that brought him the advertisements, trailers and whatever movie it might be. *Dirty Dancing* or *Cry Freedom*, Connor didn't care. It was time spent.

'Dotty! What are you doing for Christmas?' It was Ciaran calling across the kitchen. Connor hesitated. Was there a right answer?

'Heading home like, or will you be here?' Ciaran's impatience suggested he didn't care one way or the other.

'I'll be here I suppose.' He didn't imagine that anyone in Mullinmore would want to see him again this soon. The whole point of him going away was so that people might forget him and what he had done. Besides, he could hardly ask his parents to pay for his return journey and he certainly couldn't afford it himself. 'Is that OK?'

'Grand. I just wanted to know who was around. Frank is staying and Robbo will be here too.'

Inwardly Connor groaned. The only one of the men who still seemed to be suspicious of him was Robbo. Often he would catch him giving a sideways glance or looking away quickly as if he had been watching Connor. One night Robbo had started asking him exactly whereabouts in Cork he was from, but it hadn't seemed friendly, more like an interrogation. Connor wondered if some half-formed gossip had filtered through from home about the killer who had gone to work on the buildings. Whatever the reason, Robbo made him feel nervous, so the news that he would be practically alone with him for a few days wasn't welcome.

Friday was the last day of work and that night most of the housemates sat around the kitchen table drinking and telling stories of home. While the cans of lager were nothing new, these more personal tales of friends and families were less frequent. It was as if the men couldn't allow themselves to miss home, but tonight they gave themselves permission because the next day they would be getting buses and ferries back to the roads and streets where they were truly known. They would stand in pubs and look across the room at faces that all told a story of a life they knew as well as their own. Leaving home might have been a choice for most of these men but going back was as inevitable as the tides. They would always return, and if they didn't, it remained their unanswered prayer. Connor laughed at their stories and got up to pull cans out of the fridge but while he recognised everything that was being spoken of, he felt even more distant from these men than usual. How could he yearn to return to something that was no longer there? All the love and familiarity that existed for him in the streets of his home town and those few rooms above the pub were gone because he had destroyed them. Mullinmore was better off without him.

Maybe it was to do with Christmas, or perhaps it was just that he had seen every film showing in Liverpool, but on the Saturday afternoon he found himself walking down Hope Street towards the Catholic cathedral. It was an extraordinary sight, like a giant concrete shuttlecock or an umbrella blown inside out, just perched on the skyline. The closer Connor got the larger he realised the building was. It was just getting dark, so the light had begun to seep from the stained glass that pierced the tall concrete ribs that Connor assumed were the modern equivalent of a spire. The wind was blowing hard and cold, so he pulled his duffle coat tighter and made his way inside.

He wasn't religious but he had somehow hoped to find some comfort in this place. It was only now that he was standing at the edge of the immense circular room that he realised he could find no connection here to anything familiar. Yes, there was the faint smell of incense and the whisk of cassocks and whispered conversation, but he didn't feel present. It was as if he was watching a programme about architecture, when what he really wanted to do was kneel in the dark and breathe in the scent of polished wood and dusty hassocks, to be transported back to St Joseph's. His eyes took in the vast expanse of space and the giant spider structure suspended above the altar. He noticed a priest walking with purpose around the outside of the pews and realised that he was heading towards him. He hastily returned to the December chill that awaited him outside.

Looking down Hope Street he could see the other cathedral glowing in the darkness. It couldn't have looked more different, with its fat blunted spire and dark red stone turned golden by the spotlights. Connor hesitated for a moment but then reminded himself that nobody knew him here. Why shouldn't he have a look inside the Protestant church if he wanted to? His breath trailing in the early evening air, he set off. Reluctantly he had to admit that he was enjoying himself. It was as if he had a purpose.

Hope Street itself was quiet enough but at each junction he could see the crowds milling around downtown in search of friends or gifts. He found that he was strangely relieved not to be having to deal with Christmas this year. He hated the pressure of buying gifts and couldn't remember the last time one of his family had given him something he genuinely wanted or liked. It had become a formal way for his parents and sister to announce that they didn't really know him. The windows of the Philharmonic pub looked inviting and he hesitated, but then decided against going in. On the street, you had permission to be alone, but in a bar, it attracted attention or pity. He walked on.

From outside the cathedral he could hear organ music and singing. He paused, fearing he might be interrupting a mass or service but then two people walked past him into the building, so he followed. Inside the pews were empty, save for three or four people scattered around with heads bowed or staring up into the darkness of the vast vaulted ceiling. At the far end, the choir seemed to be rehearsing. Connor didn't recognise the music but it reverberated through the space, managing to sound both loud and distant. A few tourists were shuffling around the side aisles looking at tombs and peering into side chapels. One of them seemed younger than the others, with blond hair and a leather jacket worn over a denim one. He was taking pictures with what looked like an expensive camera. Without really deciding to, Connor began to walk towards him. The combination of the floor and his trainers produced a strange squeaking sound, so he stopped and pretended to be interested in various wall plaques and memorial windows as he studied the stranger. He was slim, and his jeans fitted in a way that none of Connor's did. They managed to make him seem more naked than dressed. The young man pushed a hand through his long blond fringe and his jackets rose up to reveal a thin strip of tanned skin above the waistband of his jeans. It was as if he knew he was being watched, putting on a show just for Connor.

When the man turned, Connor quickly switched his focus to a small brass panel on the wall. The blond began to walk back towards where he was standing. Although he knew it was ludicrous Connor felt his heart beating faster and he had to make a conscious effort not to hold his breath.

'Interesting?' An English accent. Not exactly posh but nor was it Scouse. Connor froze.

'Sorry?' His voice sounded like a whisper in the echoey gloom.

'What you're reading?'

Connor turned to his new English friend. He could feel his face flushing. This man wasn't handsome in the way some of the boys at school had been. This was what actors and models looked like. Symmetrical features placed carefully in blemish-free skin. He was smiling at Connor, almost laughing. His perfect mouth stretched back to reveal impossibly white, even teeth.

'I . . . I wasn't really reading it, just, like, looking at it, like.' His breathing was slightly heavy from the effort of speaking.

The Englishman cocked his head to one side. 'Looking at it. You like looking?'

Connor felt almost dizzy with embarrassment but there was an excitement as well. He managed to hold the gaze of the stranger and say, 'I do, yeah.' They both smiled.

'Matt.'

'Connor.' They shook hands. Cool and soft. He noticed a few silver rings. Connor wondered if Matt was older than he looked. There was an air of confidence about him but perhaps it just came from looking like a model.

'You're not from here, are you?'

'No. Ireland.'

'Dublin? I love Dublin.'

'No.' Connor shook his head. 'Cork.'

This provoked no response from Matt, or at least none he felt like sharing. He seemed to be looking at the young man from Cork, as if assessing him. Connor felt as though he was a new piece of furniture that Matt was unsure would fit through the door. Connor shifted from one foot to the other.

'Know anywhere nice around here to get a drink?'

A slight fear crept over Connor. Was this all moving very fast or was he the one making assumptions? Perhaps Matt just wanted a drink? Maybe he didn't even intend to invite Connor along. He remembered the warm lights spilling out onto the pavement. 'The Philharmonic isn't far from here. It looks nice.'

'Right. Can I buy a Paddy a pint?'

Connor bristled. He didn't like being called a paddy, but far more than that he didn't want to stop looking at this beautiful man.

'Yes. Thanks.'

'Great. You lead the way.' Matt put his hand on the centre of Connor's back and encouraged him towards the door.

In the lull after the concert across the street

had begun, and before the late-night drinkers had arrived, the pub was relatively quiet. Connor sat on a low stool at a table away from the windows. He watched people's eyes following Matt with his blond hair and tight jeans as he went to the bar. He nervously tore the corners off a beer mat. It was so obvious what Matt was and he was with him. He felt people looking at him, making assumptions about him, thinking they knew him. What made it worse was that they were correct.

Matt put two pints of lager on the table and then sat on the stool closest to Connor. He felt their knees touch. Had it been an accident? He shifted his leg slightly, but Matt's knee followed and pressed against him with a little more pressure.

'Cheers, Paddy!'

Connor raised his glass but couldn't look Matt in the eye.

'Cheers. Thanks.'

'You're not a Guinness fan?'

'No. No. I'm a lager man. And even if I wasn't, it's all Murphy's stout down where I'm from.'

'I see.' This information was evidently not interesting to Matt. He looked around.

'Lovely in here. I've passed it a few times but first time inside. Lovely.'

Connor agreed. This was, by quite some margin, the nicest pub he had ever been in. He felt the drink steady his nerves and his shoulders relax.

'Are you on your holidays, Matt?' He remembered being behind the bar and making stilted conversation with Europeans struggling through pints of stout they had ordered and then regretted.

'No. Working. I'm a choreographer. I was doing the panto up here. Heading home tomorrow.'

This information removed yet more tension. Whatever might happen, it was finite. He could get up right now and run off with no fear of ever bumping into this man again.

'Where's home?'

'London. South London. Brixton. You know it?'

'Never been.'

'Oh, you'll have to come visit!' They grinned and clinked their glasses but both men knew the invitation wasn't real.

Connor felt he couldn't leave after one pint because he had always been taught to buy his round, so a second pint was had. By the end of that Connor didn't want to leave. Matt had called him handsome. He had told him that he liked his freckles. The Christmas tinsel and coloured lights took on a new sparkle and while Connor might have felt nervous, even frightened, about where this evening was leading, he also felt excited and hopeful. Matt bought them shots of some brown sticky liqueur that tasted sweet, even as it was burning his throat.

'Do you want to go somewhere else?' Matt leaned across the table so that their faces were close, so close that . . . Connor jerked his head back.

'What's wrong with here?'

'Nothing. Nothing. Will you have another?'

Connor nodded and drained his pint.

After that drink, Matt tried again. 'I know a place. It's more fun than here. They play good music. You'll like it. Come on.' He was standing now, holding his coat. Connor somehow knew that by agreeing to move on to this mysterious second venue, he was making a decision beyond having another drink. He pulled his duffle coat off the stool beside him and stood up. He found he needed to steady himself against the table. 'Right, let's go.'

The cold air outside gave them both a bolt of energy and they headed off, laughing about nothing but the wind and the possibility of adventure. Matt knew where he was going and walked quickly while Connor, trying to button his coat, struggled to keep up.

'Don't worry. It's not far, Paddy.'

Connor stopped walking. Matt looked back at him quizzically. 'I don't want to be a prick about it but I'm Irish. I'm not a paddy. OK?'

'Sorry, I . . . ' For the first time Matt's confidence faltered but then he grinned and continued, 'It's not far, Irish!' He turned and began to walk away. Laughing, Connor followed him.

In the pub their conversation had mostly been a monologue from Matt about the work he did and the various shows he had been involved in. Gossip about people Connor had heard of but didn't really know. Now, his new English friend began to quiz him about back home. Where was he from? Did he have family? Why had he come over to Liverpool? Connor gave his stock answers, but he found he was tempted to say more. The combination of drink and this stranger he would never see again made him feel as if he could just blurt out the truth without consequences, like throwing a stone through a shop window and running off into the night. No. He couldn't. To tell the truth would be to relive it, and make everything real once more. For this night to continue, he had to stick to his story. The only possibility for happiness was starting over and that meant leaving everything, especially the truth, behind.

At first it looked as if Matt was just leading them down an alley but then Connor saw light spilling from a doorway with a small tattered awning above it. A thick-set woman with short hair was sitting on a stool just inside, a steep staircase behind her. A half-smoked cigarette perched on her lower lip. From somewhere above came the muffled thud of dance music. Connor glanced over his shoulder only to remember that no one knew him here. He could do what he wanted. Why then did he have a knot of anxiety?

'It's two pounds, boys. Is that all right?' The woman's voice was a disinterested monotone.

'That's fine,' Matt replied.

'Top of the stairs.'

Matt held out his wrist and the woman pressed an inky stamp against it. She kept the stamp in the air waiting for Connor. He held out his hand. Looking down at the mark it appeared to be just a dark blue smudge. Matt was already halfway up the stairs.

Past a deserted cloakroom, they padded along some sticky carpet towards black double doors. Beams of coloured lights could be seen through the twin porthole panes of glass. Matt put his hand against Connor's back and pushed him though.

After all the anticipation the greatest shock wasn't the volume of the music or the strange stench of smoke and chemicals, it was how few people there were. Two grey-haired men in leather jackets were crouched over the far end of the bar. They looked up from their pints to see who had just walked in but only for a moment. Their heads slumped in unison back to their drinks. Four younger men in T-shirts were perched on high stools smoking and all four were laughing in a way that made Connor think they were only pretending to find something funny. To their right the dance floor disappeared around the corner. A short woman draped in an unexpected silver poncho was twirling around to the music with a grim determination.

'We're early,' Matt explained over the music as he steered Connor towards the bar. 'What will you have?'

The thought of another pint made him feel queasy. He stared at the bank of brightly lit bottles. The serious-looking blonde woman behind the bar stubbed out her cigarette and stepped forward.

'You again.'

'Last night,' Matt replied with a grin. 'You'll never see me again!'

'I'm crying on the inside. One for the road?'

'Bacardi Coke please and . . . ?' Matt turned to Connor.

'The same.'

They took their twin drinks and sat at the table behind the giddy foursome. The one in the baseball cap nodded at Matt as if he knew him. Matt muttered a greeting in return and this was followed by a quartet of giggles. Connor just stared at his drink, not wanting any explanations.

Matt sat and put his hand on Connor's arm. 'This is a good last night, Irish. I'm glad I bumped into you.' He rubbed his arm and then gripped it tightly with purpose.

'Me too.'

They sipped their drinks.

Matt moved his hand under the table to stroke Connor's thigh. This was overwhelming. His jeans tightened with desire. He wanted and didn't want all and none of this. Matt was talking again.

'If you ever get to London, give me a ring. Here's my number.' And then he was writing on a beer mat and pushing it towards Connor.

'Thanks.' Connor folded it carefully and shoved it in his constricted pocket.

Matt slipped off his high stool and came around the table to Connor. He bent forward and whispered in a hoarse yell above the sound of the music, 'I've been wanting to do this all night.' And then without pause for explanation or objection, he kissed Connor. Now that it was happening, now that his tongue was inside his mouth, it all seemed so inevitable. Connor stood up and Matt, without releasing his embrace, turned him so that his back was against the wall. The kissing became more intense, their hips pressed against each other. Connor could feel the hardness. It was thrilling. Not just the kiss but also the music and even the sound of voices. People could see him kissing this man and it didn't matter. There was also a seed of panic. Even in this moment Connor's mind was racing ahead. Far from home there was no reason for this to stop, nobody to put on the brakes.

Just as abruptly as it had begun, Matt suddenly pulled away and smiled. He brushed a finger down the side of Connor's face.

'Sexy.'

Unsure how to respond to such an unprecedented compliment, Connor just smiled back. Matt half turned and looked over his shoulder. 'Dance?' he asked as he gently pulled Connor towards the dance floor. He thought he heard the boy in the baseball cap say, 'Have fun,' but he couldn't be sure.

The silver-ponchoed dancer seemed to have run out of energy and was now just stepping from side to side in the corner with her head slumped forward. The walls were lined with posters advertising a variety of club nights, strippers and drag queens. A few more people had come into the club and were standing in clumps between the bar and the dance floor. Matt pushed through them and then put his hands on Connor's hips and they swayed to some pop song that Connor didn't recognise. Matt was staring into his eyes and then they were kissing again. Matt's hands moved around Connor's hips to hold him closer and push himself forward. Connor pushed back, laughing. 'I thought you wanted to dance?'

Matt moved his head to the side and licked Connor's ear. 'I do, Irish. I want to do all sorts of things.'

Matt twirled away into the centre of the dance floor and Connor followed him. Now that he was around the corner, he could see that there were four small booths at the far end of the space and above them on a platform the DJ's thinning hair was scraping the ceiling. In the booth to the far right two men were buried in a deep embrace, their hands rubbing denim thighs. It wasn't simply that they were two men kissing that caught Connor's eye. There was something else.

As Matt grabbed Connor's hand to dance, one of the men in the booth reached forward for his drink and as he did so looked towards the dancers. Connor froze. It was Robbo from the house.

It was as if the whole world simultaneously stopped and jerked into fast forward. Their eyes locked but only for a moment, before Robbo picked his glass up and turned his back. Had he seen him? Connor pulled away from Matt, clenching and unclenching his fists. He looked around at the red and green lights that were stabbing the dance floor. Even over the music he could hear the high-pitched laughter of the foursome. His mouth was dry, and his heartbeat seemed out of control. Without even looking back at Matt he pushed his way past the drinkers at the edge of the dance floor and through the double doors. He half ran, half stumbled down the stairs. He could hear footsteps behind him. A small group were gathered at the door paying the woman with the short hair. Connor elbowed his way through them muttering, 'Excuse me.'

'She didn't like the music, did she?' A burst of laughter and jeers echoed down the alley as Connor ran towards the lights of the street at the end. He heard Matt's voice. 'Irish! Connor!' followed by another volley of whoops and catcalls.

He wasn't sure which way to turn when he hit the wider street. Nothing looked familiar. He turned left and ran up the hill. If only he could see a landmark, then he could get his bearings. He began to swing his arms to try and stay warm. He had left his duffle coat in the club. He checked his pockets. He had his keys and his wallet. The street was curving down to the right now and the buildings were becoming smaller and less lit. This couldn't be the right way. He was heading away from the centre of town. To his left there was a long straight laneway that led down towards some lock-up garages, but beyond that he could see brighter street lights. Connor crossed the street and ran as fast as he could, splashing through puddles, and hugging himself for warmth. He just needed to get back to the house. Everyone else would be gone by now so he could just sneak in, go to bed and tomorrow he would just avoid Robbo and . . . and . . . and that would be the end of it. Wouldn't it? Robbo must be as panic-stricken and embarrassed as Connor, surely?

The brighter road curved around to the left and Connor paused. His lungs were burning from the exertion and cold air. He began to switch between a brisk walk and short bursts of jogging. He pressed his hands into his eyes. There were no tears, but he felt exhausted. He wanted to sleep, crawl into bed and never emerge. Up above him in the distance he could see the top of the Anglican cathedral. He began to breathe easier. He knew where he was now. Sort of. He wasn't entirely sure how to get there but at least he had an idea of where he was heading. At the top of the steep hill he began to jog again and then he was running up Huskisson Street, looking over his shoulder and making silent deals with God that he would get inside unobserved.

The house was in darkness. Relieved, Connor slowed to a walk, trying to catch his breath. He rested against the railing for a moment before he pulled out his key and opened the door as slowly and quietly as he could. He stepped inside and with the steady caution of a burglar closed the door behind him with the quietest of clicks. He crept past the bikes and was just at the bottom of the stairs when he got a sudden heavy blow to the side of his head. He crashed against the wall and before he could begin to steady himself someone had their hands on his throat pressing him down to the floor. It was Robbo. Panting and dripping sweat onto Connor's face. There was the stench of booze and cigarettes. Robbo pushed him under the jaw so that his face scraped across the floor and was pressed into the wall. Connor didn't try to fight back but let out an involuntary whimper.

Robbo's face was glistening in the street light that spilled into the hall.

'Right, you little faggot. You are going to fuck off and you're never going to come back.' Each word exploded with a spray of spittle. 'Do you understand me? Do you?' He shook Connor, banging his head against the skirting board.

'Yes.'

Robbo pulled him to his feet by the throat and pushed him back against the wall. Connor didn't know what to say or do. It was as if he had been attacked by a wild animal. He just wanted to get away. His knees buckled and he slumped forward.

'Here's your shit. Now fuck off.' Robbo reached behind him and threw a bag at Connor's feet. Looking down he recognised it as his rucksack. He began to understand what was happening.

'You want me to go now?'

'Yes. Just fuck off out of it.' Robbo had opened the door and was standing to one side.

Connor stepped forward but then stopped.

'But I haven't a coat.'

Robbo's face contorted as he reached forward and grabbed Connor's rucksack, throwing it out onto the pavement. Then he grabbed Connor's arm and tugged him towards the door. 'Just piss off or I will fucking kill you, you disgusting little faggot,' he growled.

Connor resisted, reaching out and trying to hold on to the bikes. 'I've no coat!' he wailed. His voice sounded high and shrill in the still of the night. Robbo shoved him back and tugged an old worker's donkey jacket off a wall hook. He threw it out onto the street where it landed like a stain on the pavement.

'Well now you do, so just feck the fuck off!' He lunged at Connor who managed to step back so that Robbo just got hold of his hair. The larger man hauled him forward and then kicked his legs as he pushed him out of the front door and down the stone steps to land with a heavy thump beside his bag and new coat. The door slam echoed down the street.

With no plan or thought, Connor raised his throbbing head and felt for the jacket. He put it on. It smelled of mildew and cigarettes, but it was heavy and warm. Some T-shirts and a jumper had fallen from his rucksack, so he gathered them up and closed the top of the bag. He could feel tears coming now but he didn't care. As he heaved his bag onto his back, he was thinking about how much money he had. There was still most of his Christmas bonus in his wallet and, if Robbo hadn't found it, one of his father's fivers was in the side pocket of his bag. He put one foot in front of the other and he began to walk and cry. By the time he reached the corner of Hope Street he was howling and it almost felt like a relief, a weight lifted. Things couldn't get worse.

X.

Happiness was somehow sweeter when it was tinged with guilt. At least that's what Ellen Hayes felt as she sat with her parents at mass on Christmas Eve. The priest had said special prayers for those that had been lost that year and Maureen Bradley's crying could be heard echoing through the chapel, but all Ellen wanted to do was sneak glances at Martin Coulter sitting with his parents further up the aisle. Once, when he had caught her looking and flashed a smile, she nearly squealed out loud with delight.

After the mass, people gathered outside St Joseph's, buttoning coats and tightening scarves. Seasons greetings were exchanged, enquiries about how many people they were having to feed the next day were made, and who was going where, but the atmosphere was subdued. The usual jollity would have seemed out of place. A few people rushed to catch Maureen and Frank as they hurried away, heads bowed.

'It must be hard. The first Christmas will be the worst.' Frank thanked them for their thoughts and putting his arm around his wife headed for the steps.

A hush came over the dispersing congregation as Dee Hegarty was escorted from the chapel by Dr Coulter and his son. Head bowed, she looked like the accused being led from court. As the trio passed Ellen and her parents standing awkwardly, unsure of how to react, Martin broke away and headed towards them. His father continued to guide Dee down towards the cars.

'Merry Christmas!' Martin said brightly as if unaware that he had just being helping a grieving mother from the church. He shook hands with Dan and Chrissie. Ellen was struck by how adult he seemed.

'Poor Mrs Hegarty,' Chrissie said. 'Your family have been very good to her.'

Martin glanced over his shoulder as if to remind himself whom Mrs Hayes was referring to. 'Yes. Very hard for her. She's coming to lunch with us tomorrow, otherwise she'd have been by herself.'

Chrissie made an appreciative sound, as if he'd shown her a photograph of a puppy.

'Have you many yourselves?' he asked.

'Just my sister and brother-in-law down from Fermoy and we're taking Dan's father out for the day.'

Martin nodded, as if he knew or even cared who these people were.

Ellen became aware she was just standing there staring at him with a huge open-mouthed smile. She caught her father's expression, which suggested he feared she was ill.

'Will you be around tomorrow afternoon?' Martin asked. It took Ellen a moment to realise that the question was aimed at her.

'Yes. Yes, I'll be there.' She gave a breathy laugh.

‘Right. Well, I might pop over so. Break up the day.’

‘Well, you’ll be very welcome,’ Chrissie said with an air of finality. She obviously wanted to get home. They said their goodbyes and Martin made his way quickly down the steps to his father waiting by the car, made conspicuous by its newness.

The Hayeses walked home in silence, all occupied with their own thoughts. It was just as they entered the square that Dan cleared his throat and asked, ‘So the dance went well then?’

A blush appeared on Ellen’s cheeks. ‘It did. Yes, thanks.’ She looked at the ground, barely able to contain her all-consuming secret joy.

She had been so nervous on Thursday night. She had worn the yellow dress bought for a cousin’s wedding the year before. No one in Mullinmore had seen it, so she didn’t care that it wasn’t new. Her mother had lent her a silky cream shawl with yellow flowers that sort of matched and, Ellen imagined, made her look older. From about quarter past seven she had paced the living room because she didn’t want to crease her frock by sitting down. Every few minutes she would check the narrow mirror in the hall to see that she still had enough lipstick on and that none of it had attached itself to her teeth.

She was slightly disappointed when her father had stuck his head up the stairs to shout, ‘Ellen! Martin is waiting for you down here.’ Not for the first time in her life, she cursed living above the pub. She had wanted Martin to walk into the living room and be dazzled by the overall effect of her dress, not see her emerging hunched and squashed from the small door at the bottom of the back stairs.

She forgot everything when she saw him. He looked so . . . well, the first word that came into her mind was 'clean'. His face was freshly shaved and his hair swept back off his forehead. The extreme whiteness of his stiff-collared shirt meant that standing in the middle of the pub, he looked like an angel or gleaming apparition. When he saw her, he smiled and held out his hand.

'You look gorgeous.'

Those were the first words out of his mouth. Ellen reassured herself that this must be a date, a real date. No boy would tell you you looked gorgeous if they weren't interested.

'You look very handsome yourself.' She sounded confident enough, but Ellen could feel the heat of her face flushing.

Martin gave a shallow bow. 'Why, thank you very much.' He held his arm out towards the door with exaggerated formality. 'Shall we?'

'Have fun, you two,' Dan called from behind the bar.

Old Mr Hurley lifted his head from his pint. 'Oh, to be young.'

'You look beautiful, pet,' said a lady Ellen didn't know sitting at the table by the door.

The dance wasn't quite what she'd imagined. The crowd might have been a bit older than her but the whole thing resembled what she imagined a school dance would be like if you didn't have to smuggle in the alcohol. After an hour men were dancing on chairs wearing their ties as headbands, their shirts flapping open. The women had begun the evening with a little more restraint but soon enough some were slumped in corners with friends trying to encourage them to have a sip of water, while every bathroom cubicle appeared to be occupied by high-pitched sobs.

Throughout the evening, however, Martin remained the perfect gentleman. He never left her side and introduced her to his friends. Yes, she got a few strange looks, but it wasn't nearly as awkward as she had feared. He wouldn't hear of it when she offered to pay for her round and on the dance floor he kept his hands respectfully around her waist. If she ignored the shirtless scuffles and women outside the hall being sick, it was the perfect romantic evening.

For the short walk home Martin slipped his suit jacket over her shoulders and put his arm tightly around her to keep her warm. Outside the pub she could see a small light through the frosted glass. Her father must still be clearing up.

'Thanks for a lovely night.'

Martin put his hand under her chin. 'No, thank you.' And then he lowered his face and gave her a brief soft kiss. When he pulled away, Ellen didn't know what to do. She longed to wrap her arms around his neck and kiss him more, but she restrained herself. She didn't want to look like one of the slutty girls pushed against the wall at the end of the dance. Instead she shrugged off his jacket. 'Goodnight so.'

Martin took his coat and draped it over his

arm. He looked a little nervous. 'Would you, would you like to go out again sometime?'

Ellen felt like she had won a competition or got lucky on the slot machines. The coins were cascading noisily, lights were flashing.

'Yes! I'd love that!' She bit her lip, aware that she had inadvertently used the word 'love'. Martin didn't seem to mind. He was smiling and then he bent down and gave her another kiss. It was firmer this time, his lips opened slightly, but there were no tongues. Ellen felt relieved. She resolved to find out more about French kissing. She would ask Trinny.

Martin pushed his hair back off his face and said, 'Goodnight.' Then he was walking away putting on his jacket. Somewhere in the distance was the sound of women screaming. It wasn't clear if they were fighting or laughing. Ellen didn't care.

* * *

Christmas Day began well enough though even in his absence, it was dominated by Connor. Her aunt Brenda kept asking Chrissie how he was getting on in Liverpool despite it being very obvious that this was upsetting her. Then the talk of building sites triggered her grandfather to recall every story he knew about labourers being killed or maimed. Gory details of scaffolding poles going through brains, or arms being ripped off in cement mixers seemed to be playing on a loop in the old man's head. Ellen overheard her parents having a whispered conversation in the kitchen. 'He means no harm. He's just a gaga old fella. Don't mind him.'

Ellen was keeping one eye on the clock wondering when Martin might call over. She jumped to clear the plates the moment it looked like everyone had finished, and brought out the spoons and bowls for the plum pudding, trying to encourage her mother to get the meal over with as soon as possible. Chrissie was happy to oblige because it had been decided that after lunch they were going to phone Connor. She had suggested calling several times before but Dan had managed to dissuade her. He felt they should let the boy settle in and besides, there was no way of knowing when would be a good time to ring a house full of working lads. Today however, even Dan had to agree, seemed appropriate.

He went out into the hall and looked up the number. Chrissie was pressed close, poised to seize the phone as soon as Connor was on the line. There was some discussion about codes and then Dan carefully dialled the number.

'It's ringing,' he informed everyone.

'Hello! Hello, yes, I wanted to speak to Connor Hayes please.'

The person on the other end was speaking. Dan furrowed his brow.

'When?'

A short pause while the question was answered.

'Well, have you a number for him?'

'A forwarding address?'

Chrissie had begun to whimper by her

husband's side. Dan was very still.

'All right. Well, if he calls tell him his family want to speak with him.'

He nodded his head.

'And to you. Goodbye.' Very slowly he replaced the receiver. No one spoke for a moment. Chrissie already had tears in her eyes.

Dan spoke softly. 'He's not there. The fella on the phone says he's moved out.'

'Where? Where has he gone?' asked his wife with an edge of hysteria in her voice.

'They don't know.'

Ellen's grandfather, still sitting at the table nursing his port, called out, 'He'll be down the pub. He's a young lad. The pubs are open in England.'

'They said he'd gone. Moved,' Dan barked at his father.

Now Chrissie was sobbing in his arms. 'Oh Dan, where is he? What's happened?'

'He's probably on his way back here. To see us. For Christmas.' Her husband didn't sound wholly convinced but Chrissie looked up at him hopefully.

'Do you think so?'

'That's probably it.' His voice was steadier, more certain.

Chrissie went back to the table and was drying her eyes with a paper napkin. 'Would he not have told us?'

'Ah, it's a surprise or he just wasn't thinking. You know how scattered he is.'

Chrissie sat and studied her napkin for a moment.

'When will he get here? There'll be no ferries today and if he left yesterday, there'll be no buses for him here today. Do you think he's just stranded in Dublin somewhere?' This idea provoked horror.

Dan was sitting beside his wife and took her hand. 'Don't worry, love, he might have got a lift, or, sure we don't know. He'll probably walk through that door any moment now.'

As if on cue the doorbell on the street door rang and Chrissie leaped to her feet holding her napkin to her face. She let out a little yelp of excitement.

Ellen also jumped up. 'I think that's for me. Martin said he'd call over.'

Her mother slumped back into her chair.

Sure enough, when Ellen got to the bottom of the stairs, Martin was waiting outside the door. He was holding a small package wrapped in Christmas paper. He held it out.

'Just wanted to give you a little something.'

Ellen wished people were passing in the street to witness this magical moment, but the square was deserted.

'I'm sorry. I didn't get you anything. I didn't know we were — '

'Don't be silly. It's nothing. Just something small.'

Ellen took the parcel. It was soft. She ripped at the paper; to reveal a silky scarf, which she unfurled. The design was some green leaves on a cream background and then what looked like stirrups or horses' reins.

'It's lovely.' Ellen pressed the fabric up to her

face. It smelled of perfume. For a moment she allowed herself to consider the possibility that this gift had belonged to Mrs Coulter, but she quickly banished such thoughts. It was a lovely present from . . . could it be that this tall man looking so handsome in his heavy navy coat over a bright red jumper was her actual boyfriend? She smiled and thanked him again, before realising that Martin was looking at her expectantly.

'Oh, I'm sorry. I'd ask you up but . . . ' She considered what to tell him. To mention Connor was to bring up the subject of the crash and she knew that she didn't want to do that. 'There's some Christmas drama going on upstairs. Relatives. You know yourself.'

'Of course. Yeah, always the same.' He paused. 'Would you like to go for a walk?'

'That would be good, yes. I'll just grab my coat.'

She ran up the stairs hoping that Martin wasn't staring at her bum. As she pulled her best coat off the rack and put her new scarf on the ledge, she shouted, 'I'm going out.' Without waiting for a reply, she raced back down two steps at a time and slammed the door behind her.

They walked across the square and down towards the river. There were a few kids with new bikes on the street and Mrs Kilpatrick from the library out with her dog, but other than that Mullinmore seemed to be exclusively theirs.

Martin described what he had got for Christmas. They laughed about some of the more drunken antics the night of the dance. By now they were passing the weir and up ahead was the old railway bridge. Ellen had walked this way many times before but never with a boy. Would Martin take her as far as the bridge? They both fell silent as if each of them was waiting to see if the other suggested they turn back.

They entered the gloom under the bridge and it seemed as if their breathing had suddenly become very loud. Martin reached for Ellen's hand and their walking slowed till they were standing still. There was quite a strong smell that reminded her of the gents' toilets in the pub. Ellen did her best to try and ignore it and concentrated instead on the romantic possibilities of this hidden pause on their walk. Martin turned to face her and then they were kissing. Ellen put her arms around him and squeezed tightly. She couldn't believe that this was happening to her. He pulled his face slightly apart from hers.

'Merry Christmas,' he whispered.

Giggling with a heady mix of nerves and excitement, Ellen whispered it back at him. He kissed her again and this time she felt the damp presence of his tongue. Why hadn't she talked to Trinny? She opened her mouth and tried to mimic the movements of his tongue with her own. It wasn't that difficult, but maybe she wasn't doing it right. Martin slipped his hands under her coat and moved them around her back. She liked it. She liked it all. Martin gave a low moan. Ellen hoped he wouldn't ask her if she wanted to go all the way because she had a horrible feeling that she would say yes.

Without warning Martin pulled away and said, ‘We should be heading home.’

1988

I.

The new year began with whispered reports that Declan and Caroline O'Connell were back. They had spent a strange Christmas in a Dublin hotel near to the hospital. Linda was out of her coma, but the doctors and physiotherapists were still trying to establish what movement, if any, she might recover.

Caroline was glad not to be in their house in Mullinmore, but she almost felt as if she was hallucinating as she sat in the hotel dining room on Christmas Day. Declan was wearing the suit he'd worn to Carmel's funeral and she was wearing a maroon twinset, with her gold stud earrings. She didn't know why she had bothered. She'd even had her hair done in some trendy salon on Grafton Street. 'Up visiting family,' she had told the young hairdresser with a smile. Why should Caroline rain on some young one's Christmas parade by describing Linda lying paralysed in a hospital bed with tubes coming out of her?

Now she sat in the hotel with well-dressed families braying at bad Christmas cracker jokes, when all she wanted to do was stand up and scream at them that one of her babies was dead and that there was no real life left for the other one and that her family would never know another happy Christmas as long as they lived. Instead she placed her knife and fork together and leaned across the table.

'I can't eat this.'

'Sprouts are tough all right,' was Declan's response but she could see the water pooling in his eyes about to spill onto his plate.

After Christmas, Linda returned to Mullinmore in an ambulance. Caroline sat with her in the back. Declan had driven home the day before to set up a bed in the sitting room because it had the double doors. They hoped the front door was wide enough for the wheelchair. The medics were wonderful. They got Linda into the chair and wheeled her up the drive. The front door was wide enough, thank God, and then they helped Declan lift her into the bed.

'This is just temporary,' Caroline heard herself saying to the ambulance crew as if they cared, but it seemed as if they did. The red-haired female paramedic gave Caroline a tight hug before she drove off, leaving the three O'Connells alone.

'People can be wonderful,' Declan announced to no one in particular.

'They can,' agreed his wife.

* * *

Above the pub the Hayes family was dealing with its own loss. After three days Dan abandoned his optimistic mantra of 'You never know. He might still show up.' Finally, they all accepted that Connor wasn't just going to arrive at the door one day, his backpack piled high, his hair a tangled nest, freckles strewn across his face. The focus turned to the phone. Every time it rang, Chrissie would freeze and stare at Dan and he would walk slowly towards it saying a silent prayer. It was never the call Chrissie longed for, but she comforted herself with the thought that nor was it the call she dreaded.

There were days when she couldn't get out of bed. She saw the morning light creeping around the bedroom curtains, but she just couldn't face it. Dan brought her plates of toast that went uneaten. He began to worry for her but by the end of the week she was downstairs mopping the bar, polishing the taps, wiping out ashtrays. This was the woman he married, thought Dan, fragile but unbreakable. Chrissie insisted that they go to the guards. They were sympathetic but didn't hold out much hope. They would let the police in Liverpool know but young lads went missing all the time.

Chrissie understood that she could expect no sympathy from the town. Connor had robbed families of their children, but this waiting and not knowing still didn't seem fair. She didn't dare say it to anyone, even Dan, but she sometimes wondered if it might not be better to know your child was gone, really gone, rather than living in this purgatory. She tried to stay strong; they had a business to run and she had another child. She just wished that Ellen could be a little more sympathetic. It was lovely to see her happy, but it was as if she didn't care at all that her own brother was all alone somewhere.

What made it worse was seeing her all doe-eyed over Martin Coulter. If it hadn't been for his car and his trip to Trabinn none of this would have happened.

Ellen did her best to be sensitive around her parents, especially her mother. It was impossible to ignore their sadness and constant worry, but she struggled to share their concern. Surely anyone could see that this was all Connor's own fault? He had no one but himself to blame. Why shouldn't she be happy? She had done nothing wrong.

* * *

'Has he tried to finger you?' Trinny asked matter-of-factly as she picked some limp slices of cucumber off her sandwich.

'No!' Ellen squealed. 'He has done no such thing. He's lovely.'

'It doesn't matter how lovely they are, all men are after the same thing in the end.'

Ellen wondered how her friend had gained such worldly wisdom, but she had heard it from others as well.

'We're waiting,' she said primly, even though she and Martin had never discussed such matters. When he came home from uni for weekends they normally went somewhere in the car and then kissed each other for a while before starting the engine and heading back to Mullinmore. The last couple of times he had managed to snake his hand up her top to squeeze her breasts and she had cautiously grazed her hand over the back of his jeans, but that was the full extent of their activities.

After about a month of what neither of them had referred to as dating, Martin suggested that he meet her in the pub. She agreed, quite enjoying the thought of her father watching her having a drink with her grown-up boyfriend. Saturday was the chosen evening and he suggested nine o'clock, so that he could have dinner with his parents first.

On the night, Ellen perched on a bar stool and waited. It was unusually quiet for a Saturday. The clock ticking over the bar could clearly be heard. She was wearing a new top and was very self-conscious that her bra straps were visible. Her father had served her a gin and lemonade, and she could tell he was proud of her and how well she looked with her hair tied back and some make-up on her face. She crossed her legs and admired the way her ankle bone jutted out below her jeans.

When the door opened she saw Martin and smiled but then behind him, she spotted Dr Coulter and his wife. Instinctively she slipped down off her stool to greet them. The trio entered the bar, with Martin being the only one to smile. Ellen wondered what this was about but then she realised that they were being followed into the pub by Maureen and Frank Bradley. This could only be something bad.

'Dad!' she called to her father who was in the little office space behind the bar. Dan emerged, wiping his hands on a beer towel. 'What is . . . ' He stopped speaking when he saw the group now standing in front of the bar.

The silence was broken by Dr Coulter.

'Now, Maureen, Frank, what will you have?'

Dan stepped forward. 'Whatever it is, it's on the house. Ellen, go and get your mother.'

'That's very kind of you,' the doctor was saying as Ellen headed up the stairs.

Chrissie had insisted on brushing her hair and putting on a smear of lipstick — 'Who? What in God's name do they want?' — and when they came down a few minutes later, the group was gathered around one of the long tables against the banquette near the toilets. They all had drinks in their hands and Dan was standing by Frank Bradley. He waved his wife over.

Encouraged by Maureen, Chrissie squeezed onto the banquette beside her. Frank cleared his throat and spoke.

'I was just telling Dan, that we' — he indicated the people around the table — 'have been talking, and well, we just wanted you to know that we, well there's no problem, we have no problem.'

Maureen interjected. 'We bear you no ill will. We've all been through so much.'

'Agreed,' added the doctor.

Chrissie looked at Maureen. 'That's very good of you. That means a lot, doesn't it, Dan?'

'It does. It does.'

Maureen reached forward and pulled Chrissie into an unlikely hug. A ripple of relieved laughter went around the table.

Back at the door to the stairs Ellen was watching the scene unfold. She only had thoughts for one person. Martin Coulter. He had single-handedly saved the Hayes family. Martin Coulter. She felt as if she might burst with the love and gratitude she felt for the floppy-haired boy raising a toast with the adults at the table. Martin Coulter. In that moment she knew she would one day lift back her veil and with a slight crack in her voice, say, 'I do,' as she stared into his eyes.

And thirteen months later that is exactly what she did.

1995

I.

Melissa designed hats. She didn't make them. She had tried, but concluded that actual millinery was a quite different, somewhat challenging discipline, so now she limited herself to drawing sketches of her creations. She spread her newest batch over the large table like campaign plans. Connor sat beside her, proud that this long-necked beauty, with her severe wedge haircut and heavy eye make-up was his friend. He pointed out various details and cooed appreciatively. 'I love the height.' 'Is that metal?'

Melissa had asked to meet Connor in the Neal's Yard Tea Rooms around the corner from 'Radish', where they had both just finished a long lunch shift. Melissa had news.

'I'm having an exhibition!'

'You're kidding!'

'It's true. A gallery in Clapham. You know John's friend Peg who manages the pub?' Connor nodded encouragingly. 'Well, there.'

'Isn't that in Balham?'

'Claphammy, Balhammy,' Melissa said breezily as she gathered her drawings into a neat pile.

'And where's the gallery?'

'That room upstairs, where they had the Christmas drinks?'

'Oh yeah, I know it.'

'It's an amazing space. I'm so happy!'

'Congratulations! I'm thrilled for you.' And he was, even though he knew there was a big difference between a gallery in Clapham and a room above a pub in Balham.

Sometimes he envied people their ambitions and vocations. Practically everyone he knew had big plans for the future; photographers, actors, models, singers — nobody seemed to see their future working in restaurants. What was he going to do? This was already a world he never thought he would inhabit. It seemed greedy to dream of more. Besides, he was only twenty-seven. He suspected Melissa must be at least thirty. When he considered where he had come from, he didn't think he was doing so badly.

He rarely thought about the old Connor. If some random sight or thought or bad dream triggered a memory of the crash on Barry's roundabout, he immediately tried to shut it down. He refused to live that day over and over again. He didn't dare allow himself to go back to that moment and consider that his new life was built on regret. Sometimes he was reminded of the Connor that had left Liverpool all those years before and he almost felt like laughing. It was like looking at baby photographs. He had been so pathetic. That terrified boy lying in the street, while weird Robbo slammed the door. In his mind's eye it reminded him of the Little Match Girl. Sometimes in his memory the boy had trudged down Huskisson Street leaving a single set of footprints in the snow. That wasn't what had happened, of course. In reality, he had set off into the damp cold night and headed for the bus station, deciding that it would be cheaper than the train. The lights had been on, but the doors were locked. He had sat and waited, wrapped in his new coat. Eventually more lights flickered on and he boarded the first bus to London.

Stepping off the coach in Victoria station that day marked, for Connor, the beginning of his new life. He had walked the streets of Pimlico, his backpack weighing him down, but he had felt free, released from the past and his shame. Nobody knew him here. Of course, that was also a problem. Where was he to go? What was he going to do? By late afternoon it was dark and the weight of his backpack had become unbearable. He found a post office so he could use a phone book to look up youth hostels in London. A helpful woman on the phone explained her hostel was full but he could try the one in Earl's Court.

'Where's that?' Connor asked.

'Well, where are you now pet?'

'I don't really know.' He could feel the pressure of tears pressing behind his nose.

'Do you have an *A — Z*?'

'No.' His voice sounded like a child being brave. He longed for this kind woman to come and rescue him.

'You'll need one of those and then you can always find where you're going, all right?'

Connor squeaked his agreement.

'Do you need the number for Earl's Court or do you have a phone book?

'There's a book here.'

'All right then pet. Best of luck to you!' and the only friendly voice he had heard all day was gone.

The next morning, Connor felt desperate. He had only bought three sandwiches, a couple of coffees and paid for his night in the hostel, but already his funds were diminishing much faster than he'd hoped. Connor found himself back in a phone box clutching a folded-up beer mat.

A voice he didn't recognise answered the phone. Connor cleared his throat.

'Could I speak to Matt please?'

'Hang on.' Then shouted away from the receiver, 'Matt, it's for you!'

There was a shout in the distance, then approaching footsteps echoed down the line.

'Hello?'

'Matt?'

'Yes.'

'It's Connor.'

'Sorry?'

'Connor from the other night.' Already in his mind it might have been weeks before rather than barely forty-eight hours earlier.

'Irish? There's a surprise! What happened to you?' Connor felt pathetically grateful that this man, who was essentially little more than a stranger, hadn't just hung up.

'I'm sorry. It's a long story. It wasn't about you . . .' His voice trailed off.

'Good to know,' Matt said with a smile in his voice. 'Where are you?'

'I'm in London.'

'Oh, oh I see.' Matt sounded flustered.

Connor bowed his head and pressed his hair against the glass of the phone box. It looked as if it was causing him physical pain to articulate the truth. 'I have nowhere to go.'

'Right.' There was silence on the line. 'I know I said to come and visit but now isn't . . . I mean, tomorrow is Christmas Eve.'

'I know, I know,' Connor replied. He realised how ridiculous his request for help must seem. 'I didn't mean you. I just . . . What should I do? I stayed in a hostel last night, but I can only afford one more night.'

'All right, Mary and Joseph, don't panic just yet. Let me ask around. I can see you this afternoon for a drink in Brixton. The Prince of Wales pub — it's not far from the tube station. Do you think you can find that?'

'Yes,' Connor replied with more conviction than he actually felt.

'Around four.'

'Great.'

'You'll be all right, Irish!'

And so, after navigating the Underground with short-tempered last-minute Christmas shoppers less than thrilled to encounter his backpack, he climbed the steps up to Brixton Road.

It was a sensory overload. Not only were the pavements even more crowded than the train from which he had just escaped, but the racial diversity of the people swarming past was something he had never experienced before. Connor had never thought of himself as racist. On the contrary, he could list any number of black musicians and singers he liked, he had told his father off for making rude comments about certain athletes when they'd been watching the Los Angeles Olympic Games, he had even made a point of speaking to the African bishop who had come to give a talk at his school. But this was entirely different. He had to admit he felt intimated, even fearful. Connor tried to find an expression for his face that suggested nonchalance and then started walking. He had studied his *A — Z* earlier so he knew it was left out of the station and then the pub should be on the corner of Coldharbour Lane. Without any confusion he found The Prince of Wales, which felt like a minor victory on his path to becoming a person who really lived here.

Matt was waiting in the gloomy interior. The pub seemed to be in denial about Christmas. Connor was struck once more by Matt's glossy sheen of perfection. His hair fell in a blond swoop over one eye and his white T-shirt practically glowed. He was sitting at a small table alongside a tall thin man with a shaved head. Matt smiled and stood up.

'You found us!' He attempted to give Connor a hug but faced with the obstacle of the towering backpack, opted for an arm slap instead.

'Connor, this is Chris.' The bald man flashed his teeth and held out his hand.

* * *

The seeds of Connor's new family tree were planted that afternoon in The Prince of Wales.

The roots grew in the squat that Chris ran with three other gay men in a small terraced house beside a railway bridge in Camberwell. The arrangement was meant to be temporary, but Connor stayed on after Christmas. In fact, he lived there for almost two years, before the squat finally came to an end. From that house he met friends, found lovers and got various jobs working behind bars and waiting tables. This was the clean slate he had longed for. No one cared about his past because they were also trying to redefine themselves as artists and activists, not just boys who had attended grammar schools in Wiltshire or gone to church every Sunday in Oban. They wore clothes they would never wear in the towns of their birth, ate food their mothers would never cook, had lovers who would never be taken home at Christmas. Family had been replaced by a tribe, and Connor flourished. When he stopped failing at trying to be the man he couldn't be, he found he was able to succeed in all sorts of other ways. People liked him, he was funny, he could earn good money.

Sometimes he wondered if this new Connor could ever go home. Would his parents be able to love this Connor? He decided that they wouldn't, they couldn't. He knew what they thought of men like him. From even before he'd had suspicions about himself and who he might grow up to be, he could remember the comments. Watching a 'homosexual' speaking on *The Late Late Show*, Chrissie, shaking her head sadly, said, 'Imagine being the poor parents of that.' Sometimes in his memory Connor recalled that she had even blessed herself, as if warding off the evil spirits of perversion that stalked the earth. He remembered Dan behind the bar discussing a 'bad death'. The distant relative of a drinker living up in Cork. There had always been talk. Found swinging in the garage. Dan nodded sagely. 'God forgive me, but a fella like that, isn't he better off?' More recently, Chrissie had been listening to a mother on the radio expressing her pride in her gay son. 'Well, she's a stronger woman than I am. I don't think I could love a child like that.' Connor knew that his parents weren't monsters. The world they lived in belonged to them and he was the one at fault. Now he had found his own world and he couldn't see how the two could ever meet.

Once, very early on, he had found the courage to phone home. What was he going to say? Just the sound of his mother's voice had crushed him flat. He had sunk to the floor of the phone box, unable to speak, the dropped receiver dangling down by his ear. 'Hello? Hello? Connor? Connor, love, is that you?' He had wiped his eyes on his sleeve and hung up. It was a bridge he didn't know how to build. He sent a postcard. It was four views of London. The sort of card his mother might have chosen because it was better value than just one famous landmark. Once sent, he told himself that now they knew he was well and happy. He had told them on the back of the card. That was all they needed to know. What more was there for him to tell them?

The new family tree flourished. Connor may

have hated how he had reached this destination, but he had to admit he was so grateful. If he hadn't been forced to run away, who knows how long it would have taken to become this man? Even in Dublin, he knew he would never have felt this free, so washed clean by the rivers of anonymity that coursed through the streets of London.

He listened to his friends or men he met in bars telling their coming-out stories. Some were horrific and dark, others full of love and acceptance. Connor just skirted around the subject. 'They're fine about it now,' was his stock answer. He couldn't begin to explain that his banishment involved the deaths of three people. Because he had arrived in London only knowing Matt, there had been no question marks over his sexuality as he launched his new life. Connor was gay. Everyone he met made assumptions about him which he never had to confirm or deny. Connor almost felt guilty. It was as if he had cheated in some way. He had been springboarded into the express lane and missed all the awkward pit stops of telling school friends, people at work and family. It had all been so easy.

Had this life that he was now living been available to him all along? Could that be true?

Barry's roundabout. The smell of burning behind him. The taste of grass in his mouth. No. This Connor had risen from the ashes of that Connor and there could be no going back.

* * *

Melissa packed up her hat drawings and they air-kissed their goodbyes. She was heading off to meet her father, or 'Daddy' as she called him, somewhere in the City. Connor got the impression that Melissa would survive even if she failed to set the fashion world alight. He watched her as she cycled away unsteadily, her drawings safely stowed in the wicker basket on the handlebars. It was almost rush hour when Connor stepped out into the cobbled streets of Covent Garden. He didn't fancy heading back to the ex-council flat in Oval that he now rented with his friends Mark and Daz. The Northern Line would be hideous at this time of day, or at least that was the excuse he gave himself as he headed down St Martin's Lane. He walked with purpose past the Lumiere Cinema, and then with the speed of a conjuror, vanished into a doorway on the corner of the building. Pink and blue neon spelled out 'Brief Encounter'. Daz always referred to it as 'Briefcase Encounter' because the bar attracted more of an after-work crowd. Connor liked it because it tended to be busy earlier in the evening. With its alien mix of men in suits and curious tourists Connor felt free to cruise and flirt uninhibited by the presence of people he might know.

He headed for the lower basement and ordered a pint. He had done the same many nights before, tapping his foot to the music, casting his gaze around the room to see who was in. Nobody grabbed his attention, so he had begun to shuffle through the crowds towards the stairs when a man at the bar wearing a dark jacket turned around. Connor just stared at him. Not in order to cruise the man but simply because he couldn't stop looking. The man's eyes were the same blue as the fancy gin bottle on the glass shelf behind him. His hair was grey and close-cropped, his nose thick and masculine. There was nothing fey about him. He might have been in the wine bar a couple of doors down waiting for his girlfriend. The handsome face grinned. Connor looked over his shoulder. Who was the man smiling at? Looking back, the older man was pointing at Connor, then laughing, he beckoned him over.

'Drink?' The man had an accent. American? Canadian? Sometimes Swedish people sounded like that too.

'I'm fine thanks.' Connor lifted his almost full pint.

'A shot to perk things up?' Another smile. His eyes were unsettling. It was like being observed by a different species.

'Sure.'

'Jäger?'

'I'm easy.'

'Don't say that too loudly in here!'

Connor laughed, not because he found the banter funny but because he knew he should. This was a conversation they had both had many times before. The easy back and forth in-between drinks until one of them had the courage to make a move.

They clinked their glasses and downed their shots.

'What the fuck was that?' Connor stuck out

his tongue in disgust.

'Jägermeister. You didn't like it?'

'It's like medicine!' The two men laughed.

Timothy, 'call me Tim', was working on an opera at the ENO. He was a set designer, based in London, but he worked all over the world, mostly Europe and North America. In response Connor felt a little inadequate describing his work at Radish. 'I've been there a while now, so I get to pick and choose my shifts. The money's OK. I like it.'

Another round of drinks. Connor wanted to kiss beautiful Tim but he sensed that was not how Tim liked to play this game, so he stood by the bar like a gazelle at the watering hole feigning a limp, hoping the lion would pounce.

'Would you like to grab some dinner?'

This was not normally part of the ritual. Connor wasn't sure what to say.

'If you have plans or whatever, don't worry. I'm just enjoying our talk is all.' The smile. The eyes. Of course he was going to have dinner with him. 'My treat.'

Connor threw back the last of his pint and walked out of the bar enjoying the eyes following Tim and then the glances to see who had been the chosen one.

II.

Time was a great healer. That was what Maureen Bradley had been told her whole life, but now, eight years since her heart had been broken, she knew it wasn't true. Time might be able to numb, it could distract, but it was incapable of truly fixing anything. Being able to open the wardrobe and catch sight of Bernie's wedding dress hanging there like a ghost, without bursting into tears, might have been seen by some as progress, but for Maureen it felt as if her heart had calcified, her memories turned to ice.

She thought about Frank. Her big strong Frank. He'd never be right again. It was as if Bernie had taken all the love he had to give. When Maureen had told him about her breast cancer diagnosis the year before last, she had been so worried about how hard he would take it, but Frank had been dry-eyed throughout. 'We'll get through this too, pet,' he had reassured her with a tight smile and squeezed her hand. Maureen had thought she would never want to see her husband weep again but on that awful day, some tears, even a quivering lip, might have helped her feel more loved or worthy of saving at least. It had been completely different when their youngest, Connie, had got married. Frank had cried so much he couldn't say his few words.

Their son Kieran had to step forward and read his speech for him. They had tried to pretend he was weeping for Connie, but everyone knew his tears were for Bernie. Maureen had felt awful. Poor Connie, her special day taken over by her dead sister. Why couldn't he have been strong for the daughter he did have? She had tried to scold him afterwards, but she couldn't. He looked so pathetic, perched on the edge of the sofa, his big back bent over, swiping at his tears with his tie. Dee Hegarty's funeral was the same. Maureen had to go by herself leaving Frank at home apologising through sobs. Maureen tried, she really did, to be understanding, but she couldn't prevent herself from resenting him. His grief robbed her of her own. When he fell apart, she was left with no choice but to hold him together. He had hardened her, and she couldn't forgive him for it. Maureen thought about her own funeral. Would Frank weep at that? She doubted it.

Ellen Coulter was also thinking about time. How did some people have so much of it? Caroline O'Connell had Linda in a wheelchair and yet she was always coming into the surgery asking them to put up posters for endless meetings and charity fundraisers. Then there was Kate Sweeny next door, three kids, a husband, a Montessori school to run in the extension, and still, she was out tending to her hanging baskets or polishing her gleaming letterbox. How did they have so much more time than her?

Ellen had thought things might be easier when the kids started school, but it was just as bad. In the mornings, she managed to drag a brush through her hair, now cut short in a style which she knew made her look like her mother, but it was easy to look after. Then wrapped in her oversized dressing gown to disguise the weight she hadn't managed to lose since childbirth, she headed downstairs. She made packed lunches and put cereal in front of the children before Martin ferried them away. He liked to drop them off at the school gates personally. A public display of hands-on parenting. Wasn't he a great man? When he came back, he never even came into the house. She only knew he had returned when she heard his voice in the surgery talking to Angela, the new receptionist who had replaced little Dee Hegarty. Hearing him talk through the wall was when her day started to fall apart.

She would put the kettle on for coffee. While that was boiling she put the breakfast dishes in the sink, because the dishwasher was still full from last night. She noticed yesterday's paper on the counter. She carried it through to the living room to put on the stack by the fireplace. The dust on the coffee table caught her eye. She went back to the kitchen to get a duster but once there she noticed food stains all down the side of the bin. She should wipe them off while she thought of it. Down on her knees the state of the floor couldn't be ignored. This room needed a good sweep. The kettle must have boiled but she wasn't sure when, so she put it on again. She sat for a moment waiting for the little click, but she found that her attention drifted away. Imaginary conversations that she knew she would never have with Martin. Scenes played out in her mind of other days she thought she might live in another life. Buenos Aires. A glass of red wine in her hand, guitar music drifting across the dusty square. She was having lunch with someone, but she wasn't sure who. France. That's where Martin had taken her on their honeymoon. The ferry to Brittany. Such a disappointment. The weather had been awful. Endless rain. The whole place was just like Ireland but with smellier cigarettes. It wasn't really France at all — that was clearly somewhere else that Martin had conspired not to take her for fear she might have enjoyed it.

At some point she would snap out of her own head and remind herself of all the things that needed doing. The beds. She would make a start with the beds and then she could tackle everything else. Heading for the stairs she came across the dirty games kits from yesterday dumped in the hall. She retraced her steps to put those in the washing machine, but she found there was a load in it from yesterday that needed to go in the dryer but that was waiting to be unloaded as well. She remembered her coffee. Then she would glance at the clock on the cooker. Nearly time to take coffee through to the surgery and she was still in her dressing gown. She sighed. It was never right. Always a forgotten teaspoon or a chipped saucer. It was as if she did it on purpose. Certainly that's what Martin seemed to believe, but she honestly didn't. Even if everything did pass muster, he would still look at the small plate of shop-bought biscuits with undisguised disappointment. Every single day. Would you not get over it by now? If baking had been so high on his list of priorities when it came to choosing a wife, maybe he should have asked before the wedding rather than afterwards.

'No, my mother never taught me. She doesn't bake either!' and it was true, but Dan, her father, had savoured the slices of crayon-pink Battenberg she served up with the Sunday tea as if she had. 'Oh Chrissie, that is lovely.' Ellen had never considered her parents' marriage worthy of note but now that she was in one of her own, she couldn't help but compare it to theirs.

When she'd met Martin's mother before the wedding she had seemed a fairly nondescript little woman. Her hair was always 'just so' and she dressed nicely but it was Dr Coulter who had done all the talking. Now it transpired that the senior Mrs Coulter had in fact been some sort of superwoman all along, starching and baking her way through life. After the wedding Martin's parents had moved to a sleek newly built bungalow out on the coast road. It was the sort of house Ellen would have liked for herself. Bright and filled with simple modern furniture, rather than the high-maintenance museum of Victoriana her in-laws had left behind for the newlyweds. The dark mahogany furniture with its scrolled legs and carved edges seemed to produce its own dust. No matter how much time Ellen and Mr Sheen spent together, the very air seemed thick with it. Martin trailing a finger along the sideboard in the hall and then raising his eyebrows as he glanced at her, made her want to scream.

In the beginning she had hated the feeling that she disappointed Martin, but as the years slipped by she had grown to just hate Martin's disappointment. She had never been a wife before, why would she instantly know how to do everything? 'I don't see what's so hard. I've got you a front loader and a dryer. It's more than Mammy ever had, and she managed!' As much as Ellen tried not to cry, sometimes she couldn't help herself. Wouldn't a husband comfort his wife? Martin left the room.

She still remembered the love. It wasn't so long ago, after all. The kisses, the compliments, his desire; she had to remind herself that she hadn't imagined them. It had been real. The change was so abrupt, she doubted herself. The young bride wondered what she had done wrong. What had changed? Confused, she had asked Martin why he seemed standoffish?

'We're married now, Ellen. Things are different.'

It was as if he felt that in the simple act of saying 'I do' at the altar he had completed his side of the bargain, and now every other aspect of their marriage, all the effort, was down to Ellen.

She remembered sitting in the car as they had driven away from their reception. She had never been happier than in that moment. The guests cheering, the clatter of cans tied to the car, her father with his arm around his mother who was laughing and crying at the same time. It really had been her special day. For once the film was about her and she was its worthy star.

Her mother had tried to have a conversation about the honeymoon, but a horrified Ellen had blushed and blustered her away. She knew enough, the basics anyway, and how hard could it be when the whole world did it? Martin's tight embraces had promised so much. Sometimes when he pressed himself against her in the car, Ellen felt his sense of urgency. She had visions of their passion being unleashed on their wedding night, but like every other part of their relationship it was not what she had imagined. They had spent their first night together in an old manor house surrounded by giant pine trees on the cliffs beyond Roscoff. It had reminded Ellen of the protestant rectory in Mullinmore, though she didn't mention this to Martin as he struggled with the bags in the driving rain. They had a lovely meal — well, a French meal, bits of it were too mysterious for her to attempt, but Martin ate everything, '*Très bien*' — ing each enquiry from the waiter and sounding like a distressed cow as he ordered '*moules*'. Ellen had found it endearing, watching him make such an effort to impress her.

Afterwards they had sipped brandies in the bar. In Ellen's case, it was just one sip. The fumes of it had been enough to make her feel slightly nauseous. The manageress was a rather severe woman and Ellen could remember her standing at the bottom of the stairs with a shelf-like bust and red glasses hanging on a chain around her neck, bidding them '*Bonne nuit!*' with a wink and a throaty laugh.

Upstairs, it had all begun as Ellen had foreseen. The kisses, the way he took off her bra and touched her breasts, how he had moved himself between her legs, but once they were naked, he had sort of stabbed at her. Eventually he had managed to get himself inside her and appeared to have reached some sort of climax. For Ellen it was just painful. When he rolled off her, panting, he noticed the tears in her eyes.

'Sorry. It's not easy for the woman at first. It'll get easier.' He touched his lips to hers before rolling over to sleep.

The next night he tried again, this time pushing his fingers in first. Ellen had let out an involuntary yelp of pain. Martin had responded to this by taking hold of her hair and pulling her face downwards. She wasn't stupid. She knew what she was supposed to do and she had tried, but she had gagged until she retched. He released her and while she coughed and spluttered over the side of the bed, Martin sighed heavily and made a great show of 'going to sleep'.

On their first night back in Mullinmore, Ellen brushed her teeth and got into bed, wondering if Martin was planning to try again. Part of her hoped that he would. Maybe they would both feel more relaxed now they were home. She turned on her side to look at her new husband, but he quickly got out of bed and grabbed his dressing gown off the back of the door.

'I'll be back in a minute.'

She could hear the creak of the stairs all the way down to the ground floor. He must have gone into the surgery because when he came back into the bedroom, he was brandishing the largest tub of Vaseline that Ellen had ever seen.

'This will help,' was all he said before he got under the covers.

In one sense, he was right, it did help. It made it possible for her to endure him poking away at her, but it did not reveal what part of intercourse might be designed to give her pleasure. Was sex just for men? She knew they really liked it, but she had heard enough to know that women were meant to enjoy it too, or was that just talk?

Ellen attempted to ask her mother about it, but Chrissie was rather vague and dismissive.

'Sometimes you enjoy it and sometimes you just do it for him. You've a good man there and you want to keep him happy.'

Ellen stared at her mother. Were they talking about the same thing? Did her father paw great dollops of Vaseline between her mother's legs? It didn't bear thinking about.

Trinny was also a wife now. Her husband Dom had come to Mullinmore to work behind the counter in the bank, and being on the shorter side himself he made a perfect mate for Ellen's petite friend. 'Aren't they gorgeous together?' Ellen said to whoever would listen at their wedding reception.

She felt she could broach the subject of sex with Trinny, as a fellow newlywed bride.

'How are you finding it?'

Her friend's face burst into ecstasy. 'Isn't it great? So much better than I thought it would be.'

'Do you do it a lot?'

'Well, sometimes Dom is too tired when we get to bed but then we just do it in the morning. What about you guys?' Trinny inched closer.

'It's good,' Ellen spoke slowly, 'but do you sometimes find it a bit, a bit sore like?'

Trinny's eyes opened wide. She seemed delighted by the question. 'Oh, does Martin have a big one? He looks like he'd have a big one!'

Ellen didn't have an answer. Was it big? Bigger than what? Too big for her? Was that the problem?

She had attempted to raise her dissatisfaction with Martin and of course the conversation had turned to what her friend had said.

'Trinny!' he had barked at her. 'What does that little midget know? I am a doctor, a medically trained doctor, and I can tell you it will get better. It's just a matter of getting used to things. If you don't believe me, you can talk to my father!'

'No, no. Of course I believe you,' she said, trying to placate him.

Marriage, it seemed to Ellen, wasn't about being happy or making someone happy. It turned out it was just a matter of deciding whose unhappiness was the easiest to deal with. It was hers. Her unhappiness seemed an acceptable price to pay for not living with Martin's.

She tidied the jar of Vaseline away in the bedside locker on Martin's side of the bed, but some nights when she came back from the bathroom in her nightdress, it had reappeared, a heavy glow beneath the lamp. Her stomach sank.

III.

'Babies, baby. It'll all change when you've some little ones.' Chrissie was comforting Ellen as she sobbed in her arms at the kitchen table above the pub. Her daughter had complained to her more than once about her marriage, but she'd had no idea she was this unhappy.

'The first year is always the hardest. It's difficult for everyone.' She stroked Ellen's back, wondering to herself why these young girls with so many more choices than she'd ever had, were still in such a rush to become wives. 'You're both finding your feet, figuring things out.' She lifted Ellen's head to emphasise the point she was making. 'At first you forget why you ever got married, I remember that with your father, but then everything makes sense, it just clicks into place when you have children . . . '

Unfortunately, the mention of her own children meant that Chrissie had now made herself cry too.

Ellen sat up and swiped away her tears. Clearly this mother and daughter bonding was no longer about her. Connor. He haunted every moment of her parents' lives. Dan was forever going in to see the guards: 'You've got to keep reminding them.' They had written to some missing persons organisation in the UK but had heard nothing. Ellen lost count of the number of times she'd come into a room and her parents had stopped speaking. She knew it wasn't because they'd been talking about her. Ellen wasn't heartless. She understood that it must be sad not to know where your son was, but, seriously, had they forgotten the funerals, the loss, their own empty pub?

'I'm sorry, pet.' Chrissie was composing herself. 'It's just . . . ' Her eyes filled with tears once more.

'I understand, Mammy,' Ellen said and hugged her mother before heading down the stairs and back to her own problems.

As it happened, babies *were* a sort of fix. Not for the marriage, but for Ellen. Caring for little creatures that didn't judge you, who stopped crying when you held them, meant that Ellen could exist on a small island of contentment, only wading out into the choppy waters of criticism and regret when she was forced to. The mornings spent soaping perfect fleshy little puddings in the plastic basin she placed on the draining board made her feel half crazed with love. She wondered if any mother had actually bitten into their baby because they adored them so much. She would quite happily have had more than two, but after their daughter was born, it appeared that Martin had decided that was enough. They never spoke about it, and Ellen felt she couldn't raise the subject for fear of sounding as if she missed Martin clambering over to her side of the bed, his hot breath against her neck. It reminded her of the educational toy

Martin's father had given the children, where you matched the peg to the correct hole. She wished the old doctor had had the foresight to have bought it for his son.

Of course, as soon as he could, Martin began to erode her isle of contentment. She felt foolish for thinking it would be otherwise. She remembered a breakfast when she had burnt the toast. It wasn't her fault; she was trying to do a hundred things at once. Martin, freshly shaved, gelled-back hair, sitting in a shirt she had ironed, had turned to their son in his high chair. 'Silly Mammy burnt the toast. Silly Mammy.' He kept repeating that phrase, while Ellen tried to ignore him. She put fresh slices under the grill, she poured the tea. 'Silly Mammy, silly Mammy.' Then the little baby boy, her baby boy, banging his plastic spoon on the tray top in front of him, said, 'Silly Mammy,' or something that sounded very like it. Her heart broke as Martin let out a great braying laugh that was met with childish cackling. 'Silly Mammy.' And just like that Martin found his style of parenting. He bonded with his children through the seemingly endless mockery and fault-finding of their mother. Always done with a smile on his face, never a cross word. 'We're only having a bit of fun' said with an innocent, almost wounded expression. As if it was Ellen, by complaining, who was threatening to disrupt their family harmony.

Did she think of leaving? Of course she did. Sometimes in the mornings as she wandered around the house in her chaotic attempts at housework, she listened to the radio. Tearful voices on the phone-ins would describe their awful marriages and how they had managed to escape. The calm, concerned presenter would read out phone numbers and addresses for women in similar situations. But that was just it — her relationship wasn't like the ones on the radio. She felt that if she had called in to one of the programmes, the listeners would have rounded on her, telling her how lucky she was. Living in that lovely big house, healthy children, a doctor for a husband, and he never raised his hand nor his voice to her.

Maybe when the kids were older, she could just slip away without much fuss. Would that ever be possible? Had she the strength to be cast as the villain, the ungrateful bitch who left the man with a heart so big and forgiving that he had married Ellen Hayes?

Sometimes she wondered about her brother. He had left under such a heavy blanket of shame, but there were times when she envied him. Whatever life he was living, at least it was his own. He wasn't stuck in Mullinmore making choices based on what their parents wanted or what the neighbours might think.

She never considered the possibility that Connor was dead. Maybe that was because she had heard her father reassure her mother so much. 'They'd have found a body, Chrissie love. We'd have heard if it was the worst.' Dan sounded so plausible as he explained, 'The lad is just embarrassed and ashamed. God knows what went on in Liverpool. We should have known he'd never make a go of it on the buildings.'

Then with the inevitability of the call and response at mass Chrissie would say, 'One postcard, Dan. One postcard in all the years.' To which Dan replied with the reassurance, 'He'll be back. When he's good and ready, he'll come walking into the pub as if he's never been away. Mark my words, love, mark my words.'

After eight years the conviction in Dan's voice had faltered and faded and yet he continued to say it. To stop was to abandon hope and he couldn't do that, not for Connor, not for Chrissie.

Ellen wondered if, had she been Connor, she would ever consider coming back. Maybe after dark one night, just to reassure herself by catching a glimpse of her parents through a window, but then she would vanish before first light. She presumed that was why he'd just sent a postcard. The London postmark had told them more than his few scrawled lines. It was just a way of signalling that he was fine, but without having to engage with his parents or the town. Mullinmore might not have felt the pain so intensely any more, but no one had forgotten. When little Dee Hegarty had passed away the year before, it was as if she had been added to the death toll from the crash. Another life ruined because of Connor Hayes. No, Ellen decided, if she was her brother she would never return to Mullinmore.

2012

I.

Two Irish men walked into a bar.

The first arrived out of breath from running down the stairs from the apartment where he lived above the premises. It was three thirty and he was heading into the bar for his shift. He paused for a moment on the street to enjoy the heat and light of the New York afternoon. He cursed himself for sleeping the day away. Tomorrow he would definitely head over to sunbathe on the piers. He banged on the door of the bar and after a moment it opened.

'Hi, Judson!' he said to the grey-haired man in the tight blue T-shirt standing in the darkness.

'Afternoon, Irish. How are you after last night?'

'Grand.'

'Grand,' Judson repeated, mimicking the lilt of the Irish accent.

Finbarr still found it charming the way New Yorkers reacted to his Irishness but then he had only been in the city six weeks. He'd arrived with a J1 visa which meant he could work for the summer. His plan had been to head out to the Hamptons, where his friend Dean could get him a job. Just before he left Dublin, however, he received news that Dean had been sacked, so Finbarr needed a Plan B. Dervla, a girl he knew only vaguely from his design course in Dún Laoghaire, was working as a nanny in Brooklyn and fortunately, after a charm offensive by Finbarr via email, she and the family who employed her had agreed to let him crash for a week, no more, in the small basement granny flat Dervla lived in. The pressure was on for Finbarr to find a job and a place to live.

On his fifth day in the city, by some Manhattan miracle, he had done just that. Finbarr might have been young, just turned twenty-two, but he already knew his currency on the gay scene. Growing up he had never had any sense of his looks, good or otherwise, but when he got to Dublin, he soon understood that people found him attractive. Quickly he learned how to use this to his advantage. If he thought he was struggling in a certain course, he would wait behind and ask the lecturer, male or female, some innocuous question, peering at them with his pale brown eyes from beneath abnormally long eyelashes, feigning interest in their reply, laughing at their bon mots. If he didn't have the money for a drink, he would still go out, confident that some friendly stranger would provide a cocktail or two in return for a little harmless flirting. He might let them steal a kiss, but nothing more. He understood that desire got him what he wanted, but if he allowed them to possess him, he lost his power. Finbarr had never had a boyfriend.

On his first night in a Manhattan gay bar, he had felt intimidated. The place had been full of men with better bodies than his, chiselled features and perfect teeth. But after he had downed a couple of beers, he relaxed and realised that eyes were still glancing his way, maybe not as many as at home, but being a pretty twink still meant something, even here amongst the bodybuilders and models. His accent, which had never been a part of his arsenal in Dublin, was now proving to be one of his greatest assets. Barmen laughed at the way he pronounced the names of beers, a couple of them gave him drinks on the house, and whoever was standing next to him at the bar invariably gave him an appreciative gaze and asked, 'Where are you from?'

Finbarr had heard horror stories from friends about the hours they had spent tramping around the city filling out application forms in restaurants and cafés. Some of them never found a job and just turned the trip into a holiday, heading back home early. None of this sounded appealing. Instead, when he was ordering a drink, he would just lean across the bar and ask, 'Are there any jobs going here?' When the answer was 'no' he followed that question up with, 'Do you know anywhere that's hiring?' Often the barman would just shrug his strangely overdeveloped shoulders, but occasionally they would suggest a bar he might try. After the first three nights, Finbarr felt he must have visited every gay bar on the island, which was fun but had still not resulted in his finding a job. He was beginning to wonder if he might have to resort to looking during the day instead of just nursing his hangovers lying in Dervla's bed watching cooking shows on television.

The fourth night, about nine o' clock, he was in a small cocktail lounge. He knew from looking at the rest of the staff, with their preppy polo shirts and carefully gelled hair that this wasn't the place for him, but no harm in asking. The condescending look the barman gave Finbarr boiled his blood. The expression that said 'You wish you were good enough to work here'. Finbarr didn't want to give him the satisfaction of informing him that no bar in New York was hiring so he just picked up his vodka and soda and turned to look at the other patrons huddled at low cocktail tables facing a small area that Finbarr assumed would become a stage later in the evening.

'You looking for work?'

A man was on the bar stool next to him. Finbarr could see why he hadn't noticed him before. A cheap suit. Just beginning to go to fat around the jaw. His brow had a sheen of sweat. He was the sort of man Finbarr would normally have ignored or dismissed with a half-smile before he removed himself to another part of the bar, but tonight was different. Finbarr had new priorities.

'Yes, I am. You know somewhere hiring?'

'Well my boyfriend just walked out of Sobar an hour ago. I doubt they've replaced him already.'

'Doesn't sound like a great place to be working.' Finbarr was thinking out loud.

'Oh no,' the man reassured him, 'the bar is fine. My boyfriend is just a bit of an asshole.'

'Your boyfriend is an asshole?' He didn't really care but wanted to be sure he'd understood.

'I know.' The man shrugged. 'I keep meaning to dump him, but it's not so easy to find a boyfriend in this city.'

For you, Finbarr thought to himself. The man was now staring into the middle distance, playing with the straw in his drink.

'Where is Sobar?'

'What?' It was as if they had never spoken before, but then the man remembered. 'Oh, Sobar? It's on Twenty-fifth, I think, just off Seventh. Like six or seven blocks from here.'

'OK.' Finbarr was still unsure how you could tell if the street numbers were going to go up or down, but he could figure it out. He slurped the last of his drink. 'Thanks.' He gave the man one of his best smiles, which made Finbarr feel as if he had done the man a favour rather than the other way around.

Sobar was spelled out in red neon in front of a narrow building with blacked-out windows. He pulled open the door and was bathed in a gust of cool air. Finbarr had confided in Dervla that air conditioning was maybe his favourite thing about the city. She had laughed as if he was joking.

Inside, past a man checking IDs, Finbarr looked around. He liked the place. It was a bit rough around the edges. One of the bulbs in the lamps above the bar was broken, a patch of silver duct tape appeared to be holding the seat of a bar stool together, and the two barmen in simple jeans and T-shirts were good-looking but not so gorgeous that they would have been celebrities back home. Best of all, the clientele seemed to be older and the ones perched at the bar looked like they were more interested in their next drink than finding love. Twinks nursing single cocktails weren't great tippers. Finbarr should know.

The room was long and narrow with a bar running halfway along the side wall till it opened up into more of a lounge area. There was a large glass door at the back which seemed to lead out onto a narrow strip of patio for smokers. The dark-haired barman serving the end of the bar nearest the door raised his hand, which held a red cocktail napkin.

'What can I get you?'

Finbarr decided to waste no time.

'Actually, I'm looking for a job. Have you got anything?'

The barman lowered his head, as if disappointed he would have to deliver the usual bad news, but then his expression suddenly brightened.

'You know what — maybe.' He turned towards the far end of the bar. 'Judson! Question for you!'

An older man stepped away from the bar and came towards them. He had grey hair but such a muscular tanned body that Finbarr couldn't begin to guess what age he might be.

'Franco?'

'This young man is looking for a job.' He indicated Finbarr and moved down the bar, as if affording them some privacy.

Judson looked Finbarr up and down unapologetically. He felt like meat.

'You worked in bars before?' The question was almost barked at him. He began to see how someone might have just walked out.

'Yes. Loads, but back home.'

'Home?'

'Ireland.'

'How old are you?'

'Twenty-two.'

'Green card?'

'I have,' Finbarr was flustered, 'I have a J1 visa. It's a visa they give to students who have — '

'I've heard of them,' Judson interrupted him. Finbarr had no idea how this encounter was going but it was the closest he had got to a job so far.

'You strong?'

This was a question Finbarr hadn't considered before. Unsure of how to answer, he just grinned and said, 'Not as strong as you.' And then he poked a finger into Judson's left bicep.

The older man released a loud honk of a laugh. 'You might fit in!'

Finbarr let out a sigh of relief.

'What's your name?'

'Finbarr.'

Another loud honk from Judson. 'Finbarr at Sobar! It's perfect. Well, Finbarr, all we have right now is a bar-back position. You bus tables, stock the bar, make sure the bartenders have everything they need all night. It's hard work. We pay minimum and the barmen tip you out at the end of the shift.'

Finbarr's heart sank. This was not what he had

wanted. He had heard tales of the amazing money bartenders could make, sometimes hundreds of dollars in a night. This sounded more like McDonald's.

'Right. I'm . . . well, it's just that, I'll have to pay rent and that.'

'What's your rent?' Judson asked matter-of-factly. This was not a man for sob stories.

'I don't know.'

Judson raised an eyebrow.

'I haven't found somewhere permanent to live yet,' he added quickly so that he didn't sound like a complete fool.

'OK, Finbarr, sit up here,' Judson patted the bar stool, 'and grab a beer. I'll be back.'

'Franco.' It was the barman, arm outstretched for a handshake.

'Finbarr.'

'Most of the time.'

'Sorry?' Finbarr was confused.

'It's fun most of the time.'

'No. Finbarr. It's my name.'

Franco gave an easy laugh and slapped the bar. 'I thought you said 'fun bar'.'

'Finbarr,' he repeated, and they shook hands once more.

'So, you're joining us?'

'I don't know. He told me to get a drink and wait.'

Franco pulled a face to indicate that he didn't know if that was good news or bad.

'What'll it be?'

As he nursed his cold beer and waited, Finbarr felt nervous. It wasn't a feeling he enjoyed or was accustomed to. Even worse, he felt small. This was a dive at best, and he wouldn't even be working behind the bar, flirting and earning tips. But still, in just a matter of days, it seemed the city had humbled him. He didn't just need this job, he wanted it.

* * *

The second Irish man walked in just after seven o'clock. He wore faded jeans and a T-shirt emblazoned with a Miami Dolphins logo but there was no mistaking his face as anything other than Irish. His reddish hair had turned sandy with flecks of grey over the years but the wrinkles on his face did nothing to disguise the constellation of freckles that covered it.

Connor had never been in Sobar before, but when his boss had offered him a lift back to Manhattan, his phone had told him this was the nearest gay bar to where he had been dropped off. He didn't care. He just wanted a drink. He was hot and needed the alcohol to slow his brain down. Today of all days.

It was his and Tim's anniversary. Exactly one year since Connor had been throwing clothes into a weekend bag when the ringing of the phone had interrupted him. Tim had been out at the house on Fire Island all week and the plan had been that Connor would join him for the weekend. In the past they'd gone together, but this summer Tim had been working less and spending more time out on the island by himself.

When Connor tried to recollect the details of

the call, he presumed there had been some pleasantries but all he really remembered was Tim's voice sounding dry and even. 'I'm not sure it's a good idea you come out this weekend. I'm catching the ferry back this afternoon. We need to talk.'

He had sat on the bed with his half-packed case and allowed the dread to build until it was almost a relief when Tim came into their apartment and delivered the fatal blow to their relationship. Would he cross the room to sit with him? Hold his hand? Wrap an arm of comfort around his shoulders? No, he would just stand a few feet inside the door of their bedroom, staring at the rug they had bought together on that trip upstate to Hudson, and deliver his prepared monologue. Connor could almost see the paragraphs hanging in the air.

He wasn't an idiot. He had known there had been someone else staying at the Fire Island house. Friends had been only too eager to share their sightings of the dark-haired twink: 'Who's the hottie at your house?' Some had even met him. 'Carl seems nice . . . ' would be dropped into conversation like a depth charge. How bad were things between them? Connor had shrugged it off. There had been others before. The design assistant with the big lips in Denver. The tall intern at Tim's agents. Not to mention the one-night stands, or out-of-control parties. Connor had seen them all off. Tim had come home to him, and no matter what dalliances or sexual distractions Connor might have indulged in himself, he knew his true home was lying beside Tim listening to his breathing find the rhythm of sleep.

Now he struggled to believe that this new boy, this Carl, needed so much space in Tim's heart, his home, that there was no longer any room for Connor.

After Tim had finished speaking, Connor sat on the bed. He had questions, so many of them. 'Where did you meet him?' 'Are you sure?' 'Who is going to Betty and Karen's wedding?' He opened his mouth to speak but only a long sigh emerged. What was the point? He knew the only thing that mattered. Tim didn't love him.

He stood and continued placing folded T-shirts from the bed into the holdall,. He might not be off to Fire Island but he was going somewhere.

'No,' Tim said. Connor swung his head to look at him. Was it all a big mistake? Had he come to his senses?

'No, you stay here, Connor. I'm going back to the island. My lawyers will be in touch early next week.'

More than sixteen years together. The front door of the apartment closed with a quiet but definitive click. No drama. No raised voices. Just like their lives together, except they no longer were. No kiss or hug to mark the end of all those years. The apartment felt cold, or maybe it was just him. Connor walked from room to room, picking up photo frames, touching things they had chosen together. He knew he was being maudlin, but he couldn't help himself. It was if someone had died and then it struck him that

that person was him. Life would go on in this apartment. The same frames would house new memories of Tim with his arms around someone else. Connor would be erased. Without really deciding to, he placed every framed photograph he could find face down. He thought of it as a mark of respect.

Tim and Connor on safari, on beaches, at parties, opening nights, always together, and if these photographs were to be believed, always bursting with joy. Connor knew that wasn't true, but even now, as the rage towards Tim began to build, he remembered far more good times than bad. He had been whisked off his feet. That's what it had felt like. Their first night together sharing plates of pasta in Orso. The things that Connor had idly admired when they walked past a shop window, being handed to him gift-wrapped the next day. Trips to Vienna, Berlin, Copenhagen; wherever Tim's work took him, Connor followed. Things moved fast, but it never felt reckless. They were both so ready to embrace this. Connor moved into the house Tim rented in Islington, and in under a year had quit his job because it had become so difficult to swap shifts or take time off to fit in with Tim's schedule. At first Connor had resisted everything being paid for — it had caused some of their only rows — but slowly he accepted that the amount of money he could contribute was negligible and by insisting on working he was just complicating their lives needlessly.

Living with Tim was an education. Not just about opera but about food and wine, the correct things to wear on specific occasions. Connor learned fast. He found a copy of *Delia Smith's Winter Collection* in Tim's kitchen and began trying out recipes. Soon they were hosting dinner parties, where Tim's friends, men usually a good decade or two older than Connor, teased him, and squawked at Tim, 'Where did you find him?' 'Bargain basement, dear!' Connor could feel himself growing, evolving, and most importantly, putting even more distance between himself and the past.

Travelling so much and, when they were in London, spending more time with Tim's friends or eating in the sort of restaurants where you didn't pour your own wine, meant that Connor saw a decreasing amount of his old friends. Tim's world became his world. Moving back to New York full time had been an announcement, not a discussion. But Connor understood why, and more than that, he liked that this was what his life had become. It was never as if Tim was telling him what to do, he just let Connor know what was going to happen. It was a life without responsibility, and he enjoyed it.

In order to get a visa to live in New York, Connor was employed as Tim's assistant and he did in fact deal with a lot of their life administration. He spoke to contractors, made reservations, mapped out calendars. It gave him just enough sense of purpose so that his days had a structure but with enough free time for the gym or planning menus.

Now he was standing in an apartment that was no longer his home and waiting once more to be told what was going to happen. Through the window he could see the lights of Midtown. Each lit square a life, full of joy and despair, ambition and disappointment. Thousands, millions of people filling the hours, ticking off the days, until what? Connor felt very small. His life was just another speck, a dot of light in the skyline. The tears began to roll down his face and his body shook. Naturally he was upset that Tim had left him, but what he really felt, what was overwhelming him, was fear. After sixteen years he was going to have to decide what happened next.

On the Monday, it transpired that Connor wasn't yet making his own choices. Tim, or at least his lawyer, had some further announcements to make. Tim had purchased a small studio in Hell's Kitchen as an investment property. Why had Connor never heard about this? Had Tim been planning this break-up for years? Was this where Tim had carried on his affair with Carl while Connor was at home making a wine reduction or experimenting with sourdough? The property was to be gifted to Connor rent free for three years. He was also to receive a generous sum of money. The lawyer referred to it as a settlement. The sort of amount that if Connor was careful, meant he could probably avoid getting a job for a year, maybe longer.

Gratitude and rage are an uneasy mix but that was precisely what Connor felt as he ended the call. Huge relief that his immediate worries were over but fury at Tim. This wasn't an ex-boyfriend being generous, this was a rich man paying his way out of guilt. Tim didn't need to feel bad, because he had behaved with such largesse. Yet again, he was controlling the situation. Nobody was going to be on Team Connor. He could almost hear Tim explaining the end of their relationship to friends, dismissing it with 'Well, of course he was upset, but I've helped him out a bit, so he'll be fine.' Connor wished he was the sort of man who could just walk away. Storm into Tim's work studio and tell him where to stick his apartment and his cash, but he knew he wasn't going to do that. It seemed that as part of the divorce settlement, Tim had taken his pride.

When Connor moved up to his new studio apartment, he stood with his unpacked boxes and looked at the four walls. It was so small, and yet he knew that on his own even this was way beyond his means. Why did it feel like he was being punished when he had done nothing wrong? He allowed his self-pity free rein. He slid a Purcell CD into the stereo and turned up the volume, then while 'Dido's Lament' filled the room, he took a bottle of red wine and a glass into the bathroom. He squeezed his way out through the small window to sit on the fire escape in an attempt to make his world seem larger. Before long he was crying while simultaneously looking at Grindr.

For nearly two weeks this became his routine. Sometimes guys came over, which initially was fun, or at least a distraction, but invariably they made him think about Tim. The way they kissed, a question about his CD collection, some stupid joke. It seemed that somebody informing you it was time to stop loving them didn't mean you actually did.

One evening Connor was on Ninth Ave picking up more wine when he bumped into Daniel, a friend of Tim's. Had any of them ever been his friends? He doubted it. Certainly none of them had rushed to get in touch. Connor saw Daniel first. He was walking quickly and checking the time. When he looked up and saw Connor, he paused. Was he going to blank him and walk on? No. He smiled and stepped forward to kiss Connor on the cheek. Even on this warm evening, his skin was cool, the cologne freshly spritzed. Connor was acutely aware that he hadn't showered for more than a day.

'Connor. Good to see you.' The two men smiled at each other.

'You too.' An awkward tension made both men slightly regret that they had acknowledged each other at all. Daniel stroked his neatly trimmed goatee beard with a manicured hand. Connor noticed his heavy expensive watch and hated himself for it.

'I heard what happened. How are you doing?'

'Oh, you know. It's all a bit weird right now. I'll survive.' He shrugged.

'What are you up to? You working?'

'Not yet. I mean I will, but it's been a lot with the move and everything.' Connor wondered how much he should say. Was Daniel going to be on the phone to Tim the moment he walked away?

'Well listen, I've got to rush. I'm off to see

Mary Poppins, but — '

'*Mary Poppins*?' Connor interrupted. Daniel did not seem like the sort of man who would go to see *Mary Poppins* on Broadway.

'It's a client thing.' He rolled his eyes and laughed.

'Who's the client? Justin Bieber?'

Daniel barked another laugh and Connor felt a little glow of pleasure.

'No. Some old Disney queen, you know the type.'

'Good luck.' Connor raised his eyebrows and Daniel started to move away, but then turned back.

'What I was going to say is that there's a guy I know, an ex actually, who runs an irrigation company. It's about to get crazy busy at this time of year so he's always looking for guys. Message me on Facebook.'

'I'm not on Facebook.'

'Oh.' It took Daniel a moment to digest this information. 'Well, here's my card. Email me. I'll give you his details. That's if you're interested.'

'No. Sounds good. Thanks.'

'Nice to see you.'

'Enjoy Mary!'

A quick embrace and then he was gone. Connor looked at the business card. Was Daniel just sniffing around Tim's leftovers? If he emailed him would there then be a casual suggestion of drinks some time? Or had this something to do with Tim himself? Was he still pulling the strings? He decided that even Tim wouldn't have been able to orchestrate him bumping into Daniel on Ninth Avenue.

Later, fuelled by a few glasses of wine, Connor dug out the business card and sent a short email. He didn't have to apply for the job and, besides, maybe he wanted to go for that drink.

The reply that arrived the following morning was disappointingly formal. The contact details and nothing else. Connor felt rather deflated. It seemed people might not be fighting over Tim's hand-me-downs. Probably everyone wanted their very own brand-new Carl. Who was Connor on the dating scene now? Was he really old enough to be a daddy? If he was, it certainly wasn't one of the sugar variety. He doubted there was much demand in this city for a sugar-free daddy. A job seemed like quite a smart move.

In the event, Connor enjoyed the work. It wasn't especially taxing and he was outside most of the time with access to amazing apartments and roof terraces all over the city and a few properties out in New Jersey that to his eyes looked like stately homes. It was just a few weeks' work draining systems and making things secure for the winter, but George the boss seemed to like him. In February he had called and asked Connor to help with some new installations and then kept him on during the spring and summer for maintenance. It wasn't great money but living rent free meant that Connor didn't need to worry — well, not yet.

Driving around the city in the truck made Connor think of Liverpool. It seemed so odd to him that at just forty-four his life had straddled such change. He wondered where Knacker,

Ciaran, Robbo and the others were now. What had their lives become? The irony wasn't lost on Connor that after all the years and everything that had happened to him, he was back once more in the back of a truck as an unskilled labourer, but this time it all felt so different. Living a life without fear was a wonderful thing. The endless anxiety of trying to hide, making sure your secret was safe, had been such a huge burden. Sometimes he wondered how he had managed it. Of course, while marvelling how good life felt without a huge secret, he continued to carry another with him.

No one, not even Tim, knew about the crash on Barry's roundabout. As time had gone on and he had successfully put all that distance between him and that September day twenty-five years ago, it seemed too jarring a story to tell anyone. He knew that people would respond differently. Some would consider him a monster, while others simply think him a fool, but universally they would see him as someone else. That was the point. Opinions would shift and that wasn't right. Not fair. The only people he seriously considered talking to were those he'd left behind in Mullinmore. His parents especially. For years he had told himself that he didn't get in touch or go back to spare their feelings, but recently he had come to admit to himself that that was a lie. The real reason he hadn't gone home was because he was a coward. The crash was something that had happened. Time could help the awful hurts inflicted fade, but who he was, the openly gay man he had become, how could that person ever be welcomed back? It didn't matter how many stories he heard about conservative Christian parents in the Midwest embracing their gay sons, or Mormon mothers at lesbian weddings, Mullinmore was different. The words of his mother, 'I don't think I could love a child like that', echoed in his memory. Even if they did weep and rejoice at his return, he would always doubt them. Question their love now they knew the whole truth. Connor didn't think he could bear that. The fact was that he was blaming his parents for something he hadn't the courage to do. He still didn't feel strong enough to get off the bus in the square and push open the door to the pub. Would his father still be behind the bar polishing a glass or wiping down the counter? Were his parents even still alive? He didn't dare allow himself to imagine a world where life had gone on in Mullinmore. For him, it had stopped, frozen in time when he left. He could no more go back there than visit Brigadoon or Atlantis. In times of weakness, he could see that movie moment where they all hugged each other, sobbing their apologies and forgiveness at the same time. But he reminded himself that those moments were fiction, the stuff of fantasies. There was no returning, no way to make things right. He was resigned to never calling Mullinmore home again.

It felt almost clandestine to be in this bar he didn't know, as if he was in hiding. The gloom and air-conditioned chill banished the bright noisy heat of the street. There were two barmen. Connor headed for the end of the bar nearest the door, and to the more attractive barman, a well-built, tattooed man with dark hair.

The night began with beers, then moved on to vodka sodas. Connor felt a warm buzz and he liked it. He picked up a stack of the free magazines and papers and flicked through them. Photographs of men with impossible bodies enticing the reader to various club nights. News of bars closing or opening. Being with Tim he had always felt young, but now that he was single and in his forties he felt not old, but certainly older. Men stood or sat beside him and he chatted to them, answering questions and even asking some, but being careful not to give the impression he was interested or even flirting. That wasn't on the agenda for tonight; well, not with this crowd. Despite never being a smoker, he found he fancied the idea of a cigarette. He realised he must be a bit drunk.

At some point in the evening, the barmen swapped ends and now the twink was serving Connor. He was wearing a loose tank top that said 'Boyfriend Material' and seemed a little stressed. When people ordered drinks, he turned and scanned the shelves looking for the correct bottles where the other guy had just reached out for them. Connor felt a little sorry for him. Was he even old enough to be in here?

The muscled barman shouted down to the twink.

'Hey, Irish!'

Connor was suddenly very alert as he listened to the two men.

'What?' The younger man was stabbing at the

till, perspiration on his brow.

'Can you bring up a couple more bottles of the well vodka and a bucket of ice?'

'I'm a barman, Franco!' He sounded indignant.

'Well I guess you're the bar-back too, 'cause I don't see anyone else. You can tip yourself at the end of the night!'

'She'd enjoy that, honey!' shrieked a man who had been drinking red wine since before Connor had arrived. A few other punters laughed, while the twink, clearly not pleased, slammed the till drawer shut and marched down the bar to disappear into the basement. Connor was suddenly fascinated by him. The boy was Irish. That wasn't so unusual as to make him care, but he found he did.

* * *

Finbarr was furious. This was not his job. If Franco wanted vodka, why wasn't he getting the fucking vodka? He stomped back up the stairs with the bucket of ice and the bottles.

'There!' he announced and slammed them down beside Franco.

'Thanks, Irish.' He pressed an exaggerated kiss against his cheek. Finbarr shrugged him off and headed back to his end of the bar. He surveyed the drinks on the counter. Nobody was waiting. He took the opportunity to clear away some empties and turn on the glass washer.

The machine was making noise and the music was loud, but he could still hear a strange grunting noise. He realised it was coming from the older guy at the end of the bar: he was beckoning Finbarr over.

'What can I get you?'

The man stretched across the bar, half standing from his stool.

'Are you Irish?' He was pointing at Finbarr to clarify his question.

Finbarr sighed, but conscious of tips, tried to mask his irritation.

'Yes, I am. Just here for the summer.' He gave a weak smile and made to turn away.

'I'm Irish!' The man now pointed at himself, to aid comprehension.

'Great. Did you want another?' Finbarr wondered if he was supposed to still be serving this guy. Maybe he should ask Franco.

'They called me Irish.' The man slumped back on his stool.

'Yes. You're Irish. I'm Irish. Drink?'

'Vodka soda.'

'Any particular — '

'Goose.'

'Coming up.'

Finbarr could feel the drunk Irish guy watching him as he moved around behind the bar, so whenever he wasn't busy he moved down to Franco and waited till someone on his section gestured for service.

'Connor!' The Irish man was introducing himself now. For an older guy he was sort of attractive, but he seemed to be bathed in sadness. Tragic. Was there any other sort of drunk?

'Finbarr.'

Connor smiled and his face was transformed. Finbarr returned his smile and they shook hands.

'I haven't met a Finbarr in a hundred years.'

'Well, now you have.'

'Where,' Connor was having some difficulties with his words, 'whereabouts are you from?' he managed to ask.

There was a crash at the other end of the bar. The red-wine drinker had slipped getting off his stool and wiped out several drinks. Finbarr and Franco hurried over with bar towels.

Red wine stained the ice stored in the sink like a crime scene.

'Sorry, Irish,' Franco said with a smile that suggested he felt very little sympathy.

With a growl of frustration at the injustice of it all, Finbarr picked up two of the metal buckets they used for the ice and headed back down to the basement.

The evening had started so well. Just before five, Carlos, the barman who was working with Franco that night, had flounced out with his backpack slapping against his shoulder. Judson had told Finbarr to stop sweeping and called him out to the smoking terrace. He looked unusually stern and Finbarr wondered what he might have done wrong. Had he overstepped the mark using his design skills to print up posters for the karaoke and drag bingo nights? He thought Judson would have been pleased.

It transpired that his boss wasn't that interested in Finbarr's graphic design skills;

instead Judson had explained with the sort of grave sincerity he might have used breaking the news of a close relative's death, that Carlos had decided to leave Sobar. Later Franco explained that Carlos had wanted time off for some dubious modelling shoot, but Judson had refused.

'He'll be back,' was Franco's conclusion.

Finbarr hoped that wasn't the case because, after weeks of asking and nagging, Judson had finally agreed to give him a trial shift as a barman.

Finbarr felt as if he had arrived. Maybe now he could get enough money to move into a proper apartment. He had been very grateful when Judson had arranged for him to move into the small living quarters upstairs, but it was far from ideal. The space might have begun as an apartment but over the years had become offices and then a storeroom, before Judson had returned it to being a rough sort of living space. Three curtained-off bedrooms around a windowless central living room and beyond that an alcove that contained a shower and toilet cubicle, along with a kitchen sink unit and a microwave. The other sleeping areas were occupied by Ezra and Brian, who also worked downstairs in Sobar, along with a variety of boyfriends and potential boyfriends. Finbarr hadn't expected to stay there more than a week but soon almost two months would have slipped by. They all pretended that the curtains hung on the partitions around their mattresses were magically soundproof, but that didn't alter the grim reality of lying in bed trying to sleep while unidentified snores, farts and other more carnal sounds drifted around the room.

Finbarr was surprised at how challenging it was being a barman. He had almost begun to believe the lies he had been busy telling Judson about all his experience working in pubs back in Ireland, so tonight had been a shock. Still, he was managing to keep his head above water, and nobody expected him to know how to use the till or mix every cocktail. The regulars knew him and liked him, and with new customers it was easy to cover his mistakes with a flirty 'It's my first night' and a free shot.

The ice sink had been refreshed and the red-wine drinker had been encouraged to leave. Friday nights tended to start out busy at Sobar but then as the evening wore on people drifted off to bars that offered entertainment, a dance floor, or a more promising spot for finding a hook-up. There had been karaoke advertised but Pam Sexual, the drag queen who had been booked, failed to show up.

The drunk Irish guy was still sitting at the end of the bar. Occasionally Finbarr would think he had fallen asleep, his head slumped forward, but then like a puppet being brought back to life his head would bob up and he'd order another drink.

'Do you want a shot?'

Finbarr did want a drink but wondered if he should on his trial night. He glanced towards Franco.

'Him too!' Connor called.

'Franco, our friend here wants to buy us shots.'

Franco walked down the bar towards them.

'Sounds good, just don't tell Judson. He doesn't like it.'

'Of course. Right. What shot would you like?'

'Jäger.'

Finbarr looked confused. 'What?'

'Jägermeister,' Franco explained and reached for the bottle.

Connor's face brightened when he saw the bottle. 'It's . . . ' He searched for the right word, and to his evident relief found it: ' . . . lovely.' Then as if explaining the meaning of that word added, 'Like medicine.'

Franco laughed as he poured three shots.

The crowd thinned out till there was only Connor and another couple sat at the other end of the bar. It was almost 2 a.m. when Franco called it.

'All right, gentlemen. Home time please. Finish your drinks and we'll see you next time.'

The couple dutifully drained their glasses and headed for the door, calling goodnight to Franco.

In Finbarr's section he was trying to explain to Connor that the bar was no longer open.

'Home time, Connor!'

'One more.' Connor held up his thumb and forefinger to indicate how small and quick that drink might be.

'No more. Home time.'

He took the empty glass from in front of Connor and wiped down the counter. 'Goodnight.'

'Goodnight. Slán!'

'Slán abhaile,' Finbarr replied with a broad grin. There was something harmless, charming even, about this Irish drunk.

Connor slipped from his stool and nearly fell backwards but quickly steadied himself and moved towards the door.

'Fuck. Wait.' He turned.

'What is it?' Finbarr asked.

Connor was groping around in the pockets of his jacket. Then he pulled out some notes and slapped them on the bar.

Finbarr looked down. Three twenties. He hesitated. He could certainly do with sixty dollars but looking at Connor swaying on the other side of the bar, it seemed likely that he needed it just as much.

'No. That's crazy. You've been tipping me all night. Take this back.' He handed out forty dollars.

'No. No.' Connor waved his hands above his head in an exaggerated show of not taking the money. 'That's for you. That's for Irish.' With this, he swung himself around and lurched out the door.

'Thank God for that,' said Franco as he swiftly locked the door behind him.

'A proud day for the Irish. Still, how bad?' Finbarr said, brandishing the three twenty-dollar bills.

Franco handed out the staff beers and they set about closing down the bar. Loading grey bus trays from the basement to restock the fridges, wiping down sinks, tying up bags of garbage.

Finbarr went to the back of the bar to lock the sliding door onto the patio while Franco carried two black refuse sacks to the front door and took them into the street. A moment later he was back.

'Irish! I think you should see this.'

Finbarr flicked off the lights behind the bar.

'What?'

'Just come out here.'

On the kerbside of the pavement, nestled against a bank of garbage bags, was Connor's supine body.

'Fuck. Is he all right?'

'I think he's just sleeping.'

Finbarr stared at the man on the ground. His mouth was slung open while his eyes were pressed closed in what looked like concentration. His arms were resting with palms up on either side of his body. He didn't look like he had fallen but rather laid himself out waiting for collection with the rest of the trash.

'We can't leave him here,' Franco said.

'Has he ID in his wallet? We could find his address.'

'And then what? No cab is going to take him in this state.'

'Could we put him back in the bar to sleep it off?' Even as Finbarr suggested this it didn't sound like a good idea.

'Judson would lose his shit if we did that. And there's the alarm. No.'

'Out here a rat is just going to eat his face.' Finbarr had become mildly obsessed by the volume of large rodents he saw at night when he was coming back from the twenty-four-hour deli.

'We could just get him upstairs?' Franco raised his hands and tilted his head to suggest he knew it wasn't an ideal solution but at this point they didn't have many options.

'We don't know this guy! I don't want him in the apartment.'

'Please! How many strangers stay in the place every night of the week! You know he's harmless. He's just some dude who has had too much. He could be any of us. Come on, I'll help you.' And Franco bent forward to put his arm under Connor's armpit.

II.

When Connor woke, he was struck by two things: his hangover and the angle of the light on the floor. His dry mouth and thick head were quickly explained as he remembered staying in that bar for far too long the night before. But the light was strange and where was the rug? Then, with a jolt like finding an unexpectedly deep step, he reminded himself that he no longer lived with Tim. He hated that even after a year his foggy morning brain could play these tricks on him. He tried not to think about Tim and wondered about summoning the energy to get out of bed to go to the bathroom. The floor. It was just sheets of untreated plywood. He had dark hardwood. A panic took hold of his chest. Where the fuck was he? He sat up and looked around.

He was lying on a mattress in the corner of a small room. On the opposite wall was a stack of milk crates that contained neatly folded clothes. A peach bed sheet was pinned ineffectually at the window, allowing the morning light to stream in. Two pigeons kept sentry on the windowsill. His jeans lay crumpled by the side of the bed. He checked them. He still had his keys, cell phone and wallet. Completing that checklist made him feel calmer. He was still wearing his

Miami Dolphins T-shirt and his underwear was still on. This wasn't the worst situation he had found himself in. He really needed to go to the toilet. He crawled across the mattress and peered around the curtain that hung where a door might have been. The room beyond was gloomy, the only light seeping through other curtained doorways. A large TV sat against one wall while a battered couch filled another. A body was lying on the couch. Connor studied the figure for a moment. The rise and fall of sleep.

He stood up and crept across the room. In the far corner there was an alcove and when he rounded the corner he found the toilet. He tried to piss as quietly as possible and decided not to flush. He would just creep back, gets his jeans and boots, leave, and then figure out where the hell he was.

The figure on the couch was now facing into the room and was awake. Connor recognised him but wasn't sure how.

'You're alive.' The man was young and good-looking in a twinkish way. He was shirtless with a blanket covering his legs. He was smiling.

'Just.'

'Well, we couldn't just leave you out there for the night.'

'What?'

Finbarr explained the events of the previous night and how he and Franco had manhandled him up the stairs and dumped him on the bed because the sight of a strange man on the couch might have freaked out Ezra or Brian when they came home. As it happened, neither of them had.

Connor thanked him for his kindness. He dreaded to think what might have happened. He made a silent resolution to try and drink less. This wasn't funny or fun.

'Do you want a coffee or something?' Finbarr asked.

'Do you have any tea?'

'I do.'

'I'm away from home so long but still I haven't got into coffee first thing.'

Finbarr jumped to his feet. 'Actually. Wait a second.'

He dashed into the kitchen area and emerged a moment later with a distinctive red carton branded 'Barry's Tea'.

'A food parcel from home.' Finbarr was laughing.

'Irish mammies!' Connor replied. 'I'd love some.'

Finbarr padded past him wearing only his underwear. Connor couldn't help but look. The confidence of youth. That ripple of abs and pert ass, all probably achieved without stepping foot in a gym. Despite his hangover Connor felt a stirring in his own underwear. He followed Finbarr around the corner where he was putting water in mugs before placing them in the microwave.

'No kettle!' Finbarr gave an apologetic grin..

Connor leaned against the wall. 'Do you work out much?' Was he really doing this? He wondered if he was still drunk.

Finbarr turned from the sink to face him. 'I run a bit. Why, do I look like I work out?'

Connor reached forward and stroked the young man's stomach.

'Well, I'd call those abs.'

Finbarr giggled and stepped back.

'Easy, tiger. You're getting Barry's tea and that's all!'

Connor hung his head. 'Sorry. I think I'm still a bit drunk. Ignore me.'

'You can only blame booze for so much. Do you mind black tea? We don't have milk.'

'I'll pop out and get some.' Connor felt relieved to have something to do after his embarrassing attempt at seduction. He headed for the door. Finbarr stopped him.

'Jeans!' He was pointing at Connor's bare legs. 'Maybe you are still drunk.'

'Shit!' Connor walked back to the sleeping area where the rest of his clothes lay on the floor. He was putting on his jeans looking at the small clues to Finbarr's life that were scattered about. A glass bowl of condoms. An old-fashioned money box marked 'Fire Island House Share'. A pile of photographs. As he did up his belt he glanced at the picture on top. A younger, much neater version of Finbarr standing with a girl who was clearly his sister and a woman . . . Connor froze for a moment and then grabbed the photograph to peer at it more closely. His breathing had become fast and shallow. This wasn't possible. He was confused. The alcohol was making a fool of him. He put the photograph back down and looked around like a man trapped.

The sound of bare feet on the wooden floor.

Finbarr stood in the doorway holding out a steaming mug.

'What's wrong?' He sounded genuinely concerned.

'Nothing.' No; he couldn't just leave without knowing. 'It's just . . . Well, that photograph. Who is that woman?' He pointed and noticed that his hand was shaking slightly.

'That's my mother. Do you know my mother?' Finbarr asked incredulously.

'Ellen?'

'Yeah, that's right!'

Connor swallowed and looked directly at Finbarr.

'She's my sister.'

A hush descended on the two men as they silently recalibrated their relationship. Finbarr had an urge to put on a T-shirt. Outside, a jackhammer had begun to break ground.

'You're *that* Connor.' It wasn't really a question, but the older man nodded.

'Granny and Grandad often talked about you. They think you're in London.'

'I was.' Connor didn't like this. He felt exposed. All his secrets laid bare before this boy.

'This is amazing. Like, what are the chances? Mammy will go mental when I tell her.' He held out the tea. 'Barry's to celebrate?'

Connor took the mug with a weak smile. Should he ask him not to tell? Beg him to keep his secrets, or was this the moment to end all the hiding? He looked at the young man opposite him wearing nothing but skimpy sky-blue briefs. He had lived in Mullinmore.

'Does your mother know that you're . . . ' His voice trailed off and he just gestured vaguely towards Finbarr.

'That I'm fabulous? Of course she does.' He laughed and then in a more serious voice continued, 'Yeah, she was fine about it. Dad was a bit weird but he's OK now.'

Connor was shocked that the thought of a father hadn't even struck him till now.

'Oh my God. Your father. Who did Ellen marry?' It seemed extraordinary to him that his little sister's life had gone on in his absence, that she was now a woman in her forties with this grown-up son.

'Dr Coulter. Do you know him?'

This made no sense. 'Dr Coulter? Sure he must be about a thousand years old by now.'

'No.' Finbarr laughed. 'His son. Martin Coulter.'

Connor gasped and his mouth hinged open and closed. He felt winded, as if he had been punched. He had to leave. His only desire was to not be in this room any more.

'I've . . . I've got to go.'

'What?'

'I don't feel well. I've got to go.'

'Well, give me your number so I can get in touch.'

Connor was already at the door.

'I'll drop it into the bar,' he called over his shoulder. He slammed the door and stumbled down the stairs. Outside the heat and noise of the street accosted him and made him feel as if he was hallucinating. He wanted to sink to his knees and howl out the hurt and confusion that was coursing through him. Instead he staggered to the kerb and was violently sick.

III.

Was it good news? Yes, it was. It had to be, and yet that isn't how it felt. Ellen had left the house with such purpose and excitement, but a nagging dread was making her slow her pace. When she imagined telling her parents that Connor had been found, she had envisaged some sort of celebration: her father raising a glass, her tearful mother hugging her with joy. But now, the closer she got to the pub the more she suspected that this was all going to end with wailing and distress and, of course, it would all be her fault. She had already decided that she wasn't going to give them every gory detail about how her son had met Connor, nor mention her nauseating suspicion that there might have been some even more unsavoury elements of their encounter that she was being spared, but the problem was that she was now left with precious little information. She had grilled Finbarr over the phone but all he seemed to know was that Connor was alive and liked a drink. She knew her mother was going to want more than that.

Ellen let herself in through the street door. Hayes Bar no longer opened during the day. She called up the stairs.

'It's me!'

'Up here, love.' It was her mother's voice.

Ellen's heart sank. She really hoped her father was there as well. Maybe she wouldn't break the news without him. There was hardly any rush. After all, they had waited this long.

In the kitchen Chrissie was filling the kettle to make her daughter the tea she knew she would be having. Dan was also there but sitting in silence at the table with his paper. Chrissie complained often about his Sudoku addiction. 'He opens that paper in the morning and then I can't get a word out of him until he has finished that bloody thing. I'd get more chat out of a spoon.'

Now Dan looked up, his pen hovering in mid-air. 'Ellen,' he said, as if her name was the answer to an unasked question, and then returned to his puzzle. Chrissie sighed dramatically.

'Would you not put that bloody thing down for five minutes and talk to your own daughter? Honestly. Tea, pet?'

'I will,' Ellen said and pulled out a chair from the table.

'Biscuit?'

'No thanks.'

'I will,' Dan said without lifting his head.

'He speaks!' Chrissie exclaimed with mock delight as she poured the boiling water into the teapot.

'How's Martin?' Ellen's mother called casually over her shoulder.

'He's fine,' came the inevitable reply. Ellen had decided many years before to no longer involve her mother in the reality of her marriage. There really wasn't anything to discuss. She had made certain decisions and now, without being able to say she was happy, she quite enjoyed her life.

* * *

Her father-in-law had died in 2006. The green-keeper at the golf course had found him stretched out like a sunbather just beyond the eleventh hole. Without him, old Mrs Coulter went downhill fast with previously undiagnosed dementia. Martin had decided he would move his mother into the family home, turning the dining room into a downstairs bedroom with a small en-suite bathroom. This might have horrified Ellen save for two things. The first was that she would never have to attempt another dinner party, and secondly Martin had finally agreed she could have help in the house so that his mother would be taken care of.

Life was easier. After Finbarr and Aisling were born it seemed the Vaseline had been put away permanently. Ellen suspected that Martin might be indulging his desires elsewhere, but she honestly didn't care. There always seemed to be some medical conference or pharmaceutical sales event that he had to attend. Ellen imagined that after the PowerPoint presentations were over the delegates might continue to satisfy their keen interest in biology, but she never asked questions. Martin seemed quite content to come home and work in the surgery all day and then at night sit with his mother or head into his office and shut the door. It wasn't what anyone could have described as a happy marriage, but as a life it was very manageable. Over the years Ellen had convinced herself that her expectations had been unrealistic. It seemed nobody found the experience of being married easy. Little Dom had left Trinny for some bottle blonde from Kerry who had come to work in the bank. Her friend was now working on one of the make-up counters in Brown Thomas up in Cork and living in a shared house with girls nearly half her age. Connie Bradley had ended up in the refuge in the city and that was after the guards had been called to the house nearly every weekend for months on end. Yes, Ellen had a lot to be grateful for.

Pleasure was to be found in unlikely places. She enjoyed letting Martin think that she cooked meals from scratch. She would buy vegetables every week and leave them on display, sometimes even peeling a carrot or potato to leave the skins around the sink, but in fact she was microwaving ready meals in the back kitchen. She was confident that Martin would never check the spare fridge back there because it didn't contain milk or the bottles of Pouilly-Fuissé he ordered for himself but never shared. Her palate wasn't educated enough, apparently. Sneaking his precious French wine into her big tumblers of spritzer was another hot little secret that brought her joy. They barely spoke, but Ellen had grown to enjoy the silence. It was certainly preferable to what had at one time passed for conversation but was really just Martin complaining or quizzing her about why certain tasks had been left undone around the house.

It was astonishing to her how their lives took care of themselves. The surgery rolled on, and with Annie Lynch coming in every day to look after her mother-in-law and help out in the kitchen, it seemed the only things that needed to be communicated between them were if she was going to be out at a meeting or charity event, or if he was away at one of his conferences. Even then, sometimes they just left a note. People, many people, had much worse lives than hers so she stopped complaining. Ellen decided that being unhappy was a choice and she was no longer going to make it hers.

When Finbarr had come home from college two Christmases ago, she had known that something was wrong. The boy hadn't been himself. He walked into rooms and then, without speaking, walked out again. The unwavering self-confidence that had defined him for as long as she could remember seemed to be missing. Finally, he had sat down with her in the kitchen. She had made them both a cup of coffee and then from her secret stash produced two orange Club bars because they were his favourite and it was Christmas. She tried to help him. 'Is everything all right? In Dublin? With you?' It was that point on a winter's afternoon where you're not sure if you should have the lights on or not. In the encroaching dusk she couldn't really see his expression, but the moment she heard his voice she realised what he was about to tell her. She felt like such a fool for not realising her son was gay before now that she found it hard to concentrate on what he was saying.

Everything made sense to her. It wasn't perhaps the life she would have chosen for her son; she knew how cruel people could still be, but she understood the world was a very different place now and Finbarr had always seemed like one of those people destined for success. She doubted very much if this news was going to change that.

She tried to focus on what he was saying. There was no one special in his life yet. He was still her son. Nothing had changed. She found tears springing into her eyes. She was both touched and surprised to find that he seemed to care what she thought, that he was seeking her approval. She reached across the table to hug him and it felt like the easiest embrace they had shared for many years.

'Will you tell Dad?'

'Do you not want to?'

'It would be better coming from you.' Finbarr's face looked almost babyish. Ellen patted his hand.

'He'll be fine.'

Ellen tried to imagine how the conversation with Martin would go, but struggled. She understood why Finbarr would want her to be his proxy.

As she stood outside her husband's study door, she felt strangely alive. Her heart had begun to beat faster and she could hear her own breathing. This was better than passing off ready meals as home-made. This felt more like opening the study door and lobbing in an emotional hand grenade with the pin removed. Of course, she hoped that Martin could still accept and love their son, but she also relished the thought of telling him that his son wasn't the man he wanted him to be. Finbarr had seized the controls to his own life, and she was certain that would distress her husband. She remembered the sulking that had gone on when Finbarr announced he wasn't going to study medicine. Ellen found that she was smiling, so quickly recomposed her face and knocked on the door.

Inside, Martin sat in a pool of light from the desk lamp. He took off his glasses and peered at her as if he had just noticed rain had begun to fall. Ellen clenched her jaw. Was this what he was like with patients? She cleared her throat.

'It's about Finbarr.'

After she had passed on Finbarr's news, Martin examined his fingernails for a moment and then asked, 'When did he tell you this?' Ellen explained and then her husband just said, 'Right,' before turning back to his computer. Ellen stood silently for a moment expecting Martin to say more.

'Will you . . . will you speak to him?'

Without looking up, her husband gave a grunt which she assumed was one of agreement, so she turned and left.

Dinner was served without incident. Ellen passed around dishes with artfully placed lumps of microwaved chicken that she had carefully charred under the grill before serving. Ellen knew it probably took her more time and effort producing these fake meals, but she didn't care. It was the ownership of the secret that she enjoyed. That was hers, and hers alone. Aisling dominated the conversation with excited chatter about the ski trip she was going on after Christmas. Ellen was tight-lipped in her disapproval. It was too much money, but of course Martin had said yes. It seemed to Ellen that Aisling had always been given everything she had ever wanted. So had Finbarr, but somehow, he didn't seem quite as unappreciative. At least he would pop in and see his grandparents above the pub without being asked, whereas Aisling treated Dan and Chrissie as if they were subhuman.

Ellen glanced between her husband and her son. They both seemed unperturbed. Aisling headed back to her room, before Martin excused himself and went to sit with his mother, leaving Finbarr and Ellen alone. She wondered how Martin could bear to spend so much time with his mother. Most of the time she didn't know him and if there was a ripple of recognition it was usually because she thought he was his father. She seemed to have erased her son entirely. Ellen found little to admire about her husband, but she was touched by his devotion to his mother.

'Did you tell Dad?'

Finbarr's voice broke the silence with an accusatory tone.

'Yes, of course I did,' Ellen replied defensively. 'Why? Has he not said anything to you?'

'No. Nothing.' Finbarr ran his hand through

his hair. 'Was he very upset when you told him?'

Ellen considered this question, unsure of how to answer. The truth was that she really didn't think he was, but to just say 'No' made it sound as if his father didn't care.

'Not especially. He's concerned, obviously.'

'Concerned? What about?' His chin was thrust forward, as if spoiling for a fight, but Ellen could see the fear in his eyes.

'Oh, nothing really. You should talk to him.'

Later when she went to bed, Martin was already there, typing on his phone. Ellen occasionally wondered who he could be messaging but when she had asked, she was always told it was 'work'. Diagnosing people by text at half past eleven at night seemed unlikely to her, but she didn't care enough to pursue it. This marriage only worked if she didn't engage with it. Still she felt she should speak on Finbarr's behalf.

She sat at the dressing table and took off her earrings.

'Did you speak to him?' She addressed her husband's reflection in the mirror. It seemed easier.

'What?' He looked up, annoyed.

'Finbarr. Did you talk to him?'

Martin paused as if trying to remember who this Finbarr she spoke of was, but then he recalled.

'No. No I didn't.' He returned to his phone.

Ellen watched him as she took a small scoop of moisturiser and began rubbing it into her face. She assumed that even Martin might be compelled to say something more. Whatever their relationship might be, the one undeniable truth was that they were both parents of this young man. Surely Finbarr's revelation deserved some sort of discussion. But no, he was folding his glasses and putting the phone on the bedside table. Soon he would be asleep.

'Are you going to?'

Martin sighed heavily. 'What? What do you want me to say?'

'I just think he'd like you to say something. An acknowledgement at least.'

'His sexual proclivities are no business of mine.'

Ellen gripped the handle of her hairbrush tightly. She longed to throw it with all the force she could muster at the smug prig reshaping his pillow.

'You're his father,' she said, trying to keep her voice even.

'And you're his mother.' Martin spat the words out with an unexpected venom.

'What's that supposed to mean?' She had swivelled on the dressing-table stool to face him.

'Whatever that boy is now, you made him.' Martin had recovered his composure.

'We made him, Martin. Both of us. And we did a good job.' She meant what she said. Whatever her concerns about the children, she loved them, and their existence helped her to make sense of everything else she had endured over the years.

'This is the Hayes side of the family, that's for certain.' There was a challenge in his voice and in his eyes.

'What do you mean?' She had no idea what he was talking about. Her husband raised his eyebrows.

'Are you seriously suggesting that you didn't know Connor was a homosexual?'

The shock that Ellen felt was twofold. Hearing Martin say her brother's name seemed scandalous, dangerous even, while the subject of Connor's sexuality had never crossed her mind. Was she stupid? Had it been obvious in some way? Had her parents known?

'I . . . we . . . . Why would you say that?'

'Enough. Just go to sleep. I have house calls in the morning.' His hand shot from beneath the cover to switch off his bedside lamp. The conversation was over.

Ellen stood. She had more questions. Things she needed to say. The mound of Martin lay unmoving, his face turned away from her. She reached down and switched off her own lamp. Standing in the darkness, she could hear Martin's breathing already becoming slower. The glow of the street lights crept over the curtains and left small patches on the ceiling. Ellen reached for the duvet but then decided against it. She couldn't go to bed now. The thought of lying down next to Martin was more than she could bear. She walked across the room and out into the hallway. The stairs creaked as she descended them. On the lower landing the light was still on in Aisling's room, but Finbarr's was in darkness. Down in the kitchen Ellen nursed a cup of tea she didn't want.

Connor. Poor Connor. Could it be true? There

had been no girlfriends that she could remember, but equally he'd always had sexy posters of female pop stars on his walls. Even if it was the truth, that didn't explain why Martin had brought it up. If it was an open secret then surely she would have heard something at school, or gossip around the town? Had Martin made it up to try to hurt her?

She thought about her son sleeping in the room above her. Could he be gay in Mullinmore? She assumed that he could. She saw flamboyant kids waiting for the school bus and if they weren't gay, they certainly looked it, and they were surviving. Her parents would have to be told. She didn't want them hearing from someone else. Perhaps when they heard about their grandson, they might mention Connor, tell her something about the boy she could scarcely remember.

Sometimes she would catch a glimpse of a man in the street that reminded her of her brother, but always the man he had been when he left. Who knew what he looked like now? Maybe he had already slipped in and out of Mullinmore without telling anyone.

When she had finished her tea, she put the cup in the sink and headed to the foot of the stairs. Climbing them suddenly seemed like a task beyond her capabilities. She padded across the living room and opened the door into the former dining room. The dark shape of her mother-in-law lay in the single bed on the other side of the room, hospital bars keeping her safe. Ellen drew closer and looked down at the old woman's face.

Her jaw was slack and her breath rasped slowly through the wetness of her mouth. In the half-light Ellen saw the tongue twitch. She wondered if she still dreamed. Did she know the people in her dreams or were they, too, just nameless faces moving through forgotten scenes? Ellen was always struck by how placid old Mrs Coulter remained. She never seemed confused or frightened. Had she lost her memory or escaped it? Being untethered from your own past didn't seem like that awful a predicament to Ellen. She stroked the waxy hand that lay on the covers and crept away, back to her life.

* * *

After Finbarr had phoned with the news of Connor in New York, Ellen was reminded of the strange conversation with Martin. It seemed he had been right. Well informed rather than vindictively inventive. She should have known. It was a conversation she might have with him again, but not till Monday. Martin was off in Birmingham for the weekend at yet another medical convention.

At the kitchen table, her mother was bemoaning the state of the traffic in Mullinmore.

'Honestly, the roads are up more than they're down.'

'Says the woman who doesn't drive,' came a voice from behind the newspaper.

'I still have to get around.' Chrissie rolled her eyes at her daughter. 'Is Aisling back this weekend?'

'No. Not this weekend. I doubt that we'll see her before Christmas.'

'Isn't it well for her with all her friends? A real social butterfly, isn't she?'

'Yes,' Ellen replied without much enthusiasm. Since Aisling had unexpectedly got a place to do European Studies at Trinity, she had made it her mission to gather a group of friends that were as rich as they were ghastly. Ellen had only met them a couple of times, but she had walked away feeling sorry for all of them. Who had told her daughter that having money made people interesting? On good days Ellen told herself that it was just a phase and that Aisling would mature and discover what really mattered, but on other days, she wondered if she just didn't like her daughter very much.

'Any word from Finbarr? How's he getting on?'

As Chrissie asked the question, Dan lowered his paper, as if expecting a full update. Ellen took a deep breath. This was it. This was the moment.

She looked at her parents and suddenly the moment was gone. She realised that she didn't have the right words. Just to tell them that Connor was alive would have been a torment to them. She could hear all their questions, see her mother in tears, and herself just shrugging and saying, 'I don't know.' She resolved to get more information from Finbarr and then tell them everything. Maybe she could talk to Connor first.

'He phoned just now. He's having a great time.'

'Still in that bar?' Dan asked.

Ellen regretted ever telling them that it was a gay bar.

'Yes. I think he's making quite good money. He's a full barman now.'

'Good for him.' Dan raised his paper.

Walking home, Ellen thought about Connor and what she might say to him on the phone once Finbarr had managed to get his number, when she had an idea. Mullinmore. When she spoke to him, she would tell him to come home. That was the only thing that would satisfy her parents. Connor needed to walk into the pub one night with her at his side, like the magician's assistant revealing the most incredible trick of all time. She imagined the faces all around the bar smiling, people jumping up and slapping him on the back, all memories of the accident forgotten in their delight at Dan and Chrissie being reunited with their son. Little Dee Hegarty was gone, as was Maureen Bradley — cancer had taken her — while her husband Frank languished in a nursing home. Connie had re-married up near Port Laoise, and Kieran had been so young she doubted he could even remember his sister Bernie. Then she saw one face not smiling. It was a woman in a wheelchair. Linda O'Connell. Ellen stopped walking. She wondered what she should do. Just springing Connor's reappearance on her wouldn't be fair. The whole plan was so vague and unthought out, but there was no point going any further unless Ellen got Linda's blessing. She would go and see her, find a way to tell her the good news that the man who had paralysed her was coming home.

IV.

Franco was behind the bar slicing limes when Finbarr came through the door holding two coffees.

'I got you a latte.'

'Thanks, Irish.'

Finbarr put the cardboard cups on the counter.

'Am I still a barman?'

'Dunno,' Franco replied without turning around. 'Judson isn't in yet.'

Finbarr sat up on a stool and sipped his coffee.

'How was your Irish daddy last night?' Franco was chuckling.

'Don't even. You're not going to believe this. Turns out he's my fucking uncle!'

Franco turned around, mouth open. 'Oh my God! You didn't, did you?'

'No!' Finbarr almost shrieked his denial. 'The guy is old enough to be my — '

'Uncle!' Franco finished the sentence and the two men began to laugh.

'How big is your family? How could you not know your own uncle?'

Finbarr considered how much of the story to share. Three dead people seemed like they might spoil the mood. 'He's sort of the black sheep of the family. He left before I was born. It's mad because nobody knew where he was and then he just shows up at the bar.'

'It's a small gay world.' Franco swept the sliced limes off the chopping board into a metal bowl and placed them in the fridge. 'Are you planning on doing any work today?'

'What work? What's my job?'

'Well, I'm not the manager, but I would suggest you do bar-back prep because nobody else is going to do it.'

Finbarr groaned.

'Sorry, Irish.'

As Finbarr slipped off his bar stool the door opened and Judson staggered in carrying two heavy boxes.

'A little help please!'

Before either man could step forward, the boxes had been deposited on the bar.

'Thanks,' Judson said with a degree of sarcasm.

'What did you buy me?' Franco enquired in a breathless Marilyn Monroe voice.

'I didn't buy anything!' Judson was smiling. 'That stupid hummus restaurant below me finally shuttered, and as about their only customer I claimed all their beer glasses. Can you put them through the washer for me, Irish?'

'Sure.' Finbarr went behind the bar and opened the first box. 'So, Judson, I was wondering: am I still a barman?'

'Oh.' Clearly Judson had forgotten about the bar's staffing problems. 'I'm not sure. How did he do last night, Franco?'

'He coped.'

Finbarr quickly interjected: 'More than coped! What about the big tips, Franco?'

'True. Though most of that was your drunk Irish uncle.'

Judson turned to Finbarr. 'Oh, I think I've heard about that guy. Asleep in the garbage?'

'That's him.'

'Ben told me about him.'

'Red wine Ben?' Franco asked. 'How does he remember anything?'

Finbarr looked at one man, then the other. 'Excuse me. Forget about my uncle the lush. Am I barman?'

Judson sucked his teeth. 'For tonight, but you're also the bar-back. I'm sticking around so I'll see how you fare.'

'Great!' Finbarr couldn't pretend not to care. He went back to work with renewed enthusiasm. This was his success and he was enjoying it.

All things considered, this had been a good day. The phone call to his mother about finding Connor had been strange but also satisfying. He felt something had shifted in their relationship during the call. He wasn't sure if it was because she had treated him as an adult or if it was the first time he had ever seen his mother as a person rather than just one of his parents. The way she had reacted to his news had made her sound young and conjured up a woman who existed outside of nagging him to fold his clothes or calling the family in for dinner. His only slight regret was that he felt he had given his mother too full a picture of his life in New York. He had been liking the anonymity of his time in the city, relishing having a life that was his alone. He enjoyed not being the doctor's son and not being the most beautiful boy in the bar. He suspected that the sudden reappearance of his long-lost uncle was going to spoil all of that.

* * *

Thirty blocks north, Uncle Connor was lying face down on his bed, his face pressed into the pillow, a small stain of drool forming on the fabric. He had phoned in sick and in truth he really didn't feel very well. When he had got back to his apartment, he had peeled off his clothes, drunk two large glasses of water and collapsed on the bed like a body falling from a great height. Spread-eagled, he longed for sleep to spirit him away, but his mind would not be stilled.

Unwittingly, Finbarr had set Connor's brain on fire. His thoughts crackled with questions, while any notion of how he should respond to the news from home seemed lost in clouds of indecision and doubt. One name echoed around his mind ceaselessly. Martin Coulter. His sister had married Martin Coulter. They had children together. His parents probably spent Christmas with them. Did his mother call Martin Coulter son? It was an anger he had never felt before. Part of him wanted to get on the next plane back and show up in Mullinmore, knocking on doors, settling scores, causing trouble, but of course it was too late for that. That's what made this fury so intense. So much of it was reserved for himself. This mess was really his fault because he had run away and refused to go back. His fear and shame had allowed this unholy situation to occur. He groaned. He wanted to throw up again. He wondered if he had any painkillers. Probably not. That was Tim's department. He pulled his pillow towards himself in a childish embrace. Connor missed Tim. He wanted him to be here, holding him, telling him that everything was going to be all right. He would finally confess everything to Tim and then he would know what to do.

Connor thought of all the times he had refused to bring Tim back to West Cork. The excuses and lies, all easily accepted by Tim, who wasn't really that keen to meet Connor's family but no doubt felt he should at least seem willing. If only Connor hadn't been so short-sighted. Stupidly he had believed that this was his story and that by never returning he could make it end as it had for Bernie, David and Carmel that summer's evening at the roundabout. For the first time in many years he allowed himself to consider the others. The Bradleys with their surviving daughter Connie and the brother whose name he couldn't remember; poor little Mrs Hegarty; Linda O'Connell — was she even still alive? His own parents and Ellen, their stories continuing to be defined by what had happened. Leaving had solved nothing, had helped nobody. But going back now, what could that achieve? Surely, it would just make everything worse.

Outside, two helicopters chopped through the air, the noise bringing him back to Manhattan, back to a studio apartment that wasn't even his.

V.

Green knots of weeds were wedged beneath the stained concrete of the ramp. Ellen cautiously climbed the gentle slope to the front door and rang the bell. She was now regretting the bottle of wine she had brought. It had seemed polite when she was choosing it in the off-licence, but now standing outside the house she felt it looked like some sort of insensitive bribe. Sorry about your legs, here's an expensive bottle of Chardonnay. Oh well, too late.

When the bell rang, Caroline O'Connell at the back of the house assumed it must be Pat who came in to help with Linda. Perhaps she'd forgotten something. It was too early for Declan to be back from golf and besides he had his own key.

They didn't have many visitors these days. Caroline kept herself as busy as she could with charity work and local committees, but they were mostly in the evening. The majority of her days were spent with Linda. She loved her daughter, of course she did. There wasn't a day went by that she didn't think about poor Carmel and thank God that Linda was still alive. As well as thanks, she did mention some other things to the Almighty, mostly questions or requests. Could Linda share that gratitude? Would Declan re-join the family? Please make this a good day for her daughter. Sometimes her prayers were answered and the two of them passed pleasant hours, reading or chatting, even laughing at some bit of gossip from the town. More often, however, it was as if dark clouds had settled over the room and nothing could please Linda or remove her from the grip of gloom. She either sat in silence or if she did speak, every word was dipped in vitriol or sarcasm.

Caroline did her best to sympathise. More than anyone she knew how hard this life was for her daughter, but she just wished that Linda could see that this had happened to all three of them. She and Declan tried over and over to make the best of things, so why couldn't Linda? The ramp, the specially adapted car, all purchased at vast expense, but never used. Friends and neighbours had been wonderful at the start but one by one they had been driven away by one of Linda's bad days. Even Caroline invented more housework than there was just to avoid having to sit with her daughter. She had hoped that when Declan retired, he might have shared some of the burden, but he had simply swapped the office for the golf course. It didn't matter what the weather was like, after breakfast off he would go. Caroline suspected that some days he never made it onto a fairway but just hid in the clubhouse all day, sipping the hours away with the other men, outlaws in V-necked jumpers on the run from their own families. She wanted to be angry with him, but she understood how ill-equipped her husband was to deal with the situation. She coped with Linda because she could. Besides, he allowed her to enjoy some freedom in the evening. Of course, that was much easier. Caroline made food for him and Linda before she went out, then a couple of hours of television before Pat or someone else from the agency returned to get Linda back into bed and settled for the night. Sometimes when Caroline got home, she would bring her daughter a last cup of tea and they would sit in the soft glow of her bedside lamp and swap inconsequential snatches of conversation. Often this was the favourite moment of the day for both women.

'Ellen!' Caroline O'Connell couldn't disguise the surprise in her voice. 'Nice to see you. Will you come in?' She stepped back.

Ellen cleared her throat. 'Well, I actually wanted to have a word with Linda. Is this a good time?'

This was even more unexpected. Caroline had assumed this had something to do with the meals on wheels or the fundraising for the new defibrillators.

'Of course, of course. Come in. She'll be thrilled to see you.' Caroline hoped this was true. When she had checked in with Linda earlier, she wasn't in one of her blackest moods but that was no guarantee she would be pleased to see Ellen Coulter coming through the door with what looked like a bottle of wine.

'Just through here.' Caroline led her visitor into the front living room. 'If you want to wait a moment, I'll just make sure she's . . . ' The words

Caroline were thinking of were 'civil' and 'safe' but the one she used was 'ready'. 'Just make sure she's ready.' She slipped through the sliding double doors.

Linda was in her wheelchair by the window. A book lay pages down in her lap. She looked at her mother expectantly. 'Who's that?' Her voice gave nothing away.

'It's Ellen Coulter come to see you.' Caroline gave a smile to suggest that this was marvellous news.

'Ellen Hayes to see me? Why?'

'I've no idea, pet.' She lowered her voice to a whisper and pointed behind her to the doors. 'She's just there.' And returning to normal volume, 'Will I send her in?'

Linda sighed and shrugged her shoulders. 'I suppose.'

Caroline slid open the doors.

'Here she is now.' It wasn't clear which woman she was speaking to.

Ellen stepped forward and approached Linda. She held out her gift bag.

'I got you a little something.'

'Thanks,' Linda said, taking the gift. She peered inside the long glossy bag. 'Wine. A bit early for me.'

Caroline winced. 'That's very nice of you, Ellen. I'll just put it in the kitchen.' She reached forward and took the bag. 'You'll have a cup of tea. Linda? Another cup?'

Linda gave her mother a look that made Caroline fear she had inadvertently done the wrong thing. 'Sure. Why not? Live a little.'

'Sit down there.' Caroline indicated the low armchair she usually sat in herself and hastily left the room, grateful to escape for a few moments.

'Your mother looks great,' Ellen said as she sat down.

'Mammy's Mammy. Never changes.'

Ellen wasn't entirely sure if that was a good or bad thing, so she chose to ignore it.

'How are you yourself, Linda?' Ellen had crossed her hands in her lap. She felt very middle-aged.

Linda patted her thighs. 'Great, thanks. They say I'll be walking by Christmas.'

Ellen beamed and burst out with a 'That's great!' before she realised that Linda was being sarcastic. She had been in her chair for nearly twenty-five years. Things were not about to change. Ellen must have looked stricken because Linda took pity on her.

'Sorry. I'm just being stupid. This is how I am.' She indicated her wheelchair.

'Well, you look well,' Ellen said with an exaggerated degree of caution.

'Thank you.' Linda smiled and so did Ellen.

'How have you been? Your kids must be all grown now?'

'Yes. Aisling is up in Dublin. Final year of uni this year. Finbarr is over in New York working, but just for the summer. God knows what he'll do after that.'

'It's so odd. I still think of you as a young one going around the town in your school uniform.'

Ellen laughed. 'That was a while ago now.'

'The world keeps turning. It's just that in here

nothing really changes.'

Linda turned her head away and the light from the window cast a shadow, hiding her face.

'You don't get out much?' Ellen asked.

Linda turned back and flashed a smile.

'In the beginning I didn't want to and now, well, it's too late. They offer, but trying to get me in and out of the car would kill them.'

Ellen wasn't sure what to say. She didn't want to contradict Linda, but at the same time, it seemed so final.

'They could get help?' Ellen knew someone came in to get Linda in and out of bed.

'They could.' Linda pressed down on the arms of her wheelchair and shifted her weight. 'It just seems a lot of trouble to go to so that I can see the new café at Lawlor's garden centre or drive through the Jack Lynch Tunnel.'

Ellen nodded. The two women sat for a moment in silence, but it wasn't awkward. They knew each other, had an unspoken shared history: teachers' names, the boys that everyone had fancied, the girls that would go all the way, the blow-ins, what shop used to be where . . . These things mattered. They might look different, with streaks of grey and wider frames, but in the quiet of the room, they recognised each other.

The door opened and Caroline returned carrying a tray. She placed it on a side table beside an overly enthusiastic spider plant. Ellen noticed a photograph in a dark wooden frame that was also on the table. It was Linda and her sister Carmel. They were both wearing bright summer tops and the sky was an endless blue behind them.

'Milk?'

'Just a drop, thanks.'

'There's a biscuit there if you want one.' Caroline took a plate off the tray. 'Help yourself. Have you got everything you need, love?' Linda nodded.

'I'll leave you to it so.' She stood for a moment but neither of the younger women spoke. 'To catch up.' Her voice trailed away as she left the room.

'That's a lovely photo of the two of you.'

Linda turned and glanced towards the table.

'That was taken the day of the crash,' she said matter-of-factly.

'Really?' Ellen couldn't disguise her surprise that anything worth remembering had survived that day.

'Bernie took it. They found her camera in the car and Mrs Bradley had the film developed.'

'I wonder if she had any of Connor,' she pondered out loud and immediately regretted it.

'She might have. God knows where they'd be now though. That house has been all packed up.'

Ellen nodded in agreement and took a sip of her tea. The mention of her brother's name didn't seem to have caused any obvious upset. She knew that she should come to the point or it would just be a repeat of trying to talk to her parents. At least Linda had brought up the crash herself and it didn't seem to be taboo. She cleared her throat.

'It was sort of that day I wanted to talk to you about.'

Linda put down her cup. 'Oh.' Did she sound defensive? Ellen continued, 'It's just that, well, I've found Connor again.'

Linda seemed entirely composed. 'Found him?' she asked, her head at a slight angle.

'Well, you knew he was missing?' Surely the whole town knew that Connor Hayes had vanished?

'Sorry. Yes, of course I knew you lost track of him, but . . . ' Linda hesitated. 'I just thought that he must have made contact again at some point. Sorry. I don't know why I thought that. Where is he?'

Ellen was trying to gauge Linda's reaction but couldn't.

'New York. My Finbarr bumped into him.'

'Amazing.' It seemed as if Ellen was telling Linda a story that had nothing to do with her.

'Listen, I haven't told anyone this. I didn't say anything to Mammy and Daddy yet. My plan, and this is why I wanted to see you, my plan is to talk him into coming home.'

'Right.'

Ellen felt she needed to explain further. 'It's just my parents, well, they aren't getting any younger, and if they could see him again . . . ' She stopped speaking, hoping that Linda might be forthcoming with some form of agreement, or sign that she understood. The only expression on Linda's face was one of puzzlement.

'That sounds lovely, but what did you want from me?'

'Well,' Ellen began to speak but then wondered how to phrase the question. How did you ask someone if they'd mind the idea of confronting the person who'd killed their sister and left them paralysed?

'I just didn't want you to be upset.'

'Upset?'

'It might be hard, I don't know, knowing that the person who was driving that car will be walking around the town. I suppose I just wanted to warn you. I wouldn't want you hearing it from someone else.'

Linda sat back in her chair. She took a deep breath and then spoke very slowly.

'Connor? You think Connor was driving the car?'

Ellen felt uneasy. She knew that something was shifting. 'Yes,' she replied because it was the truth.

Linda's mouth twitched. A hint of a smile. Of sadness? Of pity? Both?

'Connor wasn't driving that day.' Her voice was soft.

Ellen was so surprised she assumed she couldn't have heard correctly.

'What?' She swallowed hard. She clutched the arms of her chair.

'Your brother. Connor. He wasn't driving. I thought you knew.'

Ellen felt as if she didn't know anything any more. Connor had killed people. He had been punished. Their lives had been blighted by his crime. How could that not be the truth? She was suddenly very frightened. She opened her mouth to ask a question, but she had an awful suspicion that she already knew the answer. She craned forward and almost whispered, 'Linda, who was driving the car?'

'You don't know?' Linda was incredulous.

'No,' Ellen snapped but in that moment she did.

'It was Martin.' Now it was Linda who looked apprehensive, frightened of the reaction this news might provoke. 'I'm sorry. I always thought you knew.'

Ellen could feel herself begin to shiver. Martin. Could it be true? Had Linda received some brain damage they didn't know about? But just as quickly as her thoughts searched for ways to make this news untrue, they had added together the pieces of her life and confirmed Linda's story. Of course it was true.

'Why, why didn't you say anything at the time?' She couldn't stop shaking.

'I was in a coma up in Dublin. When I came round, it seemed too late. Everything had been decided. Connor had gone.' She shrugged her shoulders. Ellen looked at her aghast.

'I tried to tell my parents,' she added, defensively.

'But why wouldn't any of you come forward?' Ellen was remembering her brother leaving home with his towering backpack, her sobbing mother slumped by the door. Her own eyes now filled with tears.

Linda was squirming in her chair. 'You've got to understand. My speech wasn't very good back then and they just thought I had got things mixed up. Later when I was clearer, they still didn't believe me. Connor had taken the blame so that was the only story that made sense to them. Nothing was going to bring Carmel back and . . . they just thought . . . we were busy dealing with this.' Her voice had risen as she indicated her wheelchair. With a flash of anger she added, 'We had our own problems!'

'But Connor, he was innocent.' Ellen allowed her tears to flow freely. 'Why would you let an innocent man take the blame?'

Linda was looking very distressed now, but Ellen didn't care. She wanted answers.

'I thought you'd made some sort of deal. It was none of my business.' Linda's voice sounded high-pitched, childish.

'Deal? What do you mean deal?'

'You know. Don't make me spell it out!'

'Tell me! What deal?' Both women were shouting now.

'You and Martin. I thought that was the arrangement. Connor took the blame and you . . . ' Linda sank back in her chair.

Ellen gasped as if she'd been struck, the full horror of what Linda was saying slowly dawning on her. She stood, breathing heavily. She wanted to defend herself, to shout at this woman who had been locked in a room for decades. How could she understand? How could she presume to know what had gone on between her and Martin? But then she realised that she herself didn't know. She had never known. Her life. Martin's. Connor's. All built on a lie.

'Everything all right?' Caroline peered around

the door and looked shocked at what she found. She rushed to her daughter. 'Are you all right, pet? What is it?'

Before Ellen could hear Linda's answer, she picked up her coat and stumbled to the front door through a blur of tears. Outside, she held on to the railing of the wheelchair ramp, bent almost double. She was gasping for air. Why had she walked? How could she get home without the whole town seeing her in this state?

Finally, she understood that her humiliation was complete. She had thought it was a private thing contained within the walls of her home, but now, with a mounting sense of shame and horror she realised that it was entirely public. Ellen Hayes and her whole life was just some sort of bargaining chip. She was a get-out-of-jail-free card and nothing more. Her feelings, her happiness, not worthy of consideration. Standing upright, she wiped the tears from her eyes and tentatively walked out to the road. Head bowed she put one foot in front of the other, heading back to the house she had thought of as her home, to wait for the return of the man who had married her.

1987

XI.

Bernie was panicking. Her wedding was the next day. She pulled at the straps of her light cotton top.

'Is there a mark? Carmel, will you look? Am I after burning myself?'

Her friend and bridesmaid-to-be gave a cursory glance.

'I put factor fifteen on you, you can't have burnt.'

Bernie sank down on the low wall by the parked car.

'Why did I come? This is pure stupid. If I have tan lines with my dress tomorrow, I . . . ' She waved a hand in front of her face. David, her fiancé, knew that this meant tears were not far away. He sat on the wall beside her and put a protective arm around her neck.

'You'll be perfect, Bernie. Perfect.' He kissed her shoulder and was slightly disconcerted to see the skin turn momentarily white where he had pressed his lips against it. 'Maybe slip on my T-shirt just to be sure.' He took off his top and Bernie wriggled into it.

A bit late for that, thought Linda, Carmel's sister and non-bridesmaid, watching as the sun sank towards the horizon.

'Thanks, Dave.' The couple looked into each

other's eyes and kissed.

Carmel sighed. This was supposed to be a fun day out, a last hurrah for the old gang, but really she was sorry she had come. Bernie and David all over each other, her sister Linda with a puss on her all day, and Martin, well, he was the worst of all. She knew the only reason he had been included was because he had a car. He had never really been part of their old gang, but David had insisted that they should accept the offer of a lift. Bernie had been nearly as bad — you'd have thought that they'd never been in a car before, so excited were they at the prospect. Now, Carmel was having to fight the urge to say that she'd told them so: Martin might look cooler now with his car and his floppy hair, but he was still an oddball. Why had he dragged along the kid from the pub? And then refusing to stop in Schull so they could get ice creams. He had sworn blind there was a shop with a freezer in Trabinn but there was no such thing. She was starving, and there was no sign of Martin with the keys to the car.

While the lovebirds were crouched on the low stone wall that surrounded the car park opposite the caravan park, the two sisters leaned on either side of the blue estate car. Small drifts of sand were daubed haphazardly around the dusty tarmac. For once there seemed to be no breeze and the flag announcing the entrance to the caravan park hung limply by its scratched and faded pole. Linda kicked one of the tyres. She had thought this invitation was some sort of olive branch from Bernie and Carmel, but they'd both been right cows ever since they left Mullinmore. Barely a word out of them.

'Look, should we start walking over to Crookhaven? There'll be a pub or something.'

Bernie was bent over, her hair cascading around her face like a curtain. 'I can't walk all that way!' Her voice came from beneath the hair and had an edge of hysteria. 'In case you didn't know, I'm getting married tomorrow.'

Linda looked away towards the caravan park, and almost under her breath said, 'Oh, we know you're getting married all right.'

Bernie's head sprang up. 'And what's that supposed to mean?'

Her face did look quite red.

David stroked Bernie's arm and muttered calming words into her ear.

Carmel suddenly lifted both of her arms into the air triumphantly. 'Thank fuck. Here comes Martin.' She was pointing now across the dunes where a single dark-haired figure was silhouetted against the setting sun.

'Thank Christ,' Bernie said and lowered her head once more beneath its screen of hair.

'Where's young Connor?' David asked.

Carmel had almost forgotten the Hayes lad. He had been so quiet in the car and then followed Martin to some spot where you could dive. None of the girls had wanted to get their hair wet so they had all stayed on the beach and of course David had been glued to Bernie's side.

'There he is,' said Linda, spying someone slightly shorter trailing about fifty yards behind Martin.

'The car is going to be like an oven,' Bernie lamented.

As Martin reached the far edge of the car park and made his way towards them, Linda studied him. He was undeniably good-looking and there was a confidence in the way he walked that was appealing, but at the same time there was something else. He acted as if he was older than the others, or thought he was better than everyone else in the town. Linda wasn't sure she even liked him very much.

Martin's shirt was flapping open and he had his bag slung over his shoulder. In one hand he was swinging a large nearly empty bottle.

'Is that cider?' David called to him.

'Where did you get cider?' Bernie had re-emerged from under her hair.

'Brought it with me.' Martin grinned.

'Thanks for telling us,' David said. 'We've had warm Fanta and a packet of crisps from the shop across the road.'

'Are you all right to drive?' Carmel asked.

'Of course I am,' Martin replied dismissively and drained the last of the bottle before throwing it with a clank into the bin by the wall.

By now Connor had reached the others. He looked as if he had caught the sun. He just re-joined the group without saying anything. It was a mystery to everyone why Martin had bothered to invite him to tag along. Maybe he had supplied the cider from the pub, thought David.

Martin had opened the driver's door and was rolling down the window.

'Probably want to get all the windows down. Let it cool for a minute.'

David opened the passenger side and the back door, then lowered the windows.

Bernie stood. 'Right, the bride bagsies the front seat!'

Linda rolled her eyes. The sooner this wedding was over the better.

David stood at the back, arm outstretched invitingly. 'Ladies.'

Carmel stepped forward, but then turned to Connor. 'Do you want to be in the middle this time?'

Before Connor could answer, Martin stepped to the rear of the car. 'No. Connor can get in the boot.'

'Ah, no need, there's plenty of room.' Linda stood back, to let Connor into the back seat.

'No,' Martin said firmly and took hold of Connor's shoulder. He lifted the rear door and pushed the boy forward.

'Come on, Martin. Cool it.' David looked concerned. Was Martin drunk? What was going on?

'If it's good enough for a dog, it's good enough for Connor Hayes.'

'It's fine. Honestly,' Connor said quietly and curled up in the space behind the back seat before Martin slammed the rear door of the estate.

Bernie was already in the car, but the others exchanged glances. Linda raised her eyebrows. None of them knew what was going on, but nobody cared especially. It was enough to know that they were heading home.

From the moment they drove off it was as if Martin was trying to hurt Connor. He took corners too quickly, braked suddenly behind other cars. They could hear Connor's body sliding and thumping from side to side. At first David tried to make a joke of it. He turned and grinned at Connor lying in the back. 'You better hold on there!' Connor didn't react. It was unnerving.

After about twenty minutes of what seemed to be deliberately erratic driving, Linda poked her face forward. 'Martin, would you ever slow down a bit? It's mad bumpy back here.'

'Yes!' Carmel agreed. The sisters looked at each other and shook their heads. This was madness.

'Home soon,' was the only response they got from the driver.

David could see that Bernie was frightened. Her arms were braced against the glove compartment. He decided not to say anything so as not to concern her further. There wasn't far to go.

The coast road as it reached Mullinmore was straight and flat, but even so they all knew that Martin was going too fast. From where David was sitting it looked like the car was heading full pelt towards the grass island in the centre of Barry's roundabout. He held his breath and prayed that nothing was approaching on the right. The roundabout was clear. He breathed a sigh of relief, but then one of the back tyres hit the concrete kerb of the central reservation with a loud bang.

The girls screamed and Martin shouted, 'Fuck!'

The car lurched to the left and then they were on two wheels. For a moment everything was quiet and still, before the car crashed onto its side and began to roll. Glass was smashing, metal scraping along the tarmac. Carmel was screaming the loudest, but her head smashing into the side window knocked her into silence. The last thing Bernie Bradley saw was a freshly manicured nail being torn against the dashboard and a dark drop of blood appearing on her fingertip. Her final thought was of photographs being ruined. David was pushed between the two front seats and over the destructive roar of the crashing vehicle no one heard the gristly snap as his neck was broken. There was a rush of air as the boot door sprang open, throwing Connor free, before the car continued rolling and crashing through the bushes, down the bank.

Connor felt branches scraping his face before he landed with a bone-shuddering thud. He could hear the crashes of the car as it continued to roll down the bank, and then there was silence. The smell of grass and damp soil filled his nostrils. He stared at his hand, noticing a small cut blossoming into a slash of red. He wondered if he could move. Tentatively he wriggled his feet, then his legs. He pushed his hands against the earth and lifted himself. Down below, the car had landed on its wheels. He could see the driver's door was hanging open and then Martin slithered out on to the flattened grass. He remained on his hands and knees, breathing heavily. Then he turned his head towards Connor and their eyes locked. Slowly Martin began to crawl up the bank towards him.

Connor had lifted himself to a kneeling position by the time Martin reached him.

'You OK?'

'I think so.' Truthfully Connor didn't really know. He found it hard to believe that it was possible to be thrown from a fast-moving car and walk away.

Martin held on to what remained of the low metal barrier that marked the verge and stood. Apart from a small cut above his left eye, he looked remarkably unharmed.

'The others?'

Martin glanced down towards the wreckage. 'I don't know.'

There was a low slapping sound. It was Bill Lawlor from the garden centre running towards them.

'You did this,' Martin hissed.

'What?' Connor didn't understand.

'You were driving the car.'

Before any response was possible, their rescuer had reached them.

Bill Lawlor, obviously unused to running, was gasping for air. 'Is everything all right? Is anyone . . . ' His questions dissolved into steady panting as he saw the remains of the car below them.

'Is help coming? How many are there?'

Connor waited for Martin to speak, but he didn't.

'Has someone called an ambulance?' A note of

panic and dread had crept into Bill's voice.

Connor looked up.

'Four. There are four of them.'

'Six.' Martin contradicted him. 'Six altogether. The two of us and four in the car. You're the first. Nobody has called an ambulance.' Martin's voice had become almost eerily calm. He sounded like his usual confident, certain self.

'Right. Don't move!' Bill shouted and he began to run back towards Barry's petrol station.

Connor turned and looked down at the car. He could see Bernie's head through the windscreen and an arm, he wasn't sure if it belonged to Linda or Carmel, sticking out of one of the back windows. 'We must help them.' He started to stand up, but Martin pushed him back down again.

'So that's settled then. You were driving.'

Connor stared up at Martin. He had hoped that his request had just been a moment of panic.

'But I wasn't.'

'For fuck's sake. I'm going into my last year. I can't have done this. I was drinking. I'm going to be a doctor. A doctor.' He repeated the word as if Connor was simple or didn't speak English very well.

'But Martin, I wasn't. What about the others?'

'The others will say what they're told.'

Connor was incredulous that in the midst of all the carnage Martin had already figured out a plan to save himself.

'Martin.' His voice was pleading. He must see that this was an impossible request. 'I wasn't.'

Martin crouched down and grabbed Connor's shoulders. 'What does it matter to you? You're not going anywhere. I'm going to be a doctor. I can't ruin my life for this.'

Connor could feel the heat of the other man's breath in his face. He twisted around to look at the car. The bodies weren't moving, and the smoke was getting thicker.

'You're crazy, Martin. I can't. I just can't.'

Martin pushed his face into Connor's. One of his eyes was badly bloodshot. He spat out his words.

'You say you were the driver, or I will tell everyone you're a little cocksucker.'

The change of expression on Connor's face told Martin that he had hit a nerve.

'Do you want your parents knowing you're a little queer?'

'No.' Connor's voice was quiet. He sounded frightened, defeated.

'If you don't want everyone in the town to know that you're a filthy queer, you'll say you were driving that car.'

Martin paused, trying to gauge Connor's response. Their breathing had become slow and heavy. They studied each other's faces, until Connor broke away and bent over. Martin put a hand on his shoulder. 'You weren't even drinking. You'll be grand.'

Ten minutes later the roundabout was filled with emergency vehicles and people in uniforms. Sirens and flashing lights ripped through the still of early evening, informing the world of the horror.

Sergeant Doyle was huddled with Connor and Martin.

'And boys, who was in control of the vehicle?'

Connor looked to Martin who just stared back at him with a blank expression.

'The driver. Who was driving?' The sergeant clarified.

Connor squeezed his eyes shut, took two deep breaths, and then looked at the police officer.

'I was. I was driving.'

2012

VI.

He walked. But these were not the same exploratory rambles he had gone on when he had arrived in the city with Tim years before. These were entirely aimless. A venti coffee in hand he would walk down Ninth, then head east along streets he had no recollection of ever seeing before. Past small stores with clothes in the window that seemed like the very antithesis of fashionable New York. Garish sequins, synthetic fabrics in candy colours draped into evening gowns for mannequins from other decades or other continents. Someone must buy these things, Connor reasoned, but he struggled to imagine who that might be. The wind blew cold and bracing off the East River as he hit the edge of the island and then, on he went, heading north. Tudor City, past the United Nations, up to Sutton Place. Long anonymous blocks where he had never spent time, that held no memories for him. It was as if, having been found by Finbarr, he just wanted to lose himself again. He avoided Central Park precisely because it did conjure up days spent with Tim or one or two ill-advised trysts with strangers.

Once, but only once, Connor had allowed himself to head further south into the village. He crossed Christopher Street and then headed west along his old block. It was early evening and the lights were on in Tim's apartment. Connor had to stop himself thinking of it as home. He had avoided coming here, assuming he would find it upsetting, but in fact he felt very little. It was closer to a faint nostalgia than any form of pressing jealousy or regret. Perhaps this was what closure felt like? Recognising it as an affair that had run its course, rather than some grand passion that had been cruelly cut short. He wondered who was up there but was surprised to find that he had no desire to join them. The postcard Tim had sent him of a giant tyre somewhere in Detroit was still stuffed in the kitchen window frame. Odd, he thought. If he had been Carl, that was precisely the sort of memento he would have removed.

Now that it was the end of September, there was less work. Connor missed having somewhere to be, the guys in the van to trade banter with. The paucity of friends in his life seemed very marked. The usual phone apps gave him a certain level of social interaction, but he wanted to meet someone for a drink where there was no 'hot or not' negotiation. He found he longed for a shared history, for jokes about times past. Some nights he tried to persuade himself to head out to a bar and make conversation, or text one of the few friends who wasn't specifically linked to Tim and their life together, but the thought of that effort seemed worse than the few hours alone on his couch sipping glasses of wine till he could fall asleep. Connor knew that what he really wanted was a boyfriend, someone to rescue him, but who on earth was going to fall in love with a gone-to-seed man who hadn't showered in days? The only sign of time passing or things achieved were the number of pizza crusts accumulating on the coffee table before him.

He thought about Finbarr. It was very likely that his nephew had the answers to the questions that were caught like a log jam in his mind. At first, he had considered whether the truth might have come out back in Mullinmore, but then he reminded himself that his own sister had married Martin. She couldn't have done that if she knew the truth, could she?

What version of the story did Finbarr know? It would be so simple to just head back to Sobar and swap numbers. They could meet and pick over all that he had missed. Why didn't he, then? He knew he was afraid — but of what precisely? He felt he could bear hearing about the town still blaming him for what had happened, so it wasn't that. No. It was the same reason he had never joined Facebook. He told himself that he had never signed up because he didn't want to be found, but what really terrified him was the idea of discovering that everyone had simply forgotten about him and gone on with their lives. Just considering that possibility made his eyes well up and his breath come in shallow little bursts.

One night, with the courage provided by a bottle of Malbec, he went downstairs and hailed a cab. It dropped him on Seventh Avenue, and he walked the half-block down towards the red neon sign of Sobar. Connor paused outside, questioning the wisdom of this decision. He had lived without answers for so long; why did he need them now? Of course, he hadn't known Ellen had married Martin before, but how much would this kid know about his parents' marriage? Connor was about to walk away when two older men in suits came and stood behind him, obviously waiting for him to step forward and open the door. Going in seemed the simplest thing to do. The trio, Connor and the two strangers, climbed the couple of steps up into the dark, music-filled space. The suited couple walked towards the lounge area further back. Connor looked at the staff behind the bar. No Finbarr. He felt a sense of relief tinged with regret. He was off the hook. He could just head home again knowing that he had tried. A tanned muscular barman, older, maybe a manager, was smiling and waving from behind the bar. He did look familiar, but why? Connor had no specific recollection.

Judson leaned across the countertop.

'Hi, stranger. Long time no see. What are you having?'

Connor found himself ordering a vodka and soda.

'So how have you been?' The barman was still smiling. Connor was fairly certain he hadn't slept with him. A friend of Tim's? He didn't think so. 'Fine. Good.' He returned the smile in a non-committal way.

Judson put the drink down in front of Connor and said, 'On me' when Connor reached into the back pocket of his jeans for his wallet.

'Thanks . . . '

'Judson. You don't remember me, do you?' he said with an exaggerated air of disappointment.

'I'm so sorry. I know the face, I just can't recall . . . '

'Fire Island. We had a house share next to you a couple of summers back. I lit your barbecue for you.'

'Of course, of course.' Connor did remember that summer and the way that Tim hadn't even tried to hide how he had stretched from the bedroom window to check out Judson and his friends lounging by their pool. Tim had become almost skittish when the 'hot neighbours' had accepted an invitation to their Sunday afternoon barbecue. It was a side of Tim that Connor had never liked.

Judson raised his hand to pause Connor as a young woman with her hair in bunches shouted a drinks order over the bar. The other barman, younger and tattooed, waved at Connor as he walked past to the till. This was disconcerting because it was another person Connor could not recall.

'It's Irish daddy!' Franco said with a wide grin as he gave someone their change.

'You know this guy?' Judson asked.

'You remember. Finbarr's uncle. The sleepy one.'

Connor felt himself blushing.

'That was you!' Judson slammed his hand onto the bar, clearly enjoying the coincidence.

'Irish was trying to find you,' Franco added as

he moved to the other end of the bar to take an order.

'Is he . . . ?'

'No, you missed him. He did happy hour.'

'That's a shame.' Connor knew that he sounded awkward and unconvincing.

Judson came and put his elbows on the bar in a lull between customers.

'So, how's your boyfriend? Tim, right?'

'Yes. Tim. We broke up.' Connor still found it difficult imparting this information even to people like Judson who didn't really know them. It seemed so personal somehow and it always felt to Connor as if he was announcing to the world that he was a failure, that he had been found wanting.

'I'm sorry to hear that. You guys had been together a while, right?'

'Yes. More than sixteen years.'

Judson raised his eyebrows, clearly impressed. 'Wow. Long time. That's got to suck.'

Connor shrugged. 'You could say that.'

'Was it mutual?' Judson asked.

Connor bristled. He didn't know this man — why did he think he had a right to ask something that was clearly private? 'Something like that.' He drained his glass. 'Well, I only really popped in to see Finbarr. Thanks for the drink.'

'Do you want to leave him your number?' Judson turned and picked up a pen from beside the till.

Connor hesitated. 'No.' He paused, knowing he couldn't just leave it at that. 'I'll swing by again. Good to see you.'

'You too,' Judson called after him as he picked his way through the other drinkers towards the door.

* * *

Two days later Connor was lying in bed trying to remember if he had any milk when the door buzzer went. He sighed. He was sick of having to let in every FedEx and UPS delivery driver. Why had Tim bought an apartment in a building with no doorman?

'Hello?' He pressed against the intercom.

'Connor?'

'Yes.' Connor wondered who it could be. It was too early for some forgotten trick returning to the scene of the crime. Who else would know his name and where he lived?

'It's Tim. Can I come up?'

Connor froze. He looked around the room. The unmade bed. The tinfoil dishes from the Thai restaurant downstairs. The empty bottles on the kitchen counter. It was not a portrait of a happy human being. Fuck.

'Sure.' He tried to sound bright.

He pulled a fresh T-shirt on and tried to smooth out the duvet. He was just putting the bottles on the floor by the garbage can when there was a soft knock at the door. Connor felt nervous, as if he had been caught out. But that was ridiculous. This wasn't his boyfriend waiting to come in, this was a man who had removed him from his life. Why was he here? In the moment it took Connor to cross the room and open the door, a thousand scenarios flickered through his mind, from Tim sobbing on bended knee and begging him to come back, to him serving him an eviction notice so that Carl could move in.

'Hello.'

'Hi.' Tim looked serious. It seemed unlikely that he would be asking Connor to run away with him.

'Come in.' Tim took a step forward and then they were both in the apartment. Connor closed the door.

'Sit down.' Tim moved to the couch and sat. 'Coffee? It's just Folgers, nothing fancy . . . '

'I'm fine. Don't bother.'

Connor rested against the kitchen counter.

'It's been a while. Good to see you.'

'And you.'

The atmosphere in the apartment was strained, both men clearly uneasy. Connor wondered how, after all the time they had spent together, this was now how they were in each other's company. He recognised the shirt Tim was wearing. He couldn't help taking this as a personal affront. Clothing had outlasted him. Tim loved this short-sleeved button-down with its pattern of feathery fishing hooks more than he loved him.

'I was going to call.' Tim's hands were clasped between his knees and he wasn't looking at Connor, 'but I felt it was better to do this face to face.'

'Right.' Connor's heart was racing. Was Tim dying? Had he gone bankrupt?

'I had a call from your nephew.'

Connor was completely wrong-footed. This was not one of the scenarios he had considered.

'My nephew?' was the best he could do.

'Yes. Finbarr. You know who I'm talking about?'

'I do, yes.'

'He called me — '

'Wait. Sorry. Why did my nephew call you?' This made no sense.

'He called the office. He was looking for your number. I guess I know his boss.'

Connor nodded. This made more sense. Judson must have provided the names.

'I didn't give it to him; I didn't think that was appropriate. I've got his — he wants you to call him.'

Connor nodded again. 'OK.'

Tim looked up, into Connor's face. 'I think you should.'

A pause. 'Do you?' He wanted to shut this conversation down.

Tim looked at the floor again and speaking quietly said, 'I met with him.'

Connor said nothing. He didn't know what to say next. Tim raised his head, trying to read Connor's expression.

'Why didn't you tell me?'

Connor turned away. This was the conversation he had wanted to have so many times when they were together but never dared. How could someone continue to love a man after they discovered how stupid and cowardly they had been?

'I didn't know how. There was never the right time. I don't know. I was afraid it would change how you felt about me.'

'It was an accident, Connor. You were a kid.'

The two men turned to look at each other. Connor smiled. He had forgotten that Tim only knew Finbarr's version of the story. He didn't have the truth.

'That — that's not what happened.'

VII.

She could hear the carer, Annie Lynch moving around the kitchen, probably making something for Martin's mother to eat. Ellen wanted to tell her to go but she couldn't face her in this state. Quickly, she crossed the living room and slipped into the former dining room where her mother-in-law lay glassy-eyed. She would splash some cold water on her face in the en suite. The old woman watched her come and go across the room as if she was observing a car with a stranger drive by. Ellen wondered who she imagined she was. A nurse perhaps? Whoever it was, she seemed unperturbed by her presence.

Ellen checked herself in the mirror. Her eyes were still red but that could have been from a cold wind out walking, or tiredness. What did it matter? She just wanted Annie out of the house before Martin came home.

'Mrs Coulter,' Annie greeted her as she made her way into the kitchen. A small portion of scrambled egg was being scraped onto a slice of toast.

'You go, Annie. I can take that in to her.'

'Are you sure?' Her expression suggested that she wouldn't need to be asked twice.

'It's no bother. We'll see you in the morning.'

'Thanks, Mrs Coulter.' And with that she was

gone. Her footsteps paused in the hall as she took her coat and then there was the sound of the front door slamming. Ellen sighed.

Walking back from the O'Connells' she had seriously considered the possibility that she was losing her mind. The axis of her life had shifted so catastrophically that it altered every shred of what she had considered reality. Her marriage had been arranged but without anyone telling her. Was that the price her brother Connor had demanded for taking the blame? Why? She found it hard to believe that her future had been a concern or even a thought, in Connor's mind. She listed all the little things about Martin which now seemed so much worse: the way he slept, those small sighs of contentment that escaped his lips during the night, the smirk of superiority when he spoke to her, and all the time he had the deaths of three people on his conscience. It hardly seemed credible. Her mind went full circle and she considered once more the possibility of Linda O'Connell just making the whole thing up. It was insane but then why did she find herself so ready to believe it?

She carried the small plate into Martin's mother's room and sat by her bed. The old woman opened her mouth to accommodate each approaching forkful. There wasn't a flicker of hunger or enjoyment. Her little mouth just did what it always had. Chew, swallow, pause. She reminded Ellen of a tortoise steadily consuming a lettuce leaf. The egg finished, the old woman lay back on her pillows. Ellen stood.

'Tea?'

The filmy grey eyes swivelled towards her, but nothing was said.

'Would you have a cup of tea?'

The soft eyelids opened and closed a couple of times but that was the full extent of her response. Ellen stared at her. What was the point? Why did this heart keep on beating? What did it know that nobody else could see? Surely this body should just pack up and release the woman it held captive.

'I'll put the kettle on.' Her voice sounded loud and harsh in the hush of the bedroom.

On her way back to the kitchen she glanced down the hall. She was almost certain that Martin was due back this evening. After she had made the tea, she would check the appointments for tomorrow to make sure she was correct about the date of his return. As she stood waiting for the kettle to boil, she wondered what she would say. How did one begin a conversation like that? She didn't want it to escalate into a screaming match, but what would she do if he just denied everything? All she really hoped was that she didn't lose her nerve and allow the two of them to drift on in this lie. The easy option. The one she had taken over and over again, and this is where it had led her. This needed to stop, and she had to be the one to do it.

Ellen allowed the tea to cool before holding the cup up to the wrinkled lips that seemed to slurp of their own accord. She carefully patted the mouth and chin dry in between sips. The tea finished, Ellen made her way down the corridor into the surgery. It felt strange to be padding along the carpet tiles in the half-dark like this. Ellen reminded herself that she had every right to be there and made a point of turning on the glare of the overhead lights in the small waiting room. She had nothing to hide. The computer sat on the reception desk, but she was fairly certain Martin still kept an old-fashioned appointment book on his desk as a backup. She opened the door to his surgery. This did seem clandestine. As far as she could recall she had never been in this room all alone before. Ellen walked over to the desk. It was so tidy and perfectly ordered that one might have thought Martin was expecting someone to come in and inspect it in his absence. The large desk diary was sitting out, so Ellen leafed through the pages to that day's date. It was scored out but on the page for Tuesday there was a list of names with various medical notes. So he would be home tonight.

Ellen took a deep breath and wondered where she should wait for him. She closed the diary and replaced it exactly where she had found it. A sudden burst of curiosity swept over her. She had never snooped or pried into Martin's life. Her philosophy had always been that if it didn't affect her then she didn't care, but now, she found herself wondering what might be in the drawers of the desk. Her hand took hold of the wooden knob on the top right drawer and it opened easily. The contents were disappointing. Pens, an old chequebook, an assortment of paper clips. The next drawer down promised more. It was a series of white envelopes with dates on them. Ellen quickly figured out that these must be receipts from his various weekends away. She hesitated before opening one. Perhaps she would find evidence of his affairs. In fact, it was all quite dull. Petrol receipts, one from a pharmacy and then a large one from a hotel. She was about to put them back when she noticed the name of the hotel, Hilton Dublin. Odd. Ellen didn't remember Martin having business in Dublin. She checked and saw that he had spent three nights there, last month. Hadn't that been when he said he was in Edinburgh? She opened another envelope and there was another bill from Hilton Dublin. Ellen felt a flutter of excitement tinged with anger. A third envelope, Hilton Dublin, three nights. She gathered up all the envelopes. This was evidence of something, and he couldn't deny it. She carried them back into the house and then piled them on the kitchen table. Ellen stared at them for a moment and then strode to the fridge. This called for a glass of Martin's Pouilly-Fuissé.

She was halfway through the bottle when she heard the key in the door. She stood. She sat back down. Her eyes darted around the room. Was there somewhere else she should be? By the counter? Standing in the door to the back kitchen? Too late. The door swung open and Martin entered and crossed to the sink. He didn't look at her.

'Still up?'

'Yes.' Ellen wondered if the wine had been a good idea after all.

Martin was washing his hands. The elaborate

method he used had always annoyed Ellen but now she wanted to lunge at his wrists with a bread knife. She held on to the edge of the table.

'Mammy all right?'

'Yes.'

Martin turned as he dried his hands and for the first time looked at Ellen. She saw him register the bottle of wine and the envelopes. His hands dropped to his side. She enjoyed the flicker of uncertainty that played across his face.

'Did you have a nice time in Birmingham?' Her tone was archer than she had intended.

He held her gaze for a moment and then replied, 'Yes, thank you. I did.'

A pause and she asked again, 'Birmingham?'

Martin leaned back and peered at her. 'Why are you saying the word Birmingham repeatedly?'

Ellen licked her lips and swallowed. It was happening. It would begin now, and she had no idea where it might end.

'You're sure you weren't in Dublin?'

He pushed a hand through what was left of his hair. It reminded Ellen of when he had been a young man.

'What are you talking about?' His voice was low but deliberate.

Ellen poked the pile of envelopes with her finger.

'Edinburgh, London, Zurich. Dublin, Dublin, Dublin.'

Martin's expression hardened; his brows lowered.

'Why have you been going through my desk?'

'Why shouldn't I? Have you got something to hide?'

Martin lunged across the room. Ellen flinched but he just seized the envelopes of receipts.

'Where I go is no business of yours!' he snapped.

Ellen felt much calmer than she'd thought she might. Perhaps the wine had been a good idea after all.

'I'm sure you're right.'

Martin eyed her suspiciously.

'It's just that lying about it does make it seem like you've got something to hide, don't you agree?'

Martin raised his chin. 'I have nothing to hide. Now, I'm going to see my mother.' He turned to leave but Ellen stopped him by calling out, 'Why did you marry me?'

Martin didn't turn at once. He slowly rotated his body until he was facing Ellen. She had seen this face before, a mixture of pity and disgust.

'What?'

'You heard me. What was your reason for asking me to marry you?'

'How much of my wine have you had?'

'Not enough.' She picked up her glass and took a large gulp. She was goading him now. 'Well?'

'You really want to do this now?'

'Yes. Yes, I do. You can't have loved me. You can't have wanted this.' She swung her arm between them to indicate the emotional wasteland of their relationship.

Martin looked at the ceiling and then back to

her. He was going to answer. Ellen held her breath.

'I thought . . . ' He took a deep breath and when he spoke again his voice had changed. It was tired, almost defeated. 'Of course I didn't want this. I thought . . . ' His eyes scanned the room. 'I hoped . . . no, sorry, I believed — yes, that's it, I believed we could make something better. A kind of happiness. I really did.' He crushed the envelopes into his face. Ellen wasn't certain but she thought he might be crying. Despite herself she was moved; she had the urge to comfort him. She stood.

'So, it wasn't a deal?'

He lowered the crumpled pieces of paper.

'A deal?'

Ellen suddenly didn't feel so confident.

'Yes, with Connor.'

'Connor?'

'Because you were the one that was driving the car when it crashed.'

It was only the tiniest of reactions, but in that fraction of a second Ellen saw that Linda had been telling the truth. She lowered herself back into her chair.

Martin was rubbing at his damp eyes and shaking his head now. 'What are you talking about?'

'Finbarr found Connor in New York.' She felt calm once more, certain that she knew the truth.

'Connor. Connor told him that I was driving the car?' He snorted to indicate just how ridiculous an idea this was.

'No. No, it was Linda O'Connell who told me.'

Another beat, another flash of fear on Martin's face.

'Linda? She doesn't remember anything about the crash. She was in a coma.'

Ellen paused. There was a sheen of sweat on Martin's forehead.

'Well, her memory seemed pretty good this afternoon.'

'This is rubbish, just rubbish. You can't believe any of this, can you?' He was speaking loudly now, trying to affect his practised tone of intellectual superiority, but it sounded more like bluster.

'How could you?' Ellen asked quietly. 'You saw what it did to my family. You were there. You could have stopped it all.'

Martin took a step back and threw his arms out wide. 'Ellen, this is nonsense. You are talking utter and complete rubbish. You can't believe this. You can't.'

Ellen just shook her head slowly and said his name. 'Martin.'

He turned and touched the kitchen counter before looking back at her. 'Well if that is who you think I am then I'm leaving. I can't stay here with you.' He stood up straight as if the conversation was over. He had spoken.

Ellen took a step forward. 'Excuse me. You aren't leaving. I am.' She hadn't thought this far ahead but now a plan was forming in her head. 'You're not leaving me here with your mother.'

'Where will you go?'

'Your parents' bungalow. I'll throw some things in a bag.'

Martin opened and closed his mouth. Things had moved out of his control and he wasn't enjoying it. Ellen left the room and went upstairs. She moved swiftly between the bedroom and the bathroom gathering a few toiletries and clean clothes for the next day. She kept thinking that Martin would appear at the top of the stairs and demand she stopped what she was doing, but no. She heard him moving around downstairs. The familiar click as he closed the door to his mother's room.

Back in the hallway, she opened the heavy drawer of the sideboard and took out the keys to Martin's parents' bungalow. It had been for sale ever since old Dr Coulter had died, but was still just sitting there fully furnished. Ellen suspected that Martin didn't really want to part with it. Another piece of his precious father he couldn't let go. Her car keys were in her anorak pocket. She paused at the front door. Should she call 'Goodbye!' or at least indicate that she was leaving? Deciding that silence was the best option she opened the door and stepped out into the chill of the night.

She knew she was probably over the limit, but it wasn't far. Once behind the wheel of the car, the enormity of what she was doing suddenly hit her. She was leaving. Walking out on her marriage. She gripped the steering wheel tightly to stop herself shaking. The thought of doing this had always made her think of failure. She had imagined that everyone would think of her as weak or ungrateful, certainly lacking in some way to be abandoning the man who had rescued her, the doctor who had saved her whole family. Tonight, however, felt very different. Just the idea of slipping alone into cold damp sheets out on the coast road made her feel like a winner. This was winning.

VIII.

It was extraordinary to Ellen that something as unremarkable as a window with a different view could make the whole world seem so changed, but it was true. Just lying with every blanket she could find piled on top of her, contemplating the rust and orange leaves of autumn, rather than the bare sky and clouds that normally greeted her, gave her such hope. Things didn't have to stay the same, they could even improve. Through the leaves she could glimpse a blue sky and the trees were bathed in morning sun. She felt hopeful but also, she had to admit, very cold. She wondered if it was warmer outside.

Retrieving her clothes from the floor at the side of the bed, she dressed herself beneath the blankets before emerging and grabbing her coat off the chair by the window. She headed to the kitchen to start her day with a cup of black tea. She had forgotten to get milk after leaving Martin and his mother the night before. Already she was allowing herself to feel comfortable in the little bungalow. She could imagine herself living here. A fridge stocked with things she liked, no heavy dark furniture to polish, an entirely selfish existence. She'd need to sort out the heating but apart from that it seemed perfect.

Ellen sat with her hands wrapped around the warm mug, wondering how long the world would allow her to hide from it. Any moment now, she would get a call from Martin demanding her return, or maybe from her mother asking if she'd lost her mind. The tea reminded her that she was hungry. There had been no dinner last night and no supplies here, so she would have to go out. Ellen considered going for breakfast in the café behind the jewellers but then she thought about people asking questions. The slightly raised voices remarking that they didn't often see her at this time of day. Enquiries hanging in the air, the spores of gossip. No, she would buy something in the bakery, a bottle of milk, and bring them back to the bungalow. Maybe she could get a fire going if the autumn sun didn't begin to heat the place up soon.

She had just put her mug in the sink when she felt a vibration in her coat pocket. She wondered which name would be on the phone screen, who had noticed her absence first. Whoever it was, she resolved not to answer. Let them stew. Taking the mobile out, however, it wasn't Martin or her mother, it was Annie, the help. She hesitated. Maybe something was wrong or was it just Martin asking her to call because he knew Ellen wouldn't answer him. She chose to err on the side of caution.

'Annie?'

'Oh, thank God. Where are ye all?'

Ellen's heart felt like a stone.

'What do you mean? I went out early.'

'But there's no one here. The waiting room is full and nobody's been in to Mrs Coulter. She's after spoiling the bed. She's very upset.'

'I'm sorry. I'm sorry.' How had she allowed herself to believe that she could just walk away from her life with no repercussions? 'I'll be there as soon as I can.'

'Where's the doctor?' Annie asked as if Ellen's return was irrelevant.

'I don't know,' she barked down the phone.

By the time she was parking the car in front of the surgery door, Ellen could see her mother walking, almost running, down the street towards her. She waved when she saw the car. Ellen sighed. This was not what she needed.

'Mammy. What are you — ?' But before the question could be asked Chrissie was in full flow.

'Thank God. I was that worried. Where were you? Where's Martin? Your father went out to get the paper and heard the surgery was full and the little Angela one telling everyone that the two of you had vanished.' She paused. That was all the information she had and she now required Ellen to provide her with more.

'It's fine, Mammy. I'm here now. I think Martin is just sick. You go home and I'll sort all this out.' She went to cross the footpath to the door, but her mother held her arm.

'You must let me help, darling.'

'Help with what? You're not a doctor. I'll be fine. Go home. I'll phone you later.'

Chrissie looked shocked by her daughter's forthright manner.

'Well. If you're sure.'

'I'm sure. Go home.' Ellen resisted the urge to physically shove her mother away.

'Call me later.'

'I will.'

Once inside she opened the door to the waiting room. Several faces turned expectantly, but the disappointment was palpable when they saw Ellen standing before them. She remembered that she hadn't even glanced in a mirror this morning; she had no idea how dishevelled she might be looking.

'Good morning, everyone. I'm so sorry but I'm afraid Doctor Coulter isn't feeling very well, so today's appointments have been cancelled. He is very, very sorry, but Angela here can rebook for later in the week.'

Ellen smiled weakly and indicated the receptionist who appeared to be hiding behind her computer.

A small woman stood up, clutching her handbag to her chest like a shield. 'I am in severe pain. I have to see a doctor.'

Ellen knew the face. Galvin, was she? Casey?

'I'd say your best bet would be the clinic or you could always go to the chemist.'

'The chemist?' The woman was shrill with indignation. 'I'm extremely ill.'

'Well then, maybe you're going to die.'

The whole waiting room gasped. Ellen knew she had gone too far. She couldn't quite believe the words had come out of her mouth and nor could anyone else. Flustered by her own bluntness, it was time to make a retreat. She turned to leave, calling 'Angela!' over her shoulder as if that was a command rather than the name of the ashen young woman sitting slack-jawed behind the reception desk.

Ellen strode down the corridor and opened the door into the main house. Immediately Annie was by her side.

'You're back. Any word from the doctor?'

Ellen felt like swatting her away.

'How's Martin's mother?' she asked as she made her way to the stairs.

'Better, the poor old thing. I've cleaned her up. She's had her breakfast.'

The final words were almost shouted as Ellen was now upstairs. She headed to their bedroom and threw open the wardrobe. The little weekend bag wasn't there but maybe he hadn't unpacked from last night. The bathroom told a similar story. His toothbrush and razor weren't there, but again, they could still be in his case. The car. She had forgotten to look for his car when she had arrived back. She rattled down the stairs and out of the front door. She could hear Annie's voice somewhere in the house calling 'Mrs Coulter!'

No sign of the car. She was no wiser. Leaving the front door open she hurried to the corner to see if he had parked along the side street the night before. Sometimes he left the car in the little bay beside the bookies beyond the hardware shop. She ran across the road to go and look but she knew it wouldn't be there. Where was he? She slowly walked back to the open door. Ellen had no idea what to do next. He had probably just decided to punish her by disappearing for a few hours, but . . . no, that was stupid, Martin was not the sort of man to . . . was he? She tried to block out her worst fears. Ellen decided she would see if she could organise a locum for the afternoon and tomorrow. Angela could ring patients and let them know. Annie was there for old Mrs Coulter, so Ellen wondered if she should try and look for Martin. She had no idea where to begin and she knew that the guards would just laugh at her if she went to them.

By the time she stood in the hall she had managed to calm her breathing. She slipped off her coat and put it on the chair by the telephone. All her immediate concerns were temporarily held at bay. She felt like someone arranging sandbags to block an approaching flood, without knowing the scale of the deluge or how many bags she might need.

Tea. Ellen made a pot, put some mugs on a tray and took it through to the surgery. The waiting room was now empty of patients and Angela had put a hastily written sign on the locked front door informing people that the premises would remain closed due to illness. Annie followed with a plate of digestive biscuits. The three women sat on the hard plastic chairs normally occupied by the sick. They stared awkwardly at each other. Ellen knew she would have to tell them something, but the thought of sharing personal details of her life made her feel queasy and anxious.

'Sorry about this morning.' That seemed like a good place to begin.

Angela and Annie froze and looked at her expectantly. Ellen felt too hot and stood. Positioning herself in front of the reception desk, she addressed the room as if it contained an audience greater than the two ill-at-ease women facing her. Annie was chewing a biscuit, the dry crumbs scraping against her teeth. Ellen couldn't look them in the eye so focused instead on the noticeboard at the other end of the room. While she spoke, a poster was advising her what to do if she was in the presence of someone having a stroke. There was also a raffle to raise funds for the hospice. From outside came the noise of cars and the certain rhythm of footsteps that knew where they were going. The waiting area had taken on the air of a panic room or what Ellen imagined a wartime bunker might have felt like.

'Doctor Coulter . . . ' That sounded ridiculous. 'Martin, will be back soon I'm sure, but in the meantime if you could both carry on looking after the surgery and Martin's mother, I'd be very grateful.' She finished her short statement with a smile that she hoped assured her audience that there was in fact nothing to worry about.

'Has he left you?' Annie spoke. The question sounded detached, as if she was asking about strangers or characters in a soap opera. Angela leaned forward. This was obviously the question she had been too shy to ask herself.

'No.' Ellen blurted her reply. She could feel her face flushing. 'He, Martin, he, well, he'll be back soon and then we can find out more, but, well, as I say, sorry about this morning.' Unsure of what to say next and fearful of further questions, she walked out of the room. As she made her way down the corridor to the house, she could hear Annie and Angela whispering feverishly. Let them talk.

She hesitated outside her mother-in-law's room but then crossing the living room, she picked up her coat and headed out of the front door. At once Ellen felt conspicuous. There weren't many people around, but every eye seemed to be on her. She was transported back to the days after the crash all those years before. A renewed surge of anger towards Martin coursed through her. The lies, and now to just walk out, leaving her to . . . to what? Could she tell anyone what she knew? The truth seemed redundant when neither Connor nor Martin were here in Mullinmore to take responsibility for the new version of events. It wasn't her story to share. She thought of phoning Finbarr so that she could contact Connor to tell him what she now knew, but she couldn't call her son without telling him that his father had gone missing, could she? She had to eat something. That would make her feel better. She got into her car and began to drive.

Ellen couldn't have said where she was going but it helped being behind the wheel. It gave her a sense of purpose and made it harder for her mind to drift off into her darkest fears. About twenty minutes from the town along the Cork road there was a large petrol station. If she was lucky there wouldn't be anyone she knew in the convenience store that stood brightly lit behind the pumps. She parked on the forecourt and went in, the automatic door doing its best to make her feel like a valued and welcome customer. She grabbed an egg sandwich and a bottle of water before heading to the till.

'Any fuel?' The young man spoke with an accent. Eastern European?

'No. Just these, and, oh, this as well,' she said, picking up a bar of chocolate with whole hazelnuts in it. It seemed a healthier option.

Ellen keyed her PIN into the machine. She wondered where she would go to eat her sandwich.

'Declined.'

'Sorry?' She hadn't been listening.

'The card is not go through.' The young man informed her in his bored monotone.

Ellen was instantly flustered and looked in the back of her purse where she found a lone ten-euro note and handed it over.

'Sorry. Sorry about that.'

'It happen. Sometimes it is no the card. It is machine.'

He handed her back her change.

Hunger meant she ripped the sandwich from its wrapper immediately and ate it in the car. A quick slurp of water and then she broke the chocolate bar into pieces. She sucked them soft and then crunched through the nuts. She should call her mother but what was the point when she still knew nothing?

Martin. She should call Martin. Just because he hadn't answered the calls from the surgery didn't mean he wouldn't answer her. Why hadn't she tried already? She was a fool.

It went straight to voicemail. The phone must be off or out of range. Maybe he's on a plane. No. Her husband wouldn't run away leaving everything behind. That wasn't him. Or was it? Under different circumstances she might have found it almost amusing how little she knew about the man she had been married to for over twenty years. Ellen had to admit that she couldn't begin to go and search for him because she hadn't a single idea of where he might have gone. As a family they had taken trips to various beaches, the end of Mizen Head, that holiday in a rented cottage outside Westport, the time they took the car on the ferry to Wales for a week, but she couldn't believe that any of those destinations held a special significance for Martin. She crushed the foil from her chocolate into the empty plastic wrapper from the sandwich and rammed them deep into the pocket of the car door. Martin was just trying to worry her and then he would return with some story that would discredit Linda and place Connor back in the driving seat. What about Dublin? How was he going to explain all the other lies he had been telling? The hotel! Maybe he was back at the Hilton. She dialled her directory services and asked to be put through.

'Hilton Dublin!' An educated Dublin accent suggested bored efficiency.

Ellen felt nervous.

'I was hoping to speak to a guest. Doctor Coulter. Doctor Martin Coulter?' What would she say to him if he was there? She could hear her new friend stabbing at a plastic keyboard.

'I'm sorry. I can't see a guest by that name. Am I spelling it correctly?'

She checked and she was.

'No. No Doctor Coulter. Sorry about that.'

'All right. Thank you.' Ellen hung up, deflated that her one idea of where to look had proved fruitless. She tossed the phone onto the passenger seat and started the engine. Maybe Martin was at that very moment sitting behind his desk catching up with emails. No, Annie would have called her, surely? Maybe not. She had the feeling that if Martin had returned then she would quickly slip everybody's minds. He was the head of the household. Annie and Angela probably considered her little more than just another member of staff. She shifted the gear stick out of park and her hand hovered over the indicator. Was she heading home? A pause and then she was turning right. Leaving wasn't an option for Ellen.

IX.

The story told, Tim held Connor in his arms. Connor had begun to cry quietly as he recounted his walk back across the dunes and by the time he had reached the part of the story where he and Martin were crouched by the roundabout, Tim was struggling to understand him through his sobs. This embrace felt right. He knew Connor wanted to be held and he, Tim, wanted to be needed. He enjoyed feeling strong and reliable. He liked the feel of his own hands splayed wide on Connor's back.

When Connor had managed to calm himself, they sat on the sofa together. Tim held his hand. It was easy and familiar, like a foot slipping into an old shoe.

'Why didn't you tell me all of this years ago?'

Connor was intensely aware of everything. It was almost like being high. He could sense the blood flowing through his veins, his hair growing, the movement of his eyes. It felt as though Tim was seeing him for the first time. Finally, somebody, another human being, knew everything about him. It was overwhelming.

'I felt ashamed. Embarrassed. How could you love me when I was so weak, so stupid?'

'How could you think that? You weren't weak or stupid. You were just young. You did what you thought you needed to. It's the keeping it a secret that's crazy. I feel awful that you were carrying this around all these years.' The two looked at each other and for a moment Connor thought Tim might kiss him. Was that a good idea? Well, it wasn't a bad one. It was too confusing. Connor didn't speak. He looked away across the room. This was his favourite time of the morning, when the sun found the window by the kitchen and light formed a pool at the foot of the bed.

'You must tell your parents.' Tim's voice held no judgement, only concern.

'I don't even know if they're still alive.'

'The kid didn't tell you?'

'No. I got out of there so fast. The Martin thing is just too much. How can I tell my parents, if it's just going to destroy my sister's life?'

Tim nodded. He understood.

'God, it's such a shit show. You've got to at least let them know you're alive and well.'

'I know. You're right.'

'Then what's stopping you?'

Connor pulled his hand away and rubbed his face.

'I just don't want to dig it all up again. It was awful. So awful, and the thought of making everyone go through it all over again makes me feel sick.'

'You're their son, Connor. They love you. They've got to want to know where you are, how you're doing. You owe them that, surely?'

'You're right. You're right.'

'Is it the gay thing? Is that still the problem?'

'I honestly thought it was. You have no idea what it was like back there, but little Finbarr is just out and proud, without any real dramas according to him.'

'Yeah, but he is very cute.' Tim laughed and Connor slapped his head playfully.

'This story is fucked up enough. Do not sleep with my nephew!'

'Really? It sounds like you nearly did.'

Connor blushed. 'That is not true. Is that what he told you?'

'No, but it doesn't take a genius to figure it out.'

'Well, you're not as smart as you think you are, because nothing happened.'

Tim raised one eyebrow.

'Seriously. I swear,' Connor insisted.

A laugh. 'I believe you.' Tim glanced at his watch. 'Can I take you to brunch?'

Despite the past year, Connor wanted to accept the invitation. He didn't want Tim to leave his life again, but of course he would.

'And what would Carl have to say about that?'

Tim looked blank for a moment and then repeated the name as if he had just remembered who it referred to. 'Carl! Oh, we're not together any more.'

Connor was stunned. It surprised him that no one had seen fit to pass on this information. 'Really?'

'Yeah.' Tim swiped one hand dismissively. 'We were never that serious.'

Connor felt as if he had been punched in the

stomach. Not serious?

'Well, it was serious enough for you to walk away from a sixteen-year relationship.' The atmosphere in the room had suddenly turned glacial.

Tim stood.

'Oh, Connor. Let's not have this conversation now. Come on. Let's grab some brunch. Don't overreact.'

'No. No I'm not very hungry. Thanks for the invitation.' He knew he sounded like a sullen teenager, but he didn't care. He had been dumped for a fling. Connor had no intention of letting Tim off easily.

'Fine.' Clearly exasperated, Tim bent down and picked his keys off the coffee table. 'Don't have brunch.' At the door he turned. 'Speak to your parents.' And then he was gone.

* * *

Late that afternoon Connor found himself standing outside Sobar once more. With Tim's abrupt departure he had neglected to leave Finbarr's phone number, so heading downtown to find his nephew seemed like Connor's easiest option. Showered and shaved he felt a little more in control after a day spent pin balling between anger, fear and regret.

He was furious with Tim. Initially it was because of Carl and how easily he had pushed Connor out of their life, but then, as the hours passed, he redirected his ire towards the way Tim had walked so casually into the apartment that morning and unearthed his buried feelings. He remembered sobbing in Tim's arms, and he felt so foolish. A stray dog too keen to believe that it had been re-homed. The upside of his fury was that Connor had indulged in a bout of angry cleaning, so the apartment was now spotless.

Later, when he had felt calmer, he allowed himself to pick over the carcass of his relationship once more. He had to admit that there had been problems that had nothing to do with Carl. Tensions and imbalances that neither of them had ever had the appetite to deal with. They had both used Carl to make things easier. He was an excuse for Tim, and for Connor someone to blame. The sad truth was that Tim just wanted out and a year later Connor was beginning to understand why. Yes, he had felt safe and settled but somewhere along the way he had forgotten about himself. Who was he and what did his life look like? He had just been a passenger and clearly Tim wanted more than that. He thought about the last twelve months and realised what a missed opportunity it had been. He was such an idiot. Here he was living rent free in New York, with money in the bank, and all he had done was wallow in self-pity with one eye out for someone to come along and rescue him. No more.

Talking to Finbarr again would be the beginning of change. He pushed open the door and stepped up into the bar. Judson and the same tattooed barman were behind the bar. Three or four figures were perched on stools, but the place was practically empty. He went to the end of the bar where he had sat that drunken night a few weeks earlier. Judson spotted him and smiled.

'You're a regular!'

'Not quite.'

'What can I get you?'

'Bit early for me,' Connor said, throwing a glance at the serious drinkers getting a head start on the night.

'Don't be a pussy!'

Was this the guy's attempt at flirting or just a hard-sell barman, Connor wondered.

'Oh, all right then. Give me a beer. A Bud.'

The other barman gave a lazy wave from where he was lounging next to the till. 'Hi.'

Connor acknowledged him with a nod and a smile.

'Bud.' The bottle and a glass were placed in front of him.

'Thanks. I was hoping to see Finbarr. He around?'

'Gone.'

'Gone?'

'Yeah. Gone gone. Left last night. Some family drama.'

Connor immediately assumed this was something to do with him. He must have told Ellen and Martin that he had found him in New York. Who knew what sort of reaction the news had provoked?

'Did he leave a number?'

'Franco, you got the contact deets for Irish?' Judson called down the bar.

'Sure.' Franco took a ledger from a pile of

papers shoved down the side of the till and approached Connor. 'Here you go.' He opened the large book and pointed to some writing. 'There's no cell number. He's not using his US number. He said he'd let us know when he got a new number sorted.'

Connor looked at the address. It was for an apartment in Monkstown.

'But this is Dublin.'

Franco shrugged. 'There's an email too. Want a pen?'

'Yes please. That would be great.' He scribbled the details on an empty envelope that Franco had provided.

Connor thought for a moment. 'What was the emergency? A bereavement?'

'I don't think so. He was out of here so fast. He got the message and then a couple of hours later he was heading to the airport.'

'Did he seem upset?'

These questions were starting to make Franco uneasy. He suspected that his answers could get Finbarr into trouble in some way. He picked up the ledger. 'No. A bit stressed maybe but that's all. Something to do with his father, I think.'

Franco turned and walked away, leaving Connor with his unwanted beer.

X.

'You're not to be cross.'

Ellen felt physically sick. What had her mother done?

'Why would I be cross, Mammy?' She spoke carefully, making sure not to raise her voice.

'I phoned Finbarr.'

'What?' Despite her best intentions, the volume of her voice had increased.

'Finbarr. I gave him a ring.'

'Why? Why did you do that, Mammy?'

'He has a right to know that his own father is missing.'

Ellen was speechless. Of course her mother had been bombarding her with messages and advice for the last four days, but this was something else. She had crossed a line. This was more than mere meddling.

'Mammy! I can't believe you. Why would you ruin his holiday? Why would you give him worry when there's nothing he can do? He's my son. *My* son.' Ellen was quivering with frustrated rage.

'I knew you'd be cross.'

'And yet that didn't stop you!' Angry tears filled her eyes.

'He was very glad I told him. He's coming home.' Chrissie delivered the latter piece of news with a flourish: Ellen would have to agree she had done the right thing after all.

This was not how her daughter felt.

'What? Why? Why is he coming home? What did you tell him? Does he think we're out beating bushes looking for his father? What use is him being here?'

'He'll be a comfort to you. I know where I'd like my son to be.' Chrissie's voice cracked and gave a muffled squeak.

Ellen sighed. Now she was angry and guilty. Her mother had played her trump card. Ellen could relate to what her mother had been through, especially with what she now knew. She had lost count of the number of times she had nearly relented and told Chrissie the truth about the crash and where Connor was living, but the thought of her mother's reaction had strengthened her resolve. This was not the time. 'All right, Mammy. Don't upset yourself. I'll call him now. Bye bye.'

'Love you, pet. Try not to worry.'

After Ellen ended the call, she looked down at her phone and repeated under her breath, 'Try not to worry.' The last four days had been nothing but a series of new and constantly surprising worries. When her debit card had failed to work for a second time on the Wednesday afternoon, she rang her bank. After what seemed like an eternity listening to instrumental versions of jazz standards, an eager young man informed her that there was nothing wrong with the card, it had merely exceeded the limit for cash withdrawals that day. Martin must still be alive then. Ellen wondered where the card had been used. The young man at first refused to tell her, but after she explained that it was a joint account and that surely she had a right to know where the card had been used in case of fraudulent activity, he reluctantly revealed it had taken cash from an ATM in Rathmines.

'Does that sound right?' he asked.

Ellen had no idea, but assumed that it must be Martin.

'Yes. Yes, that could be right.'

'Try your card again after midnight and you should have access to your funds again.' The man sounded even more cheerful at the prospect of ending the call. 'Anything else I can help you with today?'

The great list of things that Ellen needed help with unfurled inside her head.

'No. That's great. Thanks.'

On the Thursday morning she walked to the bank in the square to use the machine in the wall. Her card was denied once more. She stared at the screen, wondering what to do next, until a loud cough reminded her that someone was waiting. She stepped aside. The door to the bank itself was open. She hesitated. It would be quicker to wait at the counter than call up, but then more people would know her business. What did it matter? The whole town was no doubt already talking about the runaway doctor.

Ellen didn't know the thin young woman she spoke to at the counter. She barely looked old enough to have a Saturday job, never mind to sit behind a glass screen in a bank. Ellen explained her problem and, the name badge said Marion, told her that yet again the card had already been maxed out. No, not in Rathmines, it was Blanchardstown, to the north of the city. Marion suggested that Ellen cash a cheque, so she did. She felt calmer with a wedge of notes in her handbag. It gave her a sliver of control, rather than just waiting for things to happen to her.

She crossed the square to see her parents. Her mother, still in her dressing gown, looked stricken when her daughter appeared at the top of the stairs.

'What is it?' The question clearly expected an answer involving a body being dragged from the sea, or a wrecked car discovered in a ditch. All Ellen had volunteered thus far was that she and Martin had had a big fight, no further details offered or asked for, and that she had spent the night in the old bungalow, before Martin had vanished.

'It's all right, Mammy. There's no news.'

Her father, always the calmer of her parents, suggested that she should go to the guards. It was four days now. Ellen confessed about the debit card transactions. Her mother's face lit up.

'But that's wonderful, pet. They can find him in no time with that.'

Ellen nodded. She knew her mother was right, but it also struck her that Martin wasn't even bothering to hide. He was just gone. She could hardly report a missing person if she knew where he'd been at seven that morning.

'I'll go,' she said, giving the impression she was heading to the Garda barracks. In reality, when she left the pub, she slowly walked back to her house. What was Martin doing? Was he alone? How was he spending the money? Did he have plans?

She knew so little about Martin and his life. She never had, but now she was being forced to care. A deep weariness sat heavily on her shoulders. Ellen carried it home and took it back to bed.

* * *

Before long, Finbarr would be coming home, demanding answers, picking at secrets, and doubtless letting slip that he had found Connor. She was scrolling through her call log trying to find Finbarr's American number when the phone began to trill and vibrate in her hand. It was Aisling. Ellen had ignored a call from her the night before. What was she going to tell her daughter? No one wanted to know that their parents had lost control. She glanced heavenwards and pressed the green symbol.

'Hello.' Crisp, even, unconcerned. Ellen was proud of her self-control.

'Mammy! What's going on? Where's Daddy?'

Ellen swore silently.

'Have you been talking to your granny?'

'What? No! Finbarr called me. He's coming home. He said that Daddy has gone missing. Why didn't you tell me? I can't believe no one told me!'

Ellen rolled her eyes. It hadn't taken long for this family drama to somehow be about Aisling.

'Calm down. Your granny has got it all wrong and called Finbarr. Your father isn't missing. He's just gone away for a bit.'

A pause and then, 'Gone away? Is he OK?'

The truth was, of course, that Ellen had no idea how Martin was, but he was capable of spending money still, so that must mean something.

'Yes. Yes, he's fine. He just needed some time by himself, that's all. There's nothing to worry about.'

Another pause to consider how this might affect her and then, 'Has he had some sort of breakdown?' Aisling sounded more repulsed by this idea than worried.

'He's fine. Don't worry yourself. I'll tell him you called, and I'll let you know when he's home.'

'Do you need me to come back? I'm supposed to be doing a charity fashion show, but my friend Sinead is the one organising it. I'm sure she'd understand.'

How had Ellen managed to raise a daughter who had not only agreed to take part in a charity fashion show but seemed to actually want to? She blamed Martin. He had denied his daughter nothing, while he inflated her expectations of what life might provide. Obviously, it was important to be supportive of your children and their dreams, but it didn't hurt to remind them that you had to work for things. What was the point of anything if it wasn't earned? Ellen bristled when she heard parents talking about unconditional love. Is that what she had for

Aisling? She feared that it wasn't, but then how could she? She would have defended Aisling to the death, done anything for her, but she had to admit that most of the time, the girl felt like a stranger. She made an effort now to sound sweet and understanding.

'Don't be silly. Do your fashion show.'

'But Finbarr is coming home . . . '

'That's because your granny got the wrong end of the stick and, well, I feel awful he's cut his trip short. Everything is fine. Fine.' She repeated the word for emphasis.

2013

I.

This was his favourite time of year on the island. Most of the houses remained shuttered and small deer picked their way along the boardwalks unperturbed. Connor was wrapped in one of the navy pool towels and sipping a mug of coffee laced with a shot of Baileys.

'There's some heat in that sun today.' Tim stepped through the patio doors holding his own steaming mug. 'Might risk a swim later.'

'Madman.' Connor was gazing at the ocean where it pressed against the sky.

Tim sat with a small involuntary grunt.

A shared silence, both men utterly comfortable in the moment. A small sandpiper was picking its way along the side of the pool. The rope on the flagpole clanked in the light breeze. They had spent this day together so many times before. Connor wanted to ask questions but feared that he might spoil the mood. Besides, he already knew that none of the answers would be what he wanted to hear.

After the visit to the apartment in September, Tim had kept up a steady stream of texts and emails. He had regretted the way he'd spoken about Carl and hurt Connor's feelings. He just hadn't been thinking properly. Tim had forgotten that the ending he had written for their story had relied so heavily on Carl. He had apologised. They met for a drink. Dinner. More drinks. Tim's apartment. They had indulged in a half-hearted drunken fumble on the couch before Tim had left Connor snoring and headed to bed alone.

Mostly they talked. Conversations that were years overdue. What had gone wrong between them? Why hadn't they been honest with each other? But whether sober, tipsy or drunken, the thread always came back to Connor and the accident. Tim asked again and again why Connor had never told him, as if the answers made no sense. Why had he never gone back to Ireland? How could he just leave his family in the dark? As Connor tried to explain, his logic fell apart. Voicing all of his fears out loud for what seemed like the first time rendered them groundless. Listening to himself speaking he could hear the echo of the boy he had been all those years ago. The more Tim pushed him to explain, the more foolish he felt. Over the years he had debated the arguments of his teenage self, and that boy had always won. Even as he described comments his mother had made watching television, or the way his father had reacted to an occasional tourist, sounded weak and unfair. Tim's refrain became 'You must go home' and reluctantly Connor was forced to agree. He was a grown man with a life lived away from his family. He no longer knew them, and they couldn't guess at who he had become. They owed each other this second chance.

* * *

A few old photographs of them together had reappeared on the shelves of Tim's apartment. Sometimes Tim looked at their younger selves, and wondered, not why they had broken up, but how they had lasted as a couple for so long. Talking to Connor now, he realised that what had doomed their relationship was so much more than an age gap. Connor was like an emotional time capsule, forever trapped in his own adolescence. Listening to him trying to justify his self-inflicted banishment broke Tim's heart. He tried to reason with him, but he could never come right out with it and tell him the truth. It wasn't his place to play amateur psychiatrist, but the way Connor still blamed his parents and his fear of their reaction or acceptance was textbook. How many gay young men had made the same excuses, when in reality it was all about their own self-loathing? They were the ones who believed that they were lesser beings, not worthy of love. Running away meant never having to put their families or friends to the test. Although Tim hadn't met Dan and Chrissie, hearing Connor speak about them, it was so obvious to Tim that they would love their son no matter what. It was only Connor who couldn't see the truth.

Sitting with his ex-boyfriend he should have felt like a friend or maybe an enemy, but the truth was that he felt like more of a father than anything else. It wasn't sexy. The fumble on the couch had been a combination of alcohol and laziness, but it was never going to be the start of a rekindled romance. In the morning as they sat opposite each other nursing mugs of coffee and aching heads, they both seemed to understand that. It was early days, but things seemed to have shifted beyond their break-up into calmer, though as yet uncharted waters.

On Fire Island, in early spring, sitting next to each other, Tim felt confident enough to say, 'I'm going to miss you' without the fear of it being misconstrued.

Connor smiled. 'Well, I'll miss this.' He indicated the house and pool with its ocean view.

An arched eyebrow from Tim.

'And you.'

Connor was trying not to think about his trip too much. In a couple of hours, he would catch the ferry and then make his way to JFK.

Tim had been able to persuade Connor to email Finbarr. Connor had sat down and composed a short note. He felt like a time traveller sending a letter to the future. Finbarr had replied quickly, explaining his sudden departure from New York and filling Connor in on Martin's disappearance. He had ended his email with Ellen's mobile phone number. Connor told himself that it was too late to call, then the next day worried that it was lunchtime. Later he wondered if it might be easier to text his sister after all this time, but then finally, after his first glass of wine, he took out his phone and stabbed in the number, quickly pressing the small green symbol before he changed his mind.

It rang. A click and a rustle, followed by 'Hello'.

The voice sounded so Irish to Connor, as if an actress was playing the part of his sister.

'Hi, Ellen. It's Connor . . . Your brother,' he added halfheartedly as if he thought she might have forgotten.

'Oh Connor!' Ellen sounded delighted and in truth, she was. Happier than even she had thought she'd be. This was a call from beyond the grave. 'I'm so glad you called. Oh Connor, we've all missed you so much.' And then emotion overtook her and she was wiping away tears while still laughing down the line.

'You OK there, sis?' Connor was also laughing. 'I've missed you all too.' He found his throat squeezed shut as the truth of what he was saying struck him. The years, so many years, the hiding, the running, the love for these people he hadn't allowed himself to feel, all came clattering down on him, leaving him crushed. He covered his head with his free hand and sobbed.

'Connor? Connor, don't cry!' Ellen urged her brother, even though it was obvious that she was still weeping herself. 'We all love you. We all want to see you. Are you coming home? Can you?'

She could hear Connor trying to speak. It sounded like he was saying yes.

'That's great. Great. Just let us know when.'

Connor had managed to control his sobs.

'I'll sort out flights and . . . are you sure? Mammy and Daddy are fine with it? Do they know everything?' As he spoke, he realised that Ellen wasn't in possession of all the facts.

'Are you kidding? They'll be beside themselves. I haven't said anything to them yet. I wanted to be sure you were coming home before I told them. They'll be ecstatic.'

'What do you think about keeping it a secret? Making it a surprise?'

And just like that, they were brother and sister again, plotting together, as they had all those years before: getting up early to make breakfast on Mother's Day or pranking their father with cling film on the beer taps.

'That's a great idea. I'll say nothing.'

'They won't have a heart attack or anything, will they?'

Ellen laughed. 'No. I don't think so. They're both well. You'll see a big change but they're both in working order.'

Connor suddenly remembered the big family drama.

'What about Martin? Finbarr told me he's missing.'

A beat.

'No. Not missing. He's back.'

Ellen wondered how much of the story to tell her brother. Not much.

'But gone again. He's not here. You won't have to see him.'

Connor didn't speak for a moment, wondering what his sister was trying to say.

'Right,' he said slowly.

'I know, Connor. I know what Martin did.'

II.

In the end, he had been missing for nine days. It had seemed far longer, but on the ninth night when Ellen came home from checking on her parents, she saw a light on in the kitchen and the dark angle of a man's shoulder at the kitchen table. She knew it couldn't be Finbarr. He had run back to his life in Dublin as fast as he could once he'd realised that there was nothing to be done in Mullinmore apart from keep his mother company, and that had not been part of his big 'save the day' plan.

The shoulder didn't move. Ellen walked down the hall, her heels clicking across the tiles. Still the figure didn't stir.

'Martin?' she whispered. Was it a ghost? But no, as she pushed open the door, she saw that it was her husband sitting at the kitchen table wearing large headphones. They looked new. She thought of the debit card in Dublin. She felt her jaw tense. If this was to be a battle, she was ready for it.

Ellen walked past the table to the sink and turned around. Martin saw her but with no discernible reaction. He slipped off his headphones. They stared at each other across the room like two exhausted boxers heading into the final round.

'You're back.'

'I am.' He spoke quietly.

'For good?'

'No.'

'I see.'

Ellen picked up a crumpled tea towel from the counter and folded it. Martin was just staring into the distance.

'Anything you think I should know?' Ellen asked, unsure of how aggressive she should be. It felt so strange to see her husband like this. Cowed and uncertain.

'I didn't want to come back.'

Ellen waited for more. 'OK.'

Martin glanced at the ceiling and then down again, never looking at his wife. He might have been speaking to himself.

'I thought I could just disappear. I wasn't in my right mind. I wanted to vanish, escape everything. It turns out that isn't so easy.' His lips curled to form a bitter smile. 'Money. God, it's so mundane and dull, but I want to work, need to work. It turns out a doctor can't just start again. Questions. Lots of questions. They want to know who you are, where you've been.' He stopped and looked at Ellen as if only just noticing that he had an audience of one. 'So, I need a divorce.' His tone had changed. He became matter-of-fact, brittle.

Ellen felt like an employee being informed by management that they were going to be let go.

'A divorce?' Why was it him releasing them from their prison cell? Why hadn't it been her at the kitchen table asking for a divorce years before?

'I hope it won't turn into a fight.'

'No,' she replied quickly. 'No, I . . . we've no need for that.' Was that true? Why didn't she want to fight him, destroy him? This cold, petty tyrant, who had chipped away at her for years with his snide comments and eye-rolling, never crossing the line but relentless, didn't he deserve to suffer her revenge?

Ellen was surprised by the sense of calm that had overcome her. All those years of her inner voice screaming at him, ranting silently at every cruel injustice he had meted out to her, but now, when it seemed it was her time to speak, she found she had no words. It was over. He was leaving. There was nothing left to rail against. She felt as if she had spent her adult life pushing against a door that actually opened towards her. It was disorientating, but also a relief. She gripped the counter, unsure if she would fall or float away.

Martin bowed his head, placing his hand over his mouth. When had he got so old, Ellen wondered? She remembered him standing in the pub the night of the Rugby Club dance. His smile when he saw her. The kiss when he brought her home. It seemed impossible that those two people were now in this kitchen, trying to walk away from each other, worn away by the endless stream of unhappiness that had been their lives for so many years.

'Why *did* you marry me, Martin?'

He looked up at her as if she had interrupted his thoughts.

'Seriously,' she persisted, 'I'd like to know, now it's over. Why marry me?'

A deep sigh. 'Guilt? I don't know. I was young and stupid. I thought I could fix things.'

'Fix things?'

'Connor leaving. I . . . none of us are just the worst thing we ever did. We're more than that. Yes, I did what I thought I needed to, but then, then I wanted to make things . . . oh God, I don't know . . . better, I suppose. Right.'

Ellen pulled a chair away from the table and sat down.

'But you could have. You could have confessed, brought Connor back.'

Martin twisted his body in the chair.

'He'd gone. We were together. I thought I had mended everything. Trying to unpick what had happened would have just made everything worse.' He turned his head away from Ellen and she noticed the veins straining in his neck.

'And when did you realise that you hadn't fixed a thing, that you couldn't?'

Martin looked into her eyes. 'What's the point, Ellen? Do we need to do this? This is where we are. Who's happy? What does that look like? We've got two great kids. Is that so awful?'

Ellen thought for a moment, about Martin's question, but also about Finbarr and Aisling. 'Do you ever wonder how we managed to raise two children who both think they deserve better parents than us?'

Martin smiled. 'Aisling is a bit much all right.'

Ellen bent closer and in a stage whisper declared, 'I don't like her!'

They both laughed, but briefly. It was a hollow bubble of guilty good humour that each of them understood would not last for long. The burst of laughter faded away into the hush of the night and a silence fell.

Martin cleared his throat. Ellen looked up, expecting him to speak, but no, he continued to twist his fingers together and gaze at the floor. It seemed as if he had said all he was going to. If Ellen wanted answers, it was up to her to pose the questions. It had only been nine days, scarcely more than a week since she'd been forced to take charge, but it had changed her. Martin leaving had been like when the motor on the fridge cut out late at night, an unexpected peace. She wondered what she had ever been afraid of. Now that he had announced he was willing to get a divorce, all her curiosity about the past began to slip away. The only questions she wanted answered at that moment were practical ones. She began.

* * *

After the days of not knowing, suddenly there was a great deal to do. Martin and Ellen agreed to tell as few people as possible about the divorce. Ellen was relieved. She'd had quite enough of her private life being made public. It seemed that Martin had spent much of his time away planning. He had considered trying to sell his practice but decided that it would be quicker and more practical to just close it down and put it up for sale along with the house. He would split the proceeds with Ellen. She in turn asked if she could have his parents' bungalow. She expected him to ask her to pay for it with her share of the sale of the house, but no. Martin simply agreed. It all gave Ellen a mild but constant anxiety. Where was the Martin who took pleasure in humiliating her? When would he re-emerge to punish her for her unspecified sins?

Chrissie and Dan were the first to be told. A separation. Her father reacted as if she'd just told him they were getting double glazing. A nod to indicate he felt it was a good and practical step. Chrissie did manage to produce some tears but after all these years Ellen knew that she wasn't really that upset. Chrissie was probably more worried about the social embarrassment and the practicalities of her daughter's future. When Ellen explained about the bungalow, her mother dried her tears and returned to one of her favourite subjects: her dislike of stairs, and her own in particular.

Aisling, true to form, made it about Aisling. How would this affect her? Her bedroom? Her stuff? What was going to happen to everything? Apart from that, Ellen got the impression that hearing about the end of her parents' marriage was just mildly embarrassing because it reminded Aisling that they had once had a relationship.

Finbarr was surprisingly sweet. He made a special trip to Mullinmore to see her and make sure that she was coping as well as she had assured him she was. Ellen wondered what had happened to him in New York. He seemed changed. Rougher around the edges, but softer too. Was *thoughtful* the right word? She noticed that his approach to his studies had changed and he now spoke often about applying for jobs with design studios and agencies. Perhaps New York had taught him that working in bars wasn't as easy or as lucrative as he'd imagined? Ellen had worried that his time in the city might have fanned the flames of his vanity and self-interest, whereas he seemed to have lost that arch, slightly superior quality he used to have. When he gave Ellen a hug, she felt loved rather than judged.

When Connor had called, she had felt joy, true joy. It seemed like an actual miracle, and more than that she felt as if she had made it happen, even though, when she really thought about it, it had had very little to do with her. The only awkwardness came when Martin's name was mentioned. It seemed too much to talk about, especially so soon. The joy of the reunion immediately marred by talk of the past. She still didn't really know why Connor had agreed to take the blame for the accident. She had believed Martin when he explained about their marriage. Connor hadn't made a deal. He was just a weak young boy in the wrong place and Martin was a bully. Still, she knew there must be more to the story. Connor had asked, 'Do you know everything?' and she doubted that she did. She moved the conversation on. She reassured him that Martin no longer lived in Mullinmore and that seemed to be enough for him. She imagined that after the hullabaloo and excitement of his reunion with Dan and Chrissie, she would sit with her brother late into the night and he would tell her everything, and whatever it was, she would forgive him. Ellen liked this version of herself. Calm and generous. There wouldn't be any scenes or confrontations, just the Hayes family back together at last.

Initially the plan was that Connor would come around Christmas time, but then Dan was ill with gallstones and Chrissie had been going up and down to Cork to see him in the hospital. It didn't seem the right time for the reappearance of a long-lost son. Ellen prayed that she had made the right decision. What if their father didn't make it? What if he caught some sort of superbug in hospital and never got to see his son again? But Dan had bounced back. He'd lost weight and had become obsessed with walking. He looked ten years younger.

After Christmas, the house and surgery was sold to a firm of solicitors, so Ellen had been busy trying to get her mother-in-law into a home and arrange the sale of the house contents, as well as move into her own new home.

She and Connor decided to wait until early April. The weather would be better. Ellen and Connor laughed about how quickly the thrill of being reunited with his parents would wear off and he'd be glad to get out of the house.

Ellen had only been in her new bungalow for a few weeks, but already she had discovered something about herself. It transpired that she wasn't a bad housekeeper after all. She had just been an unhappy one. She took enormous pride in her new rooms. Having Connor's impending visit kept her motivated. She had got supplies from the farm centre where she had once worked. A sniffing Deirdre, now with glasses and hair a deep shade of plum, was still behind the counter. Ellen had touched up the woodwork and Finbarr, with only a little prompting, had come back one weekend to help her repaint the bathroom a bold daffodil yellow. 'It's like walking into sunshine,' she had declared proudly when the two of them had stood back to survey their work. The garden was still a mess, but that could wait. The house was clean, and everything was neat and in its place. She felt as if a weight had been lifted off her, unburdened as she was of all that dark heavy furniture and three storeys of another family's clutter. Doubtless it also helped that Martin was gone.

He had retreated to Dublin. Ellen had tried to press him on where he had been during his aborted attempt to run away, and after various evasive non-committal replies, he finally volunteered that he had been staying with an old university pal and his wife. Ellen had never heard him speak of them before, but she supposed it might be true. She felt oddly disengaged from her former husband. Where was her anger, her mother wanted to know? Ellen had no idea. Perhaps it would arrive later, after the dust had settled. For now, it seemed as if Chrissie was housing enough fury towards Martin for the both of them.

'Just walking out on his family. That's not a man. He is not the man I thought he was.'

Ellen thought about the crash and who had been responsible for those deaths. No, Martin was not the man her mother thought he was.

III.

The accents made him anxious. He couldn't remember the last time he had been around so many Irish people. All the faces lining up to board the plane looked familiar in a half-forgotten way, like actors appearing in a film he didn't know they were in. Connor instinctively looked away, examining the tag on his holdall or glancing at his phone, fearful that they would recognise him. He knew that was ludicrous. Even someone who had known Connor Hayes in 1987 would scarcely recognise the well-built man, with cropped greying hair, queuing for a night flight to Shannon.

After all the reassurances from Tim and from Ellen, he still questioned the wisdom of this trip. Connor did finally believe that his parents wanted to see him, and he knew that he longed to see them, but he also knew that he couldn't fix the past and it seemed to him that was precisely what everyone expected his reappearance to do.

Thanks to Tim's air miles, Connor found himself in business class. The matronly stewardess appeared to think it was her personal duty to ensure that the plane landed with only empty bottles, such was her enthusiasm for topping up glasses. Connor was already on his third glass of champagne before the plane had even taken off.

'My name's Karen. If there's anything you need now, just let us know. You're OK for champagne?'

'Thank you. I'm grand. Are you trying to make sure we all sleep for the duration?'

Karen gave a small yelp of laughter.

'That's right. That's right. I'm only after hearing the accent now. I had you down for a tourist, not one of our own.'

'Well, I haven't been home for a very long time.' And as he uttered the words, he felt emotion tug on his mouth, and he had to catch himself before he began to weep. He forced a smile and raised both eyebrows to indicate his own foolishness.

Karen stepped back, unsure of how to treat her overly emotional passenger. 'We should be taxi-ing shortly. Enjoy the flight.' And she shifted her professional largesse onto the passenger behind him.

Connor worried. Why had he been ambushed by his own emotions? He wasn't drunk. If this was what happened when he spoke to a friendly Irish stranger about going home, he dreaded to think what state he would be in by the time he reached Hayes Bar and the people waiting for him in those small rooms above it.

Karen's plan worked and he found himself waking up as muffled announcements were being made and breakfast plates were being cleared away. He glanced out of the window. There it was. The distinctive quilt of uneven greens with seams of rivers and roads meandering through it. He felt he knew what the inside of every small bungalow and farmhouse they flew over looked like. He had to wipe away another tear. This was ridiculous. Stupid. He would have to pull himself together.

'A quick cup of coffee? Tea?' Karen's faced loomed into view. She looked as if she had spent most of the flight re-applying make-up.

'Oh, a tea would be great, thanks.'

She smiled. 'It won't be Barry's, I'm afraid.'

They shared a smile of mutual understanding.

At first the road from Shannon Airport suggested a modern Ireland that he had no idea existed, but before long he was driving his whiter-than-white hire car along the byways of his childhood. High unruly hedges, sharp bends, farmyards smeared across the black of the tarmac. The voices on the radio were discussing the new water charges.

The world had changed but it hadn't changed at all. Connor knew this place. Not in the way that he might be familiar with parts of London or New York, but although he doubted he'd ever been on this actual stretch of road before, he had such a deep sense of understanding, of belonging. He knew what the people talking on the radio looked like; when the car came around a bend, he knew that the view would hold no surprises. This is what homecoming meant. Arriving in a place to discover you're fluent in a language you'd forgotten you ever knew.

After an hour so on the road, he began to recognise places. Signposts to villages and towns he could remember visiting or at least hearing of in stories from relatives or friends. Mullinmore eleven kilometres, then six, then two. The farm centre where Ellen had worked, down the hill, the bike shop was still there, that mini-mart was new, the trees were gone outside the bank, was that the school with a big glass and steel extension? He turned left before coming into the main square and followed the back quays. Ellen had given him directions to her new house, so he knew where he was going. Ellen had glossed over the next part: 'And then take the coast road off the roundabout and I'm about two hundred yards down on the right.'

Barry's roundabout. He couldn't help feeling disappointed. It was so much smaller than he remembered. The circle of grass in the centre, just a patch really, and the red and white signage of the garage just beyond, so large and bright. He slowed down and tried to see where the car had broken through the shrubbery. He wondered if there would be a marker or cross or something, but he could find nothing. This was the scene of such devastation, the destruction of so many lives, surely it should look more significant? Cars, oblivious to the awful history of the place, cruised past. Connor felt it was rude, disrespectful somehow. True, he had spent his whole life trying to forget what had happened on this spot, but for the town of Mullinmore to do so seemed wrong. He indicated and slipped away down the coast road.

His first thought when the door opened was that it was his mother, but then he realised that this must be his sister who had grown into a version of Chrissie. Ellen burst through her front door and almost before the bell had finished chiming, threw herself on her brother. Through sobs, she welcomed him, told him how happy she was to see him again. Connor hugged her back but felt oddly unemotional after all his trepidation. Hearing Ellen's voice on the phone was one thing, but this woman, this excitable middle-aged woman, bore so little relation to the version of his sister that he had left behind that it was hard for him to connect the two.

Finally she stepped back and, wiping at her eyes, urged him to come in.

'My God! Look at you, you're a man!'

Connor shrugged. 'You're a woman.'

'An old woman.' They both laughed and then before the pause in conversation became awkward, Ellen quickly continued, 'I've rung to make sure they're both in. All I said was that I had something to drop off.' She stopped abruptly and spread her arms wide. 'They're going to lose their minds!' She laughed and took Connor's bag.

'You're in here.' She indicated a door just off the small, square hallway. 'Do you want to have a lie-down? Cup of tea? Whatever now.'

'Tell you what I'd love is a shower.'

'Of course!' She grabbed his arm and led him a little further down the corridor. 'Bathroom is in here. The shower is one of those ones where you pull a string to turn on the . . . well, I'm not sure, but when that red light is on you can turn the water on at the wall. I'll get you a towel.' Ellen rushed off. She was an enthusiastic hostess. Connor was already relieved that he had opted to hire a car. He foresaw quite a few solitary day trips.

Dressed in fresh clothes, he found his sister in the kitchen. She seemed calmer. There was some small talk about Finbarr and Aisling. Martin's name was avoided as if by previously arranged agreement. She asked Connor nothing about his life other than how the trip had been. He had mentioned Tim to her in phone calls and talked about working on the roof gardens, but he sensed she didn't want to pry, or was afraid of what she might discover.

They took Ellen's car. Connor braced himself as they approached the roundabout, but she made no comment. Surely she hadn't forgotten? More likely that she was just trying to avoid any awkwardness. She pointed out the various changes in the town as they passed buildings that had been neglected or reborn.

'Will Daddy not be in the pub by now?'

'No. They only open at night these days. It's hardly worth it but they don't really have many options. In the boom time someone offered them a fortune for the place, but Daddy said no. He thought he'd hold on and get even more. They're sorry now.'

Ellen had to circle the square twice to find a parking space. Connor could feel the nerves beginning to build in the pit of his stomach. He made a conscious effort to keep his breathing deep and even.

'You all right?' Ellen asked before getting out of the car.

'Yes,' he replied but he didn't sound very confident.

'You'll be fine.' His little sister was in charge.

They crossed the square and none of it seemed real. It might have been a movie set or a theme park. Hayes Bar. The sign was the same. Had the door always been navy blue? It looked different. New glass? Ellen opened the street door as quietly as she could. The two of them squashed inside. This was where he had last seen his mother, floored by her grief at his leaving, her arm pressed up against the wall to steady herself. They could hear voices from above.

'I only have those brown ones from Taylors now. I don't know what's happening to my feet. I'll be leaving the house in slippers soon.'

'You have the grey slip-ons, don't you?' His father's voice.

'Those? They're more like an orthopaedic boot. I couldn't go out in them!'

Ellen rolled her eyes and grinned. A finger to her mouth to ensure he was silent and then she crept up the stairs in front of him. Connor wasn't sure what to do, so waited inside the door. He noticed the wallpaper was gone, replaced by light blue paint. He thought the mirror at the top of the stairs was new. His was aware of his heart drumming at an alarming rate. He felt like he was waiting backstage for a performance and he had no idea of his lines. Oh God. What if this was a huge mistake? What if . . .

'Oh, there you are, love. Dan. Kettle,' his mother greeted Ellen. He heard his sister cough and then say in a voice she might have used speaking to young children, 'Now, I have someone here who'd like to see you.' His parents made inarticulate sounds and Connor heard a newspaper being folded. Ellen stuck her hand out from the kitchen doorway and waved him up. Like a sleepwalker he began to climb, one foot in front of the other. Even before he had reached the top of the stairs, tears were falling down his face. Ellen caught his elbow and ushered him forward. Two old people that looked like his parents stared at him across the room.

Chrissie looked at the man in the doorway. Why was he upset? Did she know him? She did, but how . . . and then all at once a mother recognised her boy. Her face crumpled as she rose from the table and then with two strides he had crossed the room, the years and all the regrets gone, to hold her tight.

'Connor. Oh, Connor.' Her hand was in his hair, pulling this man down into her embrace. 'You're back,' she told him, as if to make sure that it was true. 'You've come back!'

'Mammy. I'm so sorry, Mammy.' His tears rained down on Chrissie's shoulder. 'I'm so so sorry.' He knew it was all that he had to say to her. It was all she needed to hear.

On the other side of the table Dan was standing, looking on in disbelief, and then the reality of what was happening finally registered on his face. His son, the son he thought he'd never see again was in the room, alive, warm, breathing. His features contorted as he fought a losing battle with the tears that burst forth. He stumbled past his chair, impatient with his legs. 'Connor. God Almighty, Connor!' And then he threw his arms around the huddled duo of his wife and son. The shared sobbing pulsed through the three entwined bodies till they looked like a single beating heart.

By the doorway, Ellen stood watching. This was good. It was wonderful. Only someone with a heart of stone could fail to be moved, so why did she feel so detached? Perhaps it was because her mother had used up all the happiness that could fit in the room. Ellen had often heard people speaking of eyes lighting up, but she had never witnessed it until now. It had reminded her of an illustration in a book she had loved when she was a little girl. Old Geppetto's face when he saw that his puppet had become a real little boy.

It was Dan who remembered that Ellen was still in the room. He broke away and went to give her a hug.

'You could have killed us! I'm only out of the hospital.'

Ellen laughed and hugged her father.

Connor stepped back from his mother and then the four of them looked at each other standing around the table beaming. These four people in this room had once been so commonplace and ordinary, but now it was akin to a miracle.

'Ellen! How long have you known?' Chrissie was fanning herself with her hand, tears still falling steadily.

'Not long. I thought you'd like the surprise. Was I wrong?'

'No. No.' Chrissie pulled Connor's hand to her mouth and kissed it. 'This is the most wonderful surprise.' She looked at Dan. 'The power of prayer.' Her husband gave a solemn nod.

Ellen wondered if her mother was at all bothered by the unhurried speed at which her prayers had been answered.

Chrissie fell back into her chair and looked at her son, now a middle-aged man.

'Where have you been, pet? How did Ellen find you?'

Before Connor could answer, Ellen said, 'It wasn't me that found him, it was Finbarr.'

'Finbarr?' Dan asked, trying to make sense of what was going on.

The Hayes family had a great deal to discuss.

IV.

Connor found himself walking again. This time it differed from his city treks in that he was no longer trying to lose himself. Instead, he was trying to reassemble the person he'd been when he had left this place. The streets, alleyways and squares of Mullinmore were literal memory lanes for him. Trying his first cigarette in the yard behind the bookies, smashing windows in the abandoned cottage above the nursing home on Shorten's Lane, the walks to and from school, the pub, the awkward kiss with Sarah Beamish — where was she now? Everything seemed second-skin familiar, and yet it was as if he was carrying around the memories of someone else. He couldn't articulate it. He knew who he was now, and he still remembered the boy he had been then, but it appeared to be beyond his imagination to connect the two.

The reunion with Chrissie and Dan had been easier than he had feared. Had Ellen done some groundwork for him? He wasn't sure, but happily he found he was never in the awkward situation of being almost forty-six years old and having to come out to his parents. They knew. They must have. Maybe it was thanks to Finbarr, or perhaps it was just 2013, but there were no questions about wives or girlfriends.

They managed to maintain composed faces when he mentioned moving to New York with Tim. Because he knew that they knew, it never had to be directly referred to or discussed. When they told him that they loved him, he believed them entirely. There were no nagging doubts. After all the needless foolish tears that had been shed, finally these were happy ones, and he could feel the tight knot of secrets and regret slowly loosen and slip away.

That first night was all about Mullinmore. What and who were long gone, as well as the changes and the new arrivals to the town. He found himself glazing over and pretending to remember names and places that only stirred the tiniest flicker of recognition in dusty corners of his memory. Late in the afternoon Ellen had slipped out to Murrays and brought back four fish suppers, the fish and vinegar steam conjuring up Connor's childhood almost as strongly as the faces that sat around the kitchen table. Afterwards, they had gone downstairs and had drinks in the pub until jet lag began to tug at his chin, bouncing it off his chest as he struggled to remain awake. Chrissie had tried to insist that he stay in his old room, and when he chose to go back to Ellen's bungalow, the children could tell that while she was disappointed, both she and Dan were proud to see them as adults behaving as grown-up children should. Brother and sister reunited.

Connor had gone straight to bed that night and passed out more than slept. It was only in the morning he felt he could raise the subject of

Martin and the crash. He asked his sister questions. Who had she spoken to? What did she know? Had Martin said anything? Did she know who had been driving? Surely Martin hadn't told her everything. He listened and then tailored the truth of his answers to the version of events that Ellen believed. All she was really interested in confirming was that there had been no pact between himself and Martin that involved marrying her. This particular scenario had never crossed Connor's mind before, though of course, now that Ellen brought it up, he could see how she might have jumped to that conclusion. Certainly hearing his sister talk about her marriage it didn't sound like a grand romance or even a lost love, just something Ellen had endured for more years than Connor could understand. Afterwards, on his walks, he wondered about Martin. What sort of man had he become?

Apparently, he was working in Southampton now, doing maternity cover in a practice there. That was all Ellen knew. It seemed so strange that both brother and sister should have had their lives so dramatically altered by this one man. Why had he married Ellen and, although he never asked his sister, why had he just run away when he'd heard that Connor had been found and might return to Mullinmore? Martin must be over fifty years old by now. Surely, he could have been man enough to stay and face Connor. He can't have thought it was suddenly going to become a police matter again after all these years. Apart from Linda, it was just a case of his word versus Martin's. No matter what he feared, why not just brazen it out? It made little sense.

Brother and sister talked about their parents. Now that the happy reunion had occurred, what more should they be told? Connor sensed that Ellen would be very happy if they never spoke about Martin and the crash again, but Connor knew that having come all this way, he wanted them to know the truth. It might have been an accident and he knew his parents had never really blamed him, but it was important that they finally understood that he had not killed those people. Reluctantly Ellen agreed, but then as they were leaving the bungalow, she put her hand on his arm.

'One thing, Connor . . . '

'Yes?'

'Do you mind if . . . and I completely understand that you . . . it's just . . . ' Ellen's face reddened as she became more flustered.

'What? What is it?' he asked in a soothing voice.

'Can we not tell the children? Finbarr and Aisling, do they have to know?'

Connor bristled. Surely this was the moment for everyone to know everything?

'Why?' He sounded more confrontational than he had intended. Softening his voice, he asked again, 'Why? Why not tell them?'

Ellen looked downwards and pushed her elbow into her waist in a way that made Connor think of his sister in her convent uniform waiting in the cold outside the pub.

'He's their father. Bad enough that he's left us. If they know this, they'll think he's some sort of monster.'

Connor nodded, not wanting to say that that was precisely what he thought Martin was.

'I just want to protect them. Is that all right? Do you mind?' There was a pleading in her eyes.

Even though he suspected the person she really wanted to protect was herself, he found himself saying, 'Yes. That's fine.' He comforted himself with the thought that surely once their grandparents knew the truth, it wouldn't be long before everyone was in possession of all the facts.

Chrissie had immediately dissolved into hunched-shouldered sobs, while Dan's face paled with shock. 'What?' he repeated with growing fury as Ellen and Connor pieced together the story of what had happened the day of the crash. Finally, Dan's question became 'Why?' and Connor found himself searching for the right words to explain why he had been willing to take the blame. As he picked his way through Martin's threat and his decision to claim he was the driver, he hoped his parents wouldn't make an extravagant show of dismissing his fears in retrospect. He didn't want to be forced to remind them of the things they had said about gay people, or even the general attitude of people in the town and beyond back in the eighties. To their credit they just stayed very quiet. Chrissie held out her hand and Dan took hold of it. Connor didn't want them to blame themselves — what was the point? They had all been different people back then.

'That's awful. Awful,' was all that Dan said.

'It's nobody's fault,' Connor almost whispered. 'It's not your fault. It's not mine.'

Chrissie's jaw tensed and she spat out, 'It's Martin Coulter's fault!'

Ellen winced. Every time she heard his name, she grew tense and wondered when this would all become her fault.

* * *

On Connor's third day back in Mullinmore, spring sunshine decided to make a promise of the summer ahead. It beamed from a laundry-fresh blue sky. Connor could feel the heat on his back as he walked along the quay. He had never imagined he would be able to stroll around the town like this. He had always thought of himself hiding in shadows, a cap pulled low, but here he was, head held high to greet the day. Daffodils that he hadn't noticed before stood along the opposite bank of the river. He found that he was smiling for no reason. He walked on up past the high walls of the convent and then out onto the old Cork road, looking up into the bare branches of the trees overhead, trying to spot buds silhouetted against the bright sky. He rubbed his hand against the damp hedges. He wondered if this was what it was like for a man just released from prison.

He thought he might walk as far as the entrance to the golf club and then turn and head down the hill back into town, but he was stopped in his tracks by the sight of one house. The

O'Connells'. Where Carmel and Linda had lived. He was transfixed by the small ramp leading along the front of the house to the door. It looked so old. The railing was mottled with patches of rust and the stained concrete was trimmed with the green of weeds. How was it possible that something that hadn't been here when he lived in Mullinmore could already look so ancient and neglected? Perhaps it was because he had been with Tim for so long that he continued to feel young, but seeing this house made it very clear that his youth was firmly in the past.

He was about to move on when a small hatchback pulled off the road and had to wait for him to clear the driveway before it could enter the gates. He waved apologetically and walked on, hoping that whoever was driving the car hadn't —

'Connor? Connor Hayes, is that you?' A woman's voice, clear and sharp.

He froze. For a moment he considered just walking on but had to accept that escape was not an option. Turning, he put his hand up to shield his eyes from the sun. He recognised the driver of the car.

'Mrs O'Connell!'

'I heard you were back. Were you coming to visit Linda?'

How could he admit that he wasn't? Tell this woman that he had forgotten their house was even on this road?

'Yes. I mean, if that's all right?'

'Of course, of course. I'll just go in and make

sure . . . ' Caroline's voice trailed away, unsure of how to finish the sentence. She edged the car forward and parked by the ramp. By the time she'd retrieved her small bag of groceries and the *Examiner* off the passenger seat and got out, Connor was waiting for her by the door.

They smiled at each other. It felt like a reunion of sorts, even though they had never really known each other.

'If I hadn't known you were back, I don't think I'd have spotted you at all. You're a grown man.'

'Overgrown!' Connor said, patting his non-existent belly. 'You haven't changed a bit.'

'Get away out of it!' Caroline laughed as she fiddled with her key in the door.

It struck Connor that this was not the welcome he had expected from a woman who blamed him for the death of one daughter and the crippling of another. Ellen had tried to tell him that Linda's parents knew who had been driving but he had assumed that she had misunderstood. If adults had been in possession of the full facts, surely they would have done something?

'Just take a seat in there.' Caroline indicated the suite of furniture that filled the small front room and she breezed down the hall with her bag of shopping. Connor sat. This was not a meeting he had planned on having. He had just wanted to see his parents, have a look at his old haunts and then return to his life in the States. One of the deciding factors for him making the trip was that Linda was in a wheelchair, so the chances of bumping into her anywhere were very slim. Now he was sitting in her house waiting, as if he was here to pick her up for a school dance. Odd how this one house could make him feel so old and yet, almost at the same time, like a teenager again.

One half of the sliding doors was inched open and Caroline stuck her head forward.

'She's ready for you, if you'd like to . . . ' She pushed the door further back.

Connor got out of his chair feeling very self-conscious and stepped forward. Linda was in her wheelchair, the sunlight streaming through the window like a spotlight on her face. All Connor noticed was how old she had become. Why was it such a surprise? He realised that foolishly he had imagined that because her life as she'd known it ended the day of the crash, she would be sitting in her wheelchair perfectly preserved, as if dipped in aspic.

'Connor.' Linda smiled and held out her hand.

He shook it. 'Linda.'

They took stock of each other for a moment. Connor could still recognise the girl from the back of the car.

'It's been a long time.'

'It has,' he agreed.

'I'm so glad you came to see me.' The sincerity in her voice gave Connor a pang of guilt, given that he'd had no intention of doing so.

'Sit down. Sit down,' Caroline said, patting the seat of the wing-backed chair by the window.

'Tea, or would you like something stronger?' Caroline asked this with the air of a woman who had entertained men before and knew what they might like.

'Tea will be fine.' He smiled at her.

'Linda, love?'

'Yes please.'

Caroline left them alone.

Connor was staring at the same photograph that Ellen had noticed in its dark wooden frame.

'Is that the day? The day of . . . ' He couldn't bring himself to say the words.

'Yes. Yes, it was.' She sounded impatient. 'Look, I'm so glad you came up. I just wanted to say sorry.'

'You?' This was not what Connor had expected her to say.

'About Ellen. I've felt awful about it ever since.'

'You weren't to know; don't feel bad about anything.'

'So I was right?'

'Right?' Connor was unclear.

Linda bit her lip. 'That it wasn't you driving?'

'No.' Connor was confused. 'But you knew that. You told Ellen.'

'I thought I knew it. That whole day was like a bad dream. All I meant to say to her was that I had never blamed you. I didn't mind if you came back.'

Connor sat back in his chair. 'So,' he was trying to piece things together, 'you told her what you thought had happened and she just immediately believed you?' He was incredulous.

'She was in such a state when she left here that time and then we heard about her and Martin. I just felt awful. I wasn't thinking. I just, well after all these years, I thought that if I was right about who had been driving, surely she'd know.'

'Of course she should have. Everyone should. If it's anyone's fault, it's mine. We were kids, Linda. Clueless kids.'

Linda nodded in agreement. 'How is she? Is she doing OK?'

Connor shrugged. 'I don't know. I mean she's my sister, but I can't pretend I know her after all this time. According to Mam and Dad she's happier than she has been in years, so don't feel bad. I think the mystery is that the marriage lasted as long as it did.'

'Martin. What a total prick.'

'You'll get no argument here.'

Caroline elbowed the door wide and brought in a tray of cups.

'Now, here we go.'

'Thanks very much, Mrs O'Connell. That's great.'

'Caroline, please.' She poured the tea and handed a cup to Linda and then put Connor's on the table beside him.

Caroline stepped back and looked down at Connor.

'Declan will be sorry he missed you. He's out at golf.'

'Perfect day for it,' Connor said, unsure if he had ever known what Declan O'Connell looked like or if he had simply forgotten.

'Every day's a perfect day for golf as far as that man is concerned.' She raised her eyebrows and headed back to the kitchen.

Connor bent forward and whispered to Linda, 'Ellen says that your parents knew who was driving.'

'Not at first. But eventually I did try to tell them.'

Connor sat back. How was that possible? He hesitated before he spoke, unsure of what he wanted to ask. 'When? And they didn't think they should — I don't know — tell somebody?'

Linda looked out of the window and when her gaze returned, her eyes didn't meet his.

'I know it seems mad, but it was after the court case. You'd gone, Carmel was gone. I could hardly put two words together. Don't blame them for not listening. It was so much easier not to believe me. I mean they were dealing with all of this.' She indicated her legs. 'My parents were all over the place. They humoured me, they never went back to Dr Coulter's practice, but there was no way they were going to go to the guards, not with me as the only witness. If I'm being honest even I wasn't entirely certain, not swear-on-a bible sure. They were trying to protect me, I think. The truth is they never really trusted my memory and they worried that if they spoke out it would all just backfire on them, but mostly on me.' Linda checked Connor's face to see how he was receiving her explanation of events. His jaw was clenched, and he seemed to be gripping the arms of the chair. Connor thought of his father's contorted face as he shut the car door at the bus station in Cork. His mother slumped on the floor. Could it all have been avoided?

'I understand,' he said, trying to.

As if sensing Connor's reproach, Linda moved the conversation on, asking him about his life. Where had he been? What did he do? For a prodigal son returned, his life, to him, sounded very dull indeed. He told her about the irrigation company, he explained about Tim and the years he had spent with him. Linda nodded along and seemed genuinely interested — he might have been Sinbad recounting tales of his travels. But then Connor considered the life that Linda had lived. Again, he felt guilty. How often had he cursed the injustice that had forced him to leave? Now he was sitting in a room with a woman who hadn't really had a life at all. Of course, he told himself, that wasn't his fault, but it still made him appreciate all the living he had managed to do.

It seemed wrong that he was doing all the talking, so for balance he asked Linda some questions. Vague enquiries about her health, what she did with her day. He was taken aback by her answers. It appeared that she did practically nothing. Reading and watching television with her father in the evening seemed about the extent of her activities. Surely there was more to her life than that? Yes, she was in a wheelchair but so were others, and he saw them doing things — working, travelling, engaging with the world. Surely, she wanted to venture out? Instead of answering him, she began to talk about her worries for the future. Her parents weren't young. Her father had suffered a mini-stroke at the end of the previous year. Her mother was great but wouldn't go on forever. What would happen to Linda then? She supposed she'd have to go into some sort of home or maybe what they called sheltered accommodation.

'I try to talk about it, but they refuse to listen, or else Mammy starts to cry, so now we just ignore it.' Linda chewed the inside of her lip. Connor had no idea what to say. It was difficult to conjure up words of comfort when Linda was clearly right. There was no easy fix for her future.

The woman in the wheelchair turned her dark eyes on Connor and it felt like she was reading his mind.

'So, your life hasn't been all that bad, has it?' Her voice had an edge to it, not quite aggressive but almost as if she was challenging him to disagree.

'I never said — ' he began defensively.

Linda broke the tension with a laugh. 'Don't be stupid. I didn't mean anything. Nobody has a chance against me in the 'I have a shit life' competition.'

Connor laughed uneasily and drained his teacup. He hoped it might be a signal that he was ready to leave. There didn't seem to be an easy way to extricate himself from this meeting. Walking out seemed like quitting, or as if he didn't care.

'I'm sure you've places to be.' Linda said, to Connor's relief. She had got the hint.

'My parents might be worried. They seem to think that I'll just disappear again.' He stood.

'Oh, before you go, I was wondering — and

tell me if it's none of my business — Ellen wasn't the reason you took the blame, was she?'

'No. No she wasn't.' Connor felt he should explain further but that seemed a step too far.

'I didn't think so. You know it wasn't that long ago when I think I figured it out.'

Connor sat back down.

'Tell me more.'

And she did, and she was right.

2015

I.

Christ, Irish men were hideous. Why would anyone wear a vest if they'd arms like that? Finbarr picked up the next photograph in the pile and winced. Could a person ever be drunk enough to sleep with him? Keep the shirt on. Just then his viewing pleasure was interrupted by a shock of blue hair coming around the door.

'Everything OK?'

Finbarr tried not to stare. The young man had so many piercings in his lips he looked like he was waiting for someone to hang curtains.

'Yes, fine, thanks. I'm nearly done for the day.'

'We're packing up downstairs, so when you leave just switch off the lights and make sure the door locks behind you. It needs a good slam.'

'Will do, Fergal. Goodnight.'

Finbarr hoped that he had understood correctly. It appeared that copious lip jewellery meant that some, if not all, diction was lost.

Finbarr thought to himself that if a fish could talk it would probably look and sound like Fergal.

The blue head disappeared, and the door shut, leaving Finbarr alone in the small attic that contained what the staff at *Wilde Times* referred to as their archive. In reality it was just an old desk with four plastic stacking chairs and boxes piled from floor to ceiling.

Finbarr felt a bit of a fraud when he had to talk to any of the staff from *Wilde Times*. They all just assumed that he was as politically engaged as they were, which was very far from the truth. When they expressed their outrage about the Pride parade in Istanbul, he just nodded grimly. He made a mental note to google it later to find out what had happened. Even the referendum on gay marriage earlier in the year had failed to inspire him. Many of his friends had campaigned tirelessly, going from door to door and posting endless calls to action on social media. Finbarr claimed that he didn't understand why anyone wanted to get married, but the reality was that he was simply too lazy to get involved. He had been surprised then to find how moved he had been when the country had voted in favour of it in May. He had thrown himself into celebrating the victory with an enthusiasm that he had never felt during the campaign. His mother had laughed as she told him that even his grandparents had put a 'Yes' poster up in the pub. He had experienced a brief pang of guilt that Dan and Chrissie had done more to fight for his rights than he had. Some of the old gang from Sobar in New York had left messages of congratulations on his Facebook page. Finbarr had hit the 'like' button.

Gay marriage was going to come into law in November and his firm had been commissioned by the National Library to design a small foyer exhibition on gay life in modern Ireland. Most of the work he did was commercial, coming up with point-of-sale displays or exhibition stands for trade shows, so Finbarr jumped at the chance of this more creative brief. Knowing that there was practically no budget, he had come up with the idea of a series of panel displays. Each one featured an image of the iconic Tá poster so blown up that it looked purely graphic. Each individual panel would then be printed in muted versions of the colours from the rainbow flag. The content was being provided by an in-house archive that had been donated to the library, but Finbarr had volunteered to look through the boxes at *Wilde Times*. He thought he might find some images he could use on the exhibition stands. Now, as he sat staring at the stacks of assorted back issues, jumbles of club flyers, community pamphlets and hundreds of old photos scattered in front of him, he wasn't so sure.

There were bars Finbarr had never heard of: Bartley Dunne's, Rice's, Lynch's, the Viking, the Hirschfeld Centre. Of course, there were also pictures from the George, which still existed, and he did know well. Drag Queens and barmen dominated most of the photographs, but occasionally he would come across an image of drinkers sitting around a table or attending a meeting. Their black and white eyes met the camera and Finbarr marvelled how brave these people must have been. What risks had they taken just to be themselves in Dublin in the seventies and eighties? They smiled at him from the past, happy despite never knowing how bright the future might become. They sat, not touching, only showing the camera what they could of their happiness. Finbarr thought of his uncle Connor in Mullinmore. Had he known these bars and men existed? He doubted it.

Finbarr thought of the boy he had been when he'd arrived in Dublin, the way he had entered into the gay scene, never questioning its existence. He wouldn't have been able to articulate it at the time, but now he could see that the boy from Mullinmore had firmly believed his pretty face and blond hair had given him the right to be desired and pursued. Looking at these pictures of unremarkable men and women, he realised how deluded and foolish he had been. He had never had the right to party. These people he would never meet, or have the opportunity to thank, had been to all the dull meetings and inconvenient demonstrations, just so that he could dance to Katy Perry and kiss men in the back of cabs.

Pictures from Pride marches, gay picnics, fundraising nights for people with AIDS, protests, petitions being handed to embarrassed-looking men in suits. Groups of people fighting for their rights. His rights. Finbarr was humbled by their courage and their commitment, especially because, if he was being totally honest, he feared that if he'd been born thirty years earlier it was extremely doubtful he would have had the energy or motivation to make the noise for change. He felt very small.

Finbarr had nearly reached the end of the box of photographs he was sorting through. These were from the early noughties, so less interesting to him. Some of the drag queens were still on the scene now. The interiors had hardly changed. He found a clump of photographs held together with an elastic band. They were all of the same crowd of people standing in the street, taken from different angles. He thought it was outside the George. Nobody was holding banners so he assumed it couldn't be a march or demonstration of any kind. He turned the first photograph over and on the back someone had written in black ink, 'Bomb scare 2008'. Finbarr turned the picture back round. He was amazed. He had come to Dublin not that long after that and he had never heard about a bomb scare in the George. He looked at the drinkers in the street; some looked stony-faced or concerned, others were still laughing as if they knew that it was all a hoax. He was about to put the pictures back when a face in the crowd caught his eye. He looked closer. Was it? He got up and turned on the overhead light and held the photo up. He saw that his hand was shaking.

He fumbled in his jacket on the back of the chair and retrieved his phone. He struggled to catch his breath. Placing the photograph on the table he zoomed in using the camera. The image captured, he stared at it in disbelief. He had to do something, tell someone, but who?

Quickly he scrolled through his contacts and texted the picture to his uncle Connor. *Is this who I think it is?*

II.

Old Mrs Coulter wouldn't have been able to recognise this place. Ellen looked at the neat garden, the edged flower beds on either side of the concrete path, the lawn of even green. Of course, she would never get to see it now.

The old lady's heart had finally grown weary and allowed her to leave the small corner of the earth that she had occupied for the last few years. Martin, for all his devotion when they had lived together in the old house, had only made the journey home from the UK to see his mother five or six times. Ellen knew that the old woman no longer recognised her son, but it still seemed heartless. It was as if, in order to start his new life in England, he had to completely erase the old one. Naturally he had come home for the funeral.

It had been a very small affair. Finbarr and Aisling had come back, and her own parents were in attendance, along with a scattering of older people from the town who would have known her back when she was the doctor's wife and at the very heart of life in Mullinmore. Dan and Chrissie had pointedly ignored their former son-in-law and Martin had given them a wide berth too. Had he guessed that Connor had told them the truth, or did he just think their blank stares were because of the divorce? Would it even cross his mind that Ellen and Connor had chosen not to tell his children about the crash to protect his relationship with them? He was inscrutable, and then, just as Ellen was beginning to think that he must be completely dead inside, all at once, at the end of the service, he had begun to cry in silent jagging sobs. Ellen wasn't sure what she should do. Chrissie had turned and rolled her eyes. It was Aisling who had gone and put an arm around her father's shoulders.

Ellen stared straight ahead at the coffin. She thought about the big old house. All the cleaning and dusting. The hours that woman must have spent, bent double, scrubbing and polishing, and now here she was being carried away in a shiny wooden box with gleaming handles she would never see. What was the point of any of it?

It struck her as cruel when Martin announced he was having his mother cremated. Ellen wasn't a believer, far from it, but she wondered how Martin could leave his father all alone in the family plot waiting for his wife who would never come. If her parents hadn't already despised Martin, this monstrous act would have sealed his fate. For that, Ellen was almost glad he had done it. Finally, everyone, the whole town, could see the sort of man he was.

It had taken Ellen longer than she liked to admit to become accustomed to a life without Martin in it. She loved her bungalow and only having herself to answer to, but it was as if a part of her was still waiting for the other shoe to drop.

After all the years she had spent with Martin, she couldn't quite trust him to just stay away. She carried with her an unspoken worry that he would find a way to return and ruin her quiet contentment. Ellen knew that Martin still messaged the children occasionally on Facebook, but unless they were lying to her, Aisling and Finbarr knew as little about his life in Southampton as she did. After the maternity cover, he had found a job in another practice and he was renting a flat with a view of the sea. They knew this because he liked to post pictures of his morning coffee on a small metal table with the waves in the background. Often Ellen was tempted to unfriend him, but that would have caused more trouble than it was worth with the children so she scrolled as quickly as she could past any of his posts. She noticed that while Finbarr continued to 'like' them, it was only Aisling who posted comments.

'Living the life, Dad!'

'Cup of joe and go!'

'Waving back!'

Ellen didn't understand any of it. The pictures, the coffee, or the comments. She knew that for Aisling this version of a father, vaguely cosmopolitan and distant, suited her reinvented version of herself far better than an overweight, middle-aged mother living in a pebble-dashed bungalow outside Mullinmore. Aisling had managed to get herself a job as a junior account manager with a PR firm in Dublin. Apart from attending an endless parade of bar and restaurant openings, Ellen wasn't really sure what the job entailed. After about six months, Aisling announced her engagement to her boss, Philip, who happened to be the son of the man who owned the firm. Ellen had only met the boy a couple of times. He was a ruddy lump of a thing, a thatch of blond hair over a face with a seemingly permanent sheen of sweat. Ellen imagined he was an ex-rugby player gone to seed. Aisling seemed more excited by the size of her new diamond than the man on her arm. It was now nearly two years since the fanfare of the engagement but still no word of an actual wedding. Finbarr claimed the question had only been popped because of an unfounded pregnancy scare. Ellen worried it would all end it tears. Still, that might be what Aisling needed to reattach her feet to the ground.

Three years on and Ellen still experienced the same thrill when she got back to the house. Every time she walked down the short path to the front door she felt like falling to her knees like the Pope kissing the airport tarmac. This weekend, however, was going to change everything. As she opened the door and stepped into the hall, she hoped, not for the first time, that she was making the right decision. She was. She was certain of it. And if it did all turn out to be a mistake, then no harm done — well, not that much. She was tempted to go and light a candle in the chapel as she had done when she was a girl. She chuckled at her own foolishness.

Walking around the house, tidying up, clearing out drawers and the wardrobe in the back bedroom, she felt almost giddy with a mixture of nerves and excitement. Naturally, she recalled when she had felt like this before, and how that had turned out, but surely this time it would be different? She wasn't a child. They weren't rushing anything.

It had been the spring of 2013 when she had walked into the shop at Lawlor's garden centre. Bill Lawlor had retired long ago and now Shane Dunphy was managing the place. He had worked there since he was a boy and grown into the son that Bill had never had. It was generally assumed that one day Shane would inherit the lot. This theory made sense given all the work he had put into the place, opening a café, expanding the shop, investing in greenhouses for exotic plants. All Ellen wanted was a recommendation for someone who could help her tackle the overgrown garden that surrounded the bungalow. She had managed to cut back the hedges and mow the grass by herself, but she had finally accepted that the job was too big for her alone and besides she hadn't the first idea about what to plant or where.

She found Shane outside, beyond the car park, pushing a wheelbarrow of plants between some raised beds. With his short legs and wide shoulders he made it look easy. His face bore the healthy tan of a life lived in all weathers. When he announced that he did the sort of work Ellen was interested in, she wasn't sure how to respond. She didn't imagine that she needed someone who knew as much as Shane did, and she feared how much it might cost. On the other hand, she couldn't very well backtrack because she had stated quite clearly that she wanted to hire someone to help her with the garden.

'Are you sure?' was the best she could manage.

Shane smiled at her reassuringly. 'Don't decide now. Why don't you check out the website? It's all on there. At the end of the day labour is labour, the real costs are the plants, and that's as long as a piece of string. You can spend as much or as little as you want.'

Ellen nodded and looked around as if already considering what to plant.

'I tell you what, would you like me to come one evening this week just to have a look and give you an idea?'

From someone else it might have seemed like a heavy sell or being pushy, but from Shane it just came across as helpful, friendly even.

'That would be great. You know where I am?'

'I do. The old Coulter bungalow.'

'That's the one. Any night except Wednesday would be grand.'

Ellen left with a spring in her step. Things were moving. The garden had been annoying her ever since she had got the inside of the house in order.

It was the next evening when the doorbell chimed. It was just starting to get dark but there was still enough light for them to walk around outside. Ellen pointed out where she thought she might like a little patio or deck. Shane listed plant names that meant little or nothing to her, but she smiled and nodded. Really, she just wanted it to be like one of those makeover shows on television where she could leave for the afternoon to come back and find that it had all magically been done.

'Let me put some costs together for you and I'll get back to you.'

She shut the door. He drove away.

It was more than she had intended to spend but if she didn't use Shane, who would she use? Besides, she liked him and whoever she used would cost something. She trusted that he'd do a good job and the money was in the bank for now, so she might as well spend it. It was an investment, she told herself. She was adding to the value of the property. She chose to ignore the fact that there hadn't been a single offer on the place when it had been on sale for all those years.

One Saturday about three weeks later, the work started. Ellen stood at the kitchen window transfixed. It was all so noisy and dramatic — trees being cut back, the lawn torn up. Shane waved and smiled at her through the window as happy as a child on Christmas morning who had asked Santa for a second-hand rotavator. Ellen wasn't sure of the etiquette, so at lunchtime she stepped out into the back garden. Shane cut the motor when he saw her and wiped his arm across a sweaty brow.

'What are you doing for lunch?' she called across the ploughed lawn.

'Don't worry about me. I have a sandwich in the van,' he said, pointing towards the front of the house as if the location of the van gave his statement more credibility.

'Will you eat it inside? I'll make a pot of tea.'

'Great job. I'll be in in a minute so.' He restarted the motor and continued pushing the rotavator to the far end of the lawn.

Ellen made her way back inside and put out a plate for Shane's sandwich. She considered a napkin. No, too much. She tore off a strip of kitchen roll and put it on the table. The kettle began to whistle.

When Shane came into the kitchen, he brought the garden in with him. The smell of freshly dug earth, the heat of a body that had been working hard. Although not very tall, his bulk seemed to fill the small room. The neat little set of table and chairs looked like doll's house furniture when he sat down.

'Would you not have a bowl of soup? There's plenty,' offered Ellen.

'No. No. Work away. This is loads for me.'

As Ellen fussed around the cooker, she studied the man tearing into his sandwich of thick, roughly cut bread. He was younger than she was but not by much. His hair was flecked with grey, and his weathered face was creased around the eyes. Still, there was something boyish about the way he sat, an awkwardness that he had clearly never grown out of.

'You have the place lovely,' he commented, looking around between mouthfuls.

'Thanks. It suits me,' she had replied modestly. She was always thrilled when someone complimented the place.

'It must make a change after the big house,' Shane said casually.

'It is, but a good one. I love it, to be honest.'

She sat with her bowl of soup.

'I was sorry to hear about your troubles.'

Ellen wondered what particular part of her life Shane might be referring to. Her dead mother-in-law, her long-lost brother, or her divorce.

'Thank you. It's not so bad,' she said vaguely.

'You have children, don't you?'

He must have been talking about the divorce.

'Yes. A boy and a girl. Grown now, both working in Dublin. What about yourself, are you . . . ?' She wasn't sure how to finish the question. Married? With someone?

'No.'

He finished his sandwich while she took another spoonful of soup. The atmosphere had become uncomfortable. Ellen cursed herself for asking a personal question. She considered what to say next, to get things back on track. Shane gave a little cough and wiped his mouth with the paper towel.

'There was someone for a long time. Long distance. Limerick. I think she got sick of waiting. Married someone else.' He shrugged, resigned to his situation.

'Oh, I'm sorry to hear that.' Ellen tried to keep her voice light. She had just wanted a bit of company for lunch, not a heart to heart.

'Well, you know I don't make that much at the moment, not till Bill goes anyway, and she wanted a house, kids, you know, stuff I couldn't give her. Not yet anyway. It doesn't look like Bill is going anywhere fast.'

'Is he well?' Ellen asked.

'Very!' They both laughed.

After that things became easy between them. Each weekend he returned to continue the work, Ellen would bring him out mugs of tea. He'd eat his lunch with her. She dropped into the garden centre during the week and they walked through the rows of plants with Shane giving her ideas for her garden. When he described the smells of jasmine or the night-scented stock, she imagined herself sitting on her new patio on a summer's evening sipping a glass of rose. Sometimes she imagined that Shane was sitting at the table opposite her. What was the harm? It was his garden as well now, wasn't it?

When he eventually made his move it all seemed so inevitable. The weeks of waiting had just been time wasted. One Saturday night Shane had knocked on the door to let her know that he was off. She thanked him and said that she'd see him the following weekend, but he hesitated on the doorstep.

'I saw you liked wine, so I picked you up a bottle.' He held out a bottle of red wine.

'Thank you.' She took it and looked at the label. Chianti.

'That's lovely. Thanks.' Shane was looking at her expectantly.

'Oh!' she exclaimed, the penny dropping. 'Would you like a glass now? One for the road?'

'If you're not busy . . . '

'No. No. It would be nice.'

'It would. Very nice. Yes.'

They hadn't even finished their first glass when his hands were on her thighs and his mouth on hers. They slipped off their chairs onto the floor. Ellen kept thinking that she would stop him or that he would pull away but that didn't happen. His hands seemed to be everywhere, her breasts, her legs, and then his fingers were inside her. She whimpered and found herself doing things she had never considered before. She was biting his ear, throwing her head back and letting out moaning sounds she didn't recognise as her own voice. Then he had pulled her to her feet and without either of them uttering a word, she had understood and led him by the hand to her bedroom.

After a life spent dreading the very idea of sex and being thankful that it wasn't a part of her marriage, she now found herself consumed by it. When she was with Shane, she just wanted to be touching him, be held by him and when she wasn't, she remembered the taste of him, the heat of him, the weight of him. The way that Shane was around her made her self-consciousness vanish, her feelings of not being attractive or desirable disappear. He wrapped his arms around her, cradled the softness of her belly, gazed down at her as if she was some rare impossible beauty. What made his adoration bearable was that she felt the same way about him. She allowed her hands to explore his body, the folds of flesh, the wiry tufts of hair, it was all just perfect in her eyes.

Soon people had noticed the garden centre van parked all night outside the bungalow and the gossip started. Before they had even had an opportunity to talk about what they were or what they were doing, they had become an item. Shane kissed her in the street before he got in the van to drive off and, just like that, they had gone public. Ellen had no idea how it might all end. It could be a fling or something far more serious, but for now she didn't care. She was as giddy as a teenager and she was happier than she could ever remember being before.

Finbarr had been pleased for her when she broke the news, although he did little to disguise his bewilderment about how she could be bothered to embark on a romance at her stage of life. Aisling had been uninterested veering towards dismissive until she figured out the identity of her mother's new love interest.

'The big man baby from the garden centre? Jesus, Mammy!' Ellen got the feeling that if Aisling bumped into her in the street with Shane, she would pretend not to know her. At least her own mother was happy for her. Chrissie still carried guilt for not fully appreciating how bad Ellen's marriage had been, so she had perhaps overcompensated on hearing the news that her daughter had met someone else. 'That's fantastic news, pet! Dan! Isn't that wonderful?' Dan lowered his paper to agree. 'It is. Shane Dunphy is a sound young fella. He's made a great job of Lawlor's, in fairness.' It sounded to Ellen as if her father thought running a garden centre was a similar task to dating his daughter. She didn't care. Shane was mad about her and she felt exactly the same about him.

The initial burst of frenzied passion settled down into something comfortable and steady.

They saw each other a couple of times a week and most weekends. Ellen cooked or they might have a meal in the hotel. He took her to the cinema. They went for drives on Sundays and sang along to songs on the radio. It was a part of life she had skipped the first time around and so this happiness seemed even sweeter, more important to savour.

Now two years later they had reached the point where Shane was going to move in. It made sense. Of course it did. He had been renting a damp little one-bedroomed flat above the bank that she had only set foot in twice. Now he would pay her rent and they could spend all the time they wanted together. They had never had a row, not yet, but Ellen still worried that this move could change everything. What if he stopped making an effort? What if he started to take her for granted? She kept thinking back to her days with Martin and how even the tiniest gesture or single word had made her loathe him more. What if that happened with Shane?

The light had begun to fade. She was on her hands and knees shoving old clothes into bin bags in the back bedroom when she heard somebody at the door. Odd. Too early for Shane and besides, he had his own key. Ellen stood and walked to the door, patting down her hair, smoothing her skirt.

'Hello.'

It was a deeply tanned, middle-aged man, with a handsome face slightly fading away into recently acquired jowls. He had an accent.

French? Italian? Ellen wasn't sure. She assumed he was lost.

'Yes. Can I help you?' She was aware of using a slightly more refined tone, to help him understand, in case his English wasn't that good.

'Ah, I hope so. I'm looking for Martin Coulter?'

Ellen was slightly taken aback.

'Martin doesn't live here. May I ask what it's regarding?' She felt uneasy. Did he owe money? Had he done something underhand with the deeds of the house?

'I'm an old friend. We lost touch when I moved away.'

'I see.' She wondered if she should give this man Martin's email address.

'The lady in the post office, she proposed that I try this house.'

'I see,' Ellen repeated.

'And you must be his . . . ' He appeared to be searching for the correct word. ' . . . sister?'

'No.' She was unsure how much she should explain, so simply stated, 'I'm Mrs Coulter.'

The foreign gentleman on the doorstep grew visibly pale.

III.

Connor heard the impatient ping of his phone but chose to ignore it. He loved afternoons like this and wanted to enjoy it uninterrupted for as long as possible. Leaning back into the creaks from the old wooden Adirondack chair on the porch, cool beer in hand, the forlorn honk of a train from the far bank of the Hudson, this was what life in America had looked like in his imagination.

A slight chill had crept into the late-afternoon breeze and hints of russet and amber were creeping through the leaves. Connor thought back to what winter had been like the previous year. The clanking of the ancient heating system keeping them all awake but never warm, watching TV wrapped in a duvet, taking showers at the gym because the thought of stripping naked in the bathroom made your flesh hug your bones with dread. He took another sip of his beer. He could worry about the future later.

Tim had offered him the chance to continue living in Hell's Kitchen at a reduced rent, but at nearly forty-eight years of age Connor finally felt he might be ready to try a little independence. His boss George had started giving him some office shifts as well as the outdoor work, so he was actually earning enough to live on if he was careful. One afternoon in the back of the truck the subject of apartments had come up and Connor had mentioned that he was going to be looking. One of the guys explained that a room in his house would be coming up in a couple of weeks. Connor asked how much the rent would be and immediately became very keen when he heard how cheap it was. The house, it transpired, was not in the city. It was in Nyack, a small town on the river about forty minutes north of the city. Connor became, just as quickly, less keen. However, when his co-worker Chad showed him some pictures of the house on his phone, Connor changed his mind again. It was irresistible. A shabby old Victorian house painted long ago in ice-cream pastels, it sat high above the road. With its mini turrets and abacus mouldings on the wraparound porch, the building seemed overdressed for the broken-down fence and potholed road that fronted the sloping lot. Immediately Connor imagined himself spending afternoons just like the one he was enjoying now, sipping his drink and watching the world amble by.

He could hear the laughter of children playing somewhere in the distance, the clank of a tool being dropped on the ground by Warren working on his car next door.

The neighbourhood was run-down and unloved, but he liked it. He recalled the look on Tim's face when they had pulled up outside on the day that Connor had moved in. 'Is this even safe?' Tim had helped carry boxes inside, peering into the antique kitchen and water-stained bathrooms with undisguised horror. 'Are you sure about this?' At the time Connor hadn't felt very certain, but he found that life in Nyack suited him. Coming back from Mullinmore, Manhattan had seemed overwhelming at times. He needed to take stock and that was easier in a small town. He could walk down the hill along Main Street, past the beer and pizza joints and turn onto South Broadway with its trendy coffee shops, nodding to familiar faces. It already felt more like home than Manhattan ever had. He found he turned down invitations to drinks or parties in the city, happy to head back to his peeling paint and weed-strewn drive. He had also discovered that opera was never really his first choice when he was listening to music and he was not as keen a chef as he had always believed. It seemed they'd just been affectations designed to help him fit into a life that was entirely Tim's.

He still enjoyed having Tim as a friend. He was as kind and generous as he had always been, but comparing their lives wasn't helpful. Connor lived and worked with people who were nearly twenty years younger than he was, but he earned what they did. Their lives measured up. Sitting on this porch looking out at the scruffy street, he didn't care about any of it, but when he was with Tim, he couldn't help feeling like a failure.

He remembered that there was a message waiting on his phone. Finbarr. He sighed. It was lovely to have family back in his life, but he was still adjusting to the pressures of having to stay in touch. It turned out that his mother Chrissie was a very enthusiastic texter, but since she had learned how to do it from her grandchildren, Connor often found it hard to understand her abbreviations and obscure acronyms. His responses tended to be upbeat but vague. The shorthand nature of texts didn't really suit people who hadn't communicated for so many years. When his sister had sent him a picture of the 'Yes' poster hanging in their parents' pub, she had added the laughing face emoji. He knew she just meant him to think it was sweet that Dan and Chrissie were supporting their son and grandson, but part of him felt that the emoji was laughing at him. *Look*, it said, *nobody ever cared about you being gay!* Progress was great, he was happy for Finbarr, but it didn't erase the past. His parents now weren't his parents then, but that didn't mean his memories weren't real.

He turned back to his phone and opened the message.

Is this who I think it is?

He clicked on the image. Weird. Why would Finbarr send him this? He quickly texted back.

What do you mean?

The response was almost instantaneous, as if Finbarr had been sitting staring at his phone, waiting for a reply.

Is it Dad???

Not seen him in thirty years! Looks like him I guess. Why?

Can you talk?

Sure.

His phone rang.

'Hello. What is this about?'

'I just found the photo and wanted to double check that it was definitely Daddy.'

'Where did you find it?'

Finbarr explained about the exhibition and trawling through the boxes at *Wilde Times*. Connor listened carefully as his nephew described the scene outside the George. He wasn't sure what to say.

'So, like, do you think that Daddy would be in a gay bar?'

Connor hesitated.

'Well do you?' his nephew pressed him.

'He might just have been passing. You don't know he was inside the George and even if he was, you can't jump to any conclusions.' He hoped he sounded measured and mature. He reminded himself that Ellen was trying to protect these children, however misguided he thought that was. Why shouldn't they know the sort of man their father was and the life their mother had endured? This, though, this was different.

'He was in that bar. He's in the middle of the crowd; there's no way he was just passing. What do you think I should do? Should I tell Mammy?'

'No.' Of that he was certain.

'Do you think I should say anything to my father?'

Connor gazed across the tops of the trees on the hill below. The sky stretched blue and endless before him. He had no answers for this boy.

'Only you can decide that, Finbarr.'

1987

XII.

This was the worst. Cleaning the toilets was gross enough, but standing on the street with a yard brush and a bucket of disinfectant-laden water trying to sweep away last night's vomit from the pavement was so public. Most of the time, having a paying job made him feel more grown up than his pals who had headed off to college, but this was humiliating. In the winter, at least the smell wasn't so bad, but on a warm summer's morning like today, Connor was afraid he might heave himself and add to the mess on the footpath.

He had finished and was pouring the bucket's contents into a drain when a car pulled up. Connor assumed it was someone parking so kept his head down to avoid any further embarrassment.

'Working hard.'

Connor's head jerked up and he fumbled with the handle of the bucket. It was the doctor's son Martin Coulter. There was something about him that always made Connor nervous. It wasn't just that he fancied him; he fancied lots of lads he saw around the town. There was an air about Martin that made him seem cooler than everyone else. Connor always felt judged and found lacking when Martin was around. Whenever they were both in the same place. Connor knew that he stared more than he wanted to, and Martin invariably caught him. The hint of a smirk always said that he knew exactly what Connor was thinking and pitied him for it.

'Not really. Just the morning clean-up.' Connor shrugged. The sun was in his eyes, but he was making an effort not to squint.

Martin had stepped out of the car and was resting against it. The top few buttons of his shirt were undone. Connor tried and failed not to look at the patch of dark chest hair and the elegant bones that slipped away beneath Martin's throat.

'You working all day?'

'No. I'm done now until tonight.' Connor was aware of the lingering smell of vomit tangled with disinfectant.

'Right.' Martin raised one arm and brushed a hand through his hair which flopped down over his brow. He glanced down the street and then back to Connor.

'Few of us are heading out to the beach later if you fancy a swim?'

Connor wasn't sure what to say. He wanted to ask questions. Why are you inviting me? Who are the others? But he felt he couldn't, so he found himself nodding his head slowly.

'Sounds good.'

* * *

Linda was lying on her bed while her sister rested against the door frame.

'Come. It'll be good fun.'

'It's a wedding thing. I'm not involved.' She was trying to sound uninterested rather than hurt.

'Ah, Linda, stop. It's not a wedding thing, thank God. Bernie might stop talking about it for five seconds. Martin is driving and he's not a best man or anything.'

'Martin Coulter?'

'Yes.'

'I thought he'd gone back to uni.'

'Not yet, no.' Carmel tilted her head. 'What do you say?'

Linda pushed herself up to sitting. A trip to the beach did sound like good fun, but she wasn't willing to let the snub of not being a bridesmaid go so easily.

'I dunno.'

'Well, look, I can't make you.' Carmel stood away from the door frame. Clearly she wasn't going to beg. 'Martin said he'd pick us up after lunch.'

Linda threw her legs over the side of her bed. A physical declaration that she was coming.

'Do you like that Martin Coulter?'

'*Like* him, like him?' Carmel responded.

'I mean, he's good-looking and that, but do you not think there's something about him?'

'I suppose. What, like a bit pleased with himself like?'

'Yeah. That. A bit creepy or something?'

'I dunno. All I know is he's got a car and it's a great day for a swim.' Carmel stepped onto the landing to return to her own room.

Linda called after her. 'I'm not getting my hair wet.'

Carmel laughed. 'And like I am! Salon Yvonne would kill me!'

The two sisters laughed.

* * *

Bernie was playing with David's hair. He was willing her to stop but knew that if he actually asked her to, a row of some sort would ensue. He blamed the wedding. Christ, he hoped it was the wedding and that the Bernie of the last few weeks wasn't going to be the woman he ended up married to. That was why he had been so keen when he had bumped into Martin and they had come up with the idea of a trip to Trabinn.

'It's the day before the wedding. We must have things to do,' Bernie fretted.

'It's all done,' David reassured her. 'It'll be good for us to just have some fun. Take our minds off it.'

'Do you not like thinking about our wedding?' Her face darkened.

David took a deep breath to avoid snapping at his bride-to-be. This was a minefield. 'Of course I do. But I just want to enjoy tomorrow. You know. Come to it fresh.'

Bernie looked semi-convinced. He pushed on.

'A sea breeze. A bit of a laugh.' He looked into her face and she smiled back. They did love each other.

'You might even risk an ice cream,' David

giggled, hoping Bernie might still be able to take a joke.

'David Hegarty!' she shrieked and punched his shoulder, but she was laughing too and then his face was touching hers and they were kissing.

* * *

There are moments in any life that are to be treasured, but only sometimes are they recognised as they happen. That was how the five people in the blue estate car felt that day. The windows down, an optimistic glow about the town, two of their number about to embark on a whole new life together. It felt special. This was not a day to be forgotten or confused with all the others.

The song of the summer, 'La Bamba', was bursting out of the radio and all the shoulders were swaying in unison. As they drove down the back quay, some kids playing down by the river stopped and looked up at the car and Carmel, Linda, Bernie, David and Martin fully understood that they were to be envied.

Turning into the square, Martin said over the music, 'We just need to pick up Connor Hayes.'

Carmel leaned over the front seat from the back. 'Who?'

'Connor Hayes from the pub. I bumped into him earlier. Felt a bit sorry for him. You guys don't mind, do you?'

Truthfully, they didn't but nor did they understand why this boy they didn't really know was joining the party. Martin pulled up outside the pub and Connor emerged from the side door.

'Jump in the back there with *les filles*,' Martin called through his window, with a heavy accent on the French. Linda tried to catch Carmel's eye to exchange a look, but her sister was busy opening her door. Connor squeezed onto the back seat and they drove away.

The atmosphere in the car changed. The radio was playing Pet Shop Boys and the lack of chat amongst the passengers now seemed awkward. Linda tried to ask Bernie some questions about the following day.

'Don't. I just want a day where my head isn't destroyed from thinking about the wedding.'

A tight-lipped Linda studied the passing hedgerows. She'd only asked to be nice and demonstrate that there were no hard feelings about the whole bridesmaid drama. Linda was more than happy not to mention the stupid wedding. Then Carmel's voice.

'Mammy is having to head up to Cork. I must have forgotten to mention the red and white and didn't she only go and buy a red and white dress. She was fuming!'

Bernie laughed. 'You should see the size of Mammy's hat. It's mental! Isn't it, David?'

Her fiancé turned around from the passenger seat. 'It's a fair size all right. I'd say if you wire her up she could contact outer space.'

Everyone laughed, apart from Linda who maintained her keen interest in roadside maintenance. Apparently, she was the only one who couldn't mention the wedding. Fine. She'd say nothing at all.

Connor was squeezing his backpack between his knees. He had borrowed one of the good towels from the hot press. The hope was he could return it without his mother noticing. When he'd tried on the togs he had from school, they seemed a bit tight and skimpy, so he'd brought an old pair of football shorts. He wondered what sort of swimwear Martin would be wearing. He looked at the back of the driver's head, where his hair touched the collar and the thin slice of pink from an ear that edged through. It looked intimate, almost raw, and Connor imagined running his finger along the ridge of flesh, tracing the skin with his tongue. He could feel himself become aroused and looked down to hide his blushing cheeks. Carmel was asking about ice cream.

'Can we stop in Schull for ice creams, Martin?'

'No need. We can get them in the shop at the caravan park.' He didn't sound like the others. His voice had an authority that made him seem almost like a parent.

'Does that shop have a freezer?' Carmel didn't sound convinced.

'I thought you had to wait for the ice-cream van out at Trabinn,' David added.

'What sort of a shop at a caravan park doesn't sell ice cream? Trust me.'

They had driven through Schull.

The trees thinned out and there were glimpses of the sea beyond the faded green of the fields.

'Nearly there,' Bernie said to fill the silence.

The car came down a steep incline and then

around a corner before Martin turned into the dusty car park.

'It's not as busy as I thought it would be,' David said, looking out at the cars dotted around with no sense of order.

'Schools have gone back,' Martin said. The others made various noises to indicate the logic of this but also to confirm how little school timetables impinged on their lives now. Connor felt self-conscious. Even though his schooldays were also behind him, the others being a couple of years older meant they had an air of adulthood that made him feel as if he was still the schoolboy. He pawed at the door handle and let himself out.

The group stood beside the car, unsure of how to proceed. Without the breeze blowing through the car windows the afternoon heat seemed to have taken them all by surprise. Martin addressed the others as if issuing a statement.

'I want to head over to the other side below the cliffs. I'm going to dive.'

Bernie emitted a guttural moan to indicate her revulsion at this suggestion.

'I'm not getting my hair wet. I already said. A bit of sunbathing down on the sand will do me, thank you very much.' She folded her arms and looked at David expectantly.

'I'll stay here with you, pet.' He took Bernie's hand.

'Me too,' Carmel chimed in.

Linda said nothing. Neither option was appealing at this point but at least the beach didn't involve a hike across the dunes and clambering over rocks.

'Please yourselves. Has everyone got everything?' Martin asked.

David reached into the back seat and grabbed some towels.

'That's us.'

'Right.' Martin locked the car and started to walk towards the dunes while the others shuffled in the direction of the beach.

Connor stood and looked both ways, unsure of what he was meant to do.

'Connor?' It was Martin, looking over his shoulder. 'Fancy a swim?'

'Yeah, sure.' He jogged the few paces to catch up with the older boy, who had kept walking. They made their way in single file. Connor could hear Martin whistling tunelessly as he swung his bag.

At the far end of the dunes there was a ridge of dark rocks.

'Mind yourself,' Martin cautioned as he began to pick his way down towards the thin strip of pebble beach that led towards the low cliffs. Connor had been here only once before. He had been no more than nine or ten years old and his father had brought him to see the seals sunning themselves on the rocks. He remembered their laboured breathing as they rolled themselves into the sea and the way their slick black bodies had become one with the swell of the ocean as it pulled back and forth from the cliffs.

Now Martin reached the end of the pebble beach and climbed up a seaweed-covered escarpment of rocks that looked like a stack of torn pages. He turned and called back to Connor, 'It's just here.' And then he disappeared down the other side.

Connor followed and when he reached the top of the rocks, he saw the dark rolling sea nudging the impressive boulders at the foot of the cliff. Martin was standing on a large flat rock with his bag at his feet. Had he seen something? He was standing very still, but then in one smooth movement he had removed his shirt and let it fall to the ground. Connor stopped and stared. Next Martin kicked off his shoes before undoing his belt and sliding down his jeans and underwear as one. First his right leg, then the left. The jeans sat squat and empty to one side while a tall naked Martin, legs slightly apart, stood staring out at the sea. Connor followed the line of the spine down the pale smooth back to the crack of the ass, and then the dark shadow between the gap of the thighs. He had seen naked men before in the changing rooms at school, but this was something entirely different. This wasn't someone going through a practical routine of swapping one set of clothes for another, it was a display. Martin had to know that Connor had climbed the rocks by now, that he was watching, running his eyes across every contour of shameless flesh. Connor wasn't sure what he should do. Cough, to remind Martin he was there? Continue down the rocks as if he hadn't noticed the nakedness? Before he had to decide, Martin bent down to his bag, retrieved a pair of red swimming togs and peeled them on.

Relieved, Connor carefully climbed down to the flat rock.

'There you are!' Martin smiled, as if he had been wondering where he had got to. Maybe he hadn't been putting on a show? Perhaps this had nothing to do with Connor at all? It might be that this was just a man being entirely comfortable about putting on his swimsuit in public.

'It's great here. You dive in from this bit and then you can climb out over there.' Martin pointed at the far end of the flat rock they were standing on. Then, without warning, he dived into the black sea and disappeared. Connor scanned the water, looking for him. He thought he spotted a pale sliver of flesh just below the surface. It reminded him of trying to find the remains of the soap in murky bathwater. Then with a plume of spray Martin's dark hair emerged. He manoeuvred his body around to grin at Connor.

'It's amazing. Get in!' he called back to the rock.

Connor slipped his feet out of his trainers and took off his rugby shirt. He tried to forget that Martin was looking at him. The weird hairs around his nipples. The soft swell of his belly. Quickly he sat and peeled off his socks. From his rucksack he pulled out the towel and draped it over his lap. Wriggling, he pulled down his jeans and Y-fronts. Untangling them from his feet he was very aware of being naked below his towel. He willed himself not to get an erection. Martin was laughing.

'Shy, are we?'

Connor had no idea how to respond so he just bent his head to his bag and pretended he hadn't heard. He got his shorts on as fast as he could and then stood, letting the towel fall. It felt like a mini-triumph to have got changed in front of Martin Coulter without humiliating himself. He walked to the edge of the rock and dived in.

The chill of the water was delicious. He swam beneath the surface for a few strokes and then poked his head through the slow swell of the water. The sea looked like ink and watching his own arms and hands cutting through it felt unexpectedly sensuous. He scanned the waves for Martin but couldn't see him. Connor swam a little bit and then rolled his body in the water, enjoying how free it made him feel. He saw now that Martin was lying on the rock, head thrown back, drinking from a bottle. The sun bounced from his pale wet body making it look glossy, almost plastic. Connor plunged below the surface once more, not wanting to seem overly keen to sit with Martin. He tried opening his eyes but couldn't see anything apart from a sepia mist.

Slowly he swam back to the end of the rock Martin had shown him. He placed his arms carefully above his head and back into the water, remembering his swimming lessons, conscious that he was being watched.

The rock was warm beneath his feet and he picked his way over to where Martin lay beside their bags. He stretched his towel out a couple of feet away from Martin.

'Cider?' The bottle was held aloft.

'No thanks.'

'Please yourself,' Martin said and took another long draught.

Connor wondered if he should explain that he had made himself violently sick when he was around eleven or twelve drinking stolen cider with his friend Fergal. Now, just the smell of it was enough to make him feel a little queasy. He decided against sharing the story. Let Martin think he wasn't thirsty.

They lay in silence for a few minutes. Connor had a theory that he couldn't get sunburnt while he was still wet. Once he dried off, he would dive into the sea again. The heat was wonderful. He could feel his body relaxing into his towel.

'So, who are you?'

Martin's voice broke the silence. He raised the bottle to his lips again and drained it. Connor wasn't sure if he understood the question, so chose to repeat it.

'Who am I?'

'Yeah. Like what do you want to do? Are you happy in Mullinmore? Do you like music? Do you read books? What's your story?' Martin was squinting at him but then reached for a second bottle of cider from his bag and twisted it open.

Connor considered his answer. He knew that Martin was studying medicine so whatever he said was going to sound lacklustre in comparison.

'I don't know. I did the leaving last year. Didn't do brilliant. I thought I might move to Cork.'

'Oh, the big smoke.' Martin's tone was gently mocking.

'For starters like. Then maybe Dublin,' Connor said defensively.

Martin took another drink and propped himself on his elbows, allowing his face to be bathed by the sunlight.

'Have you a girlfriend, Connor?'

With that question the mood shifted. Connor felt himself redden but Martin was still looking skyward.

'No.' He hoped that he sounded nonchalant but there was a dryness in his voice.

The water lapped at the edge of the rock and somewhere in the distance seagulls sounded mildly alarmed. Connor thought he should go for another swim, but before he could get up, Martin spoke.

'Are you still a virgin, Connor?' He continued to face the sky, his neck arched backwards.

'Yes.' That sounded pathetic. 'Sort of.' Connor added, hoping that it made him sound less prudish and a little more worldly.

Martin turned his head and smiled.

'I'd say you do a mad lot of wanking then.' He laughed.

Connor joined in, glad that Martin didn't seem to be judging him.

'A fair bit all right.'

In their jollity, it felt like a shared moment. Boys together.

Martin rolled onto his front and used his hands to hold up his head.

'Did you ever have a blow job?' His voice

sounded lower. A secret was being shared. There was a glint in his eye. Connor wanted this conversation to end but he was also enjoying it. Just talking about these forbidden things felt like a sexual act.

'What?' He edged a little closer.

'A blow job. Please tell me you know what a blow job is?' Martin grinned and playfully reached across to slap Connor on the shoulder.

'Yes. Yes of course I do.' He had heard boys talking and laughing about blowies.

'Well?'

'Well, what?'

'Did you ever have one?'

Connor paused as if trying to remember any blow jobs that might have slipped his mind.

'Not really, no.' He felt this was fair. He had been loosely connected to an actual blow job because a boy he knew had played in a match against the Presentation Brothers up in Cork, and afterwards a girl from Mount Mercy gave him a blowie in Fitzgerald Park.

Martin rolled onto his back again and closed his eyes to the sun.

'They're amazing. The best.'

Connor imagined a head of long lustrous hair moving between Martin's legs. He pulled the corner of his towel up to hide his obvious erection.

'Yeah.'

It became very silent. Their breathing seemed to be the only sound. Even the waves appeared to have been stilled. Connor could see that Martin was also aroused, but he seemed utterly unembarrassed. What should Connor do? Was he meant to say something? An involuntary tremble rippled through his body. He hated how excited he was. He knew he should just get up and walk away.

Martin, his eyes still closed, wet his lips and then said, 'I have an idea.'

Connor held his breath, waiting to hear what it was.

'If you give me one, I'll give you one.'

Connor felt like he was caught in a trap. Martin was trying to trick him. He looked around anxiously to see who else was in on the joke.

'Nobody can see us down here. Don't worry.' Martin was looking into his face now. 'Come on. Just lads messing. It feels fantastic. Come on.'

It was too much. This couldn't actually be happening. It was the stuff of his fantasies.

Connor shook his head. 'I don't know.'

'Come on. Help a lad out.' With one hand Martin tugged down the front of his trunks and with the other took a firm hold of his erection and pointed it at Connor. Connor just stared, frozen, unable to decide what the best course of action might be. Was there any way this could end well?

'Just do it for a bit.' Martin paused. 'Then I'll do you.'

Slowly, like a wild animal being tempted from its lair, Connor found himself leaning forward.

'Yeah, that's it,' Martin encouraged him.

Then it was in his mouth. It was colder than he thought it would be. He could taste the salt water and an unfamiliar mannish musk.

'Oh my God,' Martin groaned and threw back his head.

Connor moved up and down. He wondered if he was doing it right.

Martin flinched. 'Mind your teeth.'

After a couple more movements Connor felt he had done enough and tried to get up, but Martin held his hair. 'Just a bit more. A bit more.'

Connor shifted on his knees and continued.

'Good boy,' Martin sighed and it struck Connor that it sounded as if he was being spoken to like a dog, but he still enjoyed it as praise. He was doing it well.

'Take the whole thing.' More groaning.

The gagging was sudden and unpleasant. Connor wanted to stop, but his hair was being clenched too tightly. The way that Martin was thrusting himself into Connor's mouth was making him feel sick. He tried to pull back but, Martin just intensified his grip. His jaw ached and he squirmed to get away, but the pounding just got faster and more violent. Despite the unpleasantness, though, Connor was still being careful with his teeth, trying his best, wanting to please this man. The intense breathing through his nose meant it had started to run and he could feel his eyes beginning to water. Suddenly he heard Martin almost whimper, 'Jesus. Jesus. Fuck.' And then Connor's mouth was full of hot acrid liquid. Martin released his hold and fell back. 'Oh my God.'

Connor reached for his towel and as he wiped

his face, spat what he could into it, though the bitter taste stayed in his mouth. He was relieved it was over but also excited because now it was his turn. He got up on his knees and pushed down his shorts. Martin glanced at him.

'Well, you look like you really enjoyed that.' He sounded mildly disgusted.

Connor was unsure of how to proceed. Had Martin forgotten their bargain?

'You said you'd do me,' he said quietly.

'What?' Martin was incredulous. 'I'm not putting my mouth on that fucking thing.'

'But you said . . . ' Connor's voice trailed away.

'I'm not some stinking poofter like you. I'm not going to suck anybody's cock.' He was pulling on his shirt.

'But you . . . ' Connor struggled to understand how what he had done made him gay but that somehow Martin remained firmly heterosexual.

'Look, we both know that you wanted to do that. You're a little cocksucker. You got what you wanted, so now you can fuck off.' Martin stood up with his jeans in his hands.

'No,' was all Connor could think of to say. Martin was lying. This wasn't fair. The sense of the injustice was physical. It rose from his stomach. He felt that tears were not far away, but he knew he mustn't cry. 'No,' he repeated, this time a little louder. Panic was overtaking him. He felt sick. 'You're not going to tell anyone, are you?'

Martin was zipping up his flies.

'Tell anyone? Why would I? They'll all know

soon enough. You'll go to Cork, get AIDS and die. Sure, everyone will know you're a little queer then.' He bent and picked up his bag and the half-drunk bottle of cider. 'Now hurry up. The others will be waiting.'

Connor watched him pick his way over the seaweed-covered rocks and then disappear down the other side. He looked around and noticed that it was getting late. The colour had drained from the sky and the sea had turned to liquid slate. Connor slumped by his rucksack and wept harder than he had since he was a little boy. This was, without doubt, the worst thing that had ever happened to him.

2019

I.

It wasn't to his taste, but Bill had to admire the work that young Shane Dunphy had put into the place. The little café he had opened back in his day was long gone and replaced by this much larger structure designed to look as if it was sprung from nature. Twisted tree trunks were dotted about as pillars supporting a ceiling of honey-coloured rough wooden planks. Outside, the walls were covered in bark and ivy and the roof was a sloping lawn of grass. It looked more like Middle-earth than Mullinmore. Through the misshapen panes of glass in the window he could see people in their finery starting to arrive. He should make a move.

'A cheeky glass of prosecco, Bill?'

It was Ellen Coulter at his elbow holding up a thin flute of golden bubbles.

'I won't, Ellen. Thanks all the same. The doctor has me off the sauce entirely.'

'You're sure?'

'I am, I am. Shane just wanted me to see the place all decked out. You've done a fantastic job.'

Ellen and old Bill Lawlor looked across the room, each round table topped with stylish hurricane lanterns waiting to be lit and surrounded by a riot of flowers.

'It wasn't me really. It was Finbarr and Luke

did all the work. I don't know what time they must have got out of here last night. Oh, there's Shane, I have to talk to him, will you — '

'Away you go. Have a great night. All of you.' Bill turned to leave, unsure of what else might be appropriate to say on such an occasion. A gay wedding. Had he ever thought he would live to see the day?

Bill might have been perplexed, but Finbarr was truly shocked that this day had come. Over the years he had never stopped looking for *the one*, but his commitment to the dating game was similar to the way he approached most areas of his life. Effort suggested he cared and that way lay failure and disappointment. Nobody had lasted more than a month or two. Having spent so many years swatting away unwelcome attention it had begun to chip away at his granite cliff of confidence that perhaps he wasn't capable of having a relationship now that he felt ready for one.

When he first met Luke, it had not been promising. He was a mature student who had left his family business, a chain of high-end homeware stores, to do a masters in art history at Trinity College. They had met through the exhibition at the National Library. Luke knew the archivist and had been on hand to help during the installation. It was as if Luke was actively afraid someone might find him attractive. He hid his tall thin frame inside oversized corduroy suit jackets, while thick curtains of hair fell to hide his pale face. Finbarr instantly dismissed him as some sort of sexless geek. The first hint he had that Luke might be something else was one morning when they arrived together and without warning Luke began to do an impression of Jack, the small boy from the movie *Room*.

'Good morning, door. Good morning, lamp. Good morning, exhibition. Good morning, marriage equality.'

Finbarr laughed and Luke glanced at him shyly and smiled. As the morning went on, they found themselves kneeling together as they assembled the support poles for the exhibition stands. Finbarr was humming a song by The Weeknd and suddenly Luke joined in singing, 'I can't feel my face when I'm with you, but I love it.'

Finbarr rocked back on his heels and laughed again. 'Nice voice.'

'Why, thank you very much.' Luke tucked a lock of hair behind an ear and looked at him. He had high cheekbones and dark brown eyes. His face reminded Finbarr of a portrait he loved in the National Gallery next door; he thought it was by Goya. The two young men began to chat and learn about each other's lives. Finbarr was surprised to discover that at thirty-two, Luke was older than him, but he was also knowledgeable and funny, talking about all sorts of things from new movies to obscure books. By lunchtime Finbarr had a strong sense that he would develop feelings for this man. They ate their sandwiches together, went for a drink after they had finished for the day, and had been more or less inseparable ever since.

Finbarr had assumed that there would come a day after the first couple of months when he would grow bored or meet somebody new to tempt him away. But every day when he woke up he found he was as happy as the morning before to find Luke on the next pillow. After six months Finbarr gave up his room in the flat he shared and moved in with Luke, who lived in a smart two-bedroomed apartment in Rathmines that he freely admitted had been bought for him by his parents. After Luke got his MA in art history, he was lured back to the family business with the ego-boosting job title of brand director and an appropriately generous pay cheque. While this news pleased Finbarr, he soon grew tired of friends rolling their eyes or giving knowing looks, as if it was inevitable that he was dating someone with money. While he was happy to admit that it was indeed a part of the attraction, he failed to see how that was a bad thing. He noticed that none of these friends observing him from the moral high ground were going out with some hot homeless guy, but he would never say such a thing out loud. He just laughed off his reputation as a kept man, never attempting to defend himself. He could have pointed out that he hadn't given up his job; in fact he was working harder than ever because he occasionally did freelance jobs for Luke. But what was the point?

Getting married had never been part of the plan. One Sunday evening they had decided to walk out to the Poolbeg Lighthouse. They were about halfway along the South Wall, heads down against the wind blasting in from Dublin Bay, and Finbarr was silently cursing his boyfriend and his big 'let's go for a walk' idea. He could tell that Luke was saying something but it was hard to hear him with the wind rattling through the hood of his waterproof jacket. Finally, Luke tugged at his sleeve and brought the walk to a halt. His face peered in at Finbarr. 'Well?' His voice was raised against the storm and the surf.

'Well what?' Finbarr sounded mildly irritated. This walk was going to take long enough without stopping for no good reason.

'Were you not listening to me?'

'Not really. The wind. This hood. What is it?'

Luke shook his head and smiled. He spoke slowly and clearly.

'I am asking you, Finbarr Coulter, if you would like to marry me?'

A gasp of surprise and then a wave of certainty that Finbarr had never thought he'd feel. There was not a hint of doubt in his mind as he looked at the man opposite, with the long unkempt hair dancing about his face, and the dark eyes that had only ever showed him kindness and love.

'Yes.' Yes, he did want to spend the rest of his life with this man.

Luke's eyes welled up and they kissed each other as the wind and spray pummelled them from either side.

Now here they were, ten months later in matching suits, greeting guests as they arrived at the garden centre. It probably wouldn't have been Finbarr's first choice as a venue, but Luke was a devoted Tolkien geek and fell in love with Shane's new café. The tables were all named after various locations in the books. Finbarr had drawn the line at the suggestion of fancy dress. 'I want to be able to look at these wedding photographs in years to come and not be embarrassed.'

The invitations had been printed on mock parchment, with a pen and ink drawing of Luke and Finbarr above some elvish script that declared them 'The Lords of the Rings'. Connor had howled with laughter when he had opened the envelope. He wasn't going to let Finbarr forget this in a hurry. That boy must really love Luke to send this out to all their friends and family. Connor had happily accepted the invitation. It was a good excuse to head back to Mullinmore and see his family again, though he did wonder how the town was going to react to an actual gay wedding. The invitation was a plus one, but Connor thought it best he go alone. He was still technically single (he felt a semi-regular Grindr hook-up didn't qualify as a relationship) so to bring Tim or a friend would just have confused his parents. Besides, he was flying using Tim's air miles so asking for two seats might have been pushing his luck.

It was Ellen who suggested that he ask Linda: 'Even if she doesn't want to come, she'll appreciate being asked.' Connor had sent her an email assuming that she would decline but in fact the response was an enthusiastic yes. It seemed that Linda had finally begun to turn her life around. She had discovered that one of the taxis in town was wheelchair-friendly and the mere thought of not having to rely on her parents had spurred her on to go out. She had been to see Ellen and Shane in the bungalow and went to the Historical Society once a month. Her life was hardly a social whirl but even those few outings gave her things to talk about with her mother. The atmosphere in the house had shifted, lightened.

At the beginning of August, about five weeks before the wedding, Connor was enjoying his first beer on his balcony. He still lived in Nyack but now rented a small one-bedroomed apartment in a new development. He missed the grand old house, but this was in a better part of town, had both heating and air conditioning and, on nights like this one, a better view of the Palisades stretching away towards the city. His phone rang. It was Finbarr. He immediately assumed it was going to be something to do with the wedding. As he answered he was trying to think of reasonable excuses for refusing to make a speech or even raise a toast.

'Uncle Connor?'

'Hi, Finbarr. How's it going?'

'Good. Luke has agreed that we can wear shoes, so that's something.'

Connor chuckled. 'Is he calling you his 'precious' in the vows?'

'Shut up! The invitation was as bad as it's going to get. He's really normal, I swear. You're going to like him.'

'Of course I will.' It was sweet. Connor could tell that his nephew was completely besotted by this Luke. 'So, what can I do for you?'

There was a worrying silence.

'Mmmm. Something's happened and I just wanted to let you know. Give you a heads-up, I suppose.'

'Right.' Connor wondered what on earth this piece of news could be.

'It's Daddy. He asked if he can come to the wedding.'

'Really?'

'I know. I know. I told him about it, and he asked if I wanted him to be there and I couldn't really say no, could I?'

Connor thought that was precisely what he should have said, but instead replied, 'Of course. I understand. How does your mother feel about it?'

'She's OK. She understands.'

Connor wondered if she really did.

In fact, when Finbarr had broken the news to Ellen, she had only asked one question. 'Is he bringing anyone?'

Her son had looked surprised, as if the thought of his father having a new partner had never crossed his mind.

'No. No, I don't think so.'

Ellen had nodded, hoping that she looked unconcerned. Inwardly she was relieved. At least it meant Martin wasn't going to upstage Finbarr and Luke with the revelation of some shiny new life he had acquired in Britain. She watched her son scrolling through emails at her kitchen table. Should she tell him everything she knew about Martin's life? No. What was the point? If his father ever decided to be open or honest then it was his decision. Ellen was not going to be the messenger who was shot. She had had enough of being painted as the baddie in dramas that had nothing to do with her. She had already had this conversation with Shane, and he agreed.

Shane's face had been a perfect mixture of fear and confusion, quickly followed by relief, when he had come home four years earlier to find Ellen sitting with a handsome man, sharing a bottle of red wine. His girlfriend's eyes had glittered with a hint of mania when she saw him and announced, 'This is Gilles. He's an old friend of Martin's.'

Earlier that afternoon, when Ellen had invited Gilles in from the doorstep, the truth had emerged fairly quickly. Her visitor had asked all the right questions, clearly not wanting to cause too much upset — 'Are you still married?' 'Where does Martin live now?' — and Ellen had done her own detective work: 'Were you friends in Dublin?' 'Was it the Hilton you stayed at?'

Martin and Gilles had met on a website. Gilles had not known he was married. He had known he was a doctor and he remembered he had spoken about his practice in Mullinmore. The Frenchman worked for a finance company in Paris and had made frequent business trips to Dublin. Soon, seeing Martin became a regular part of those visits. Gilles blushed and looked away into the corner of the room as he spoke. His accent was charming, giving his story an air of romance it really didn't deserve. In an effort to use the English pronunciation, when he said Martin's name the 'i' became an elongated 'e'. Ellen thought it made the controlling prick she had been married to sound feminine and exotic. She found herself feeling sorry for the man in her front room. A fool who had allowed himself to develop feelings for Martin Coulter, in the belief that he was capable of returning them.

'I thought that Martin was my boyfriend. We talked of a life together. I was moving to Dublin to be with him.'

Ellen just listened, trying not to let her face betray any shock or surprise. Perhaps she didn't feel either of those things. Maybe this was the story she had been waiting to hear all along. She sat very still as if any sudden movement might spook this timid creature that had unexpectedly found itself in her house. Ellen needn't have worried. Having begun to share his story, Gilles felt compelled to continue.

Martin had suddenly been very keen for their new life to begin. He had called Gilles and told him that he had moved to Dublin and that he was waiting for him. The Frenchman shook his head and laughed softly at his own foolishness.

'I ran. I came back to Dublin as fast as possible, but Martin was already gone. I called, sent emails, but nothing. I found the number for his clinic here, I think. I left messages. My heart, it was broken. You understand how stupid I felt?'

'Oh yes,' Ellen confirmed with feeling. She understood only too well.

'I went home. I tried to forget. I even changed jobs so I would have no trips to Dublin. Finally, I met someone else. We are still together. We are happy.'

Ellen smiled. 'Good. That's good.'

His story seemed at an end, but Ellen still didn't know why he was sitting in her front room.

Gilles exhaled and gave an exaggerated shrug, like someone doing an impersonation of a French person. 'So now, these years later, I'm back in Dublin on business and I'm thinking about Martin. I thought finally he might be able to see me, to explain what happened, so I hired a car and . . . ' He indicated Ellen. She was what he had discovered.

Glancing at her watch, she asked, 'Would you like a glass of wine?'

Gilles' face suggested he thought that was an excellent suggestion.

'Red OK?'

'Yes please. It's very kind of you.'

When she returned from the kitchen, she was holding two very full glasses. She had deliberately chosen the new ones with the different-coloured stems. Was it wrong that she wanted her ex-husband's ex-boyfriend to notice, to admire them?

'It's not French. South African, I think,' she apologised.

'*Santé!*'

'Yes. And to you,' Ellen said uncertainly.

Once she was settled back in her chair, she felt she should try and fill in some of the blanks for this man.

'All I know is that Martin is in Southampton, in England, working. We're divorced, finally. I can't really tell you anything more.'

'Did he talk about me? How much did you

know about this side of his life?'

A sip of wine. 'Nothing. He never spoke of anyone else. I didn't even know he was in Dublin. I know that makes me seem very stupid, but . . . ' How could she explain it? 'But I just wasn't curious. Our marriage, it wasn't what you might imagine. Now . . . ' She thought about her life with Shane. 'Now, I understand how unhappy I was but at the time I didn't, not really.'

Gilles nodded as if he understood. Ellen wondered if he did.

'I hope you don't mind me saying this, but I think you were very lucky,' she said.

A raised eyebrow. 'Sorry?'

'A lucky escape. You had a lucky escape.'

Gilles laughed. 'Yes. Yes, now I think this too.'

There was a click at the door and then in walked a startled Shane.

If someone had asked Ellen years before how she would feel if she discovered she was married to a gay man, she would have said that she'd feel humiliated and betrayed. Oddly, when it finally happened, what she felt was vindicated. She wanted to tell everyone the truth about Martin, so that they might understand the oddness of her marriage and how its failure had nothing to do with her. It was Shane who had talked her out of any mass announcements. He had no desire for Martin and Ellen's old life to take centre stage again. 'What's the point, love?' he had asked her. 'We're happy, aren't we? So, just leave it.' She knew that he was right, and she stayed silent.

Afterwards she thought of Connor. If Martin

had known about him, had her brother known about Martin? Had they ever? No. Surely not. She wondered if she should ask Connor, but without airing her suspicions, not even to Shane, she had decided not to. Just to ask the question would be forcing her brother to lie and then she would never know the answer, not really, and that would be worse, wouldn't it? She had heard enough, learned all she wanted to about the marriage she had survived. She had Shane, and finally there was a second chance for her with a man who actually cared about her and their happiness.

Now, here she stood, clutching Shane's arm. Everyone was gathered in their wedding finery, making a fuss of the happy couple, but some eyes kept darting to the door. Was that him? Would he have changed very much? When he did finally appear, it was behind a group of people so that there was no grand reveal, just a man looking older than his years, stepping away from some other bodies. His hair had thinned considerably, really it was more like the suggestion of hair, and the skin of his face had begun to sag. Connor found himself staring for a moment, shocked to see how the years had turned Martin into a faded version of his father. Even his dark suit looked old-fashioned and ill-fitting. It was Aisling who had rushed up to him with a squeal of 'Daddy!' Ellen caught Connor's eye and they smirked at one another.

Connor wondered what she thought of her daughter. Her hair was so blond and heavy with extensions that it looked like a wig. The dress she had chosen was a pretty shade of cornflower blue, but the shoulder straps were biting into the extra flesh she had gained following the end of her engagement. She had discovered that Philip, the ex-rugby player, didn't fully understand the concept of monogamy. In fact, it seemed he hadn't understood it with every woman under forty who worked for the firm. Aisling had comforted herself by keeping the ring and treating herself to desserts. It had also helped that his parents, out of embarrassment she assumed, had given her a bright red Mini Cooper. It was astonishing how a new car could help you move on.

Ellen felt guilty for preferring this version of her daughter; or maybe it was that after Aisling's humiliation, she felt more connected to her mother. Whatever the reason, the two women found they were closer than they had been since she was a little girl. Aisling had even, voluntarily, spent a few weekends in Mullinmore, staying in the bungalow with her mother and Shane. Ellen felt there might be hope for her daughter now that she seemed to understand that there was more to life than collecting shiny things and party invitations. When she heard Aisling enthusing about her new car, however, she did think that her daughter might still have some room for improvement.

At the door, a taxi driver was delivering Linda in her chair. Connor hurried over.

'You look stunning!' And she did. with her face made up and her hair swept into a roll held by a diamante-covered clasp.

Linda laughed. 'Thanks.' She looked around the room. 'Jesus, we all look like our parents!'

'Speak for yourself!'

'You most of all, Dan Hayes junior! Now steer me to the bar.'

'There's just prosecco for now. That OK?'

Linda was about to answer when her expression changed abruptly.

'Fuck.'

'What is it?' Connor asked, concerned.

'He's here.'

Connor followed Linda's gaze to where Martin was standing with Aisling.

When Connor had emailed to warn her that the father of the groom would be in attendance, she had immediately replied, 'Like I give a shit,' but now that she was in the same room as him, she really wasn't sure how he made her feel. Connor was just pushing the chair away from the door when Martin saw them, seemed to freeze for a fraction of a second and then looked back at Aisling, a half-smile toying with his lips.

'He saw us,' she hissed.

'Prosecco, here we come,' Connor replied.

'He looked embarrassed. He was blushing.'

Connor wasn't sure. Had he reddened slightly or was that just Linda's imagination? Was she trying to project normal human responses onto a man who didn't seem to have any? He was reminded of pet owners describing the complex emotions their dogs were feeling when in fact they were just staring blankly waiting for another treat.

Long shadows stretched through the room as

the sun left the sky and strings of fairy lights on the polished branches of the twisted pillars came to life. The waiters wove through the tables lighting the thick white candles in the glass hurricane lanterns. The place took on an air of magic. It was nearly time.

The crowd gathered in the area that would be the dance floor later on and Finbarr and Luke stood in front of a low table. The woman conducting the service had been a babysitter for Luke when he was a boy. Ellen gripped Shane's rough paw and braced herself for some hippie nonsense, but in fact, apart from some extended metaphors concerning a happy marriage and the fellowship struggling against the threat of Sauron, the ceremony was straightforward and ultimately moving. Ellen had never imagined this sort of easy domesticity for her son, and that was even before she knew he was gay. He had always struck her as too brittle and self-involved to be capable of sharing his life, and yet here he was weeping openly as he stumbled through his vows. Ellen wept too and Shane squeezed her hand a little tighter.

After the happy couple had kissed, the crowd had cheered and rushed to the bar. Connor overheard an older lady with tightly permed hair say to her friend, 'It was just like a normal wedding.' She sounded disappointed. He and Linda were already sitting at their table, 'Rivendell'.

'Is that good?' Connor had asked.

'Well it's better than Mordor,' Linda replied, 'or Mount Doom.'

Connor laughed. 'Oh, please tell me some people are sitting on Mount Doom.'

He reached for one of the bottles of red wine on the table and looked enquiringly at Linda.

'Please.'

Patricia, a friend of Finbarr and Luke, was acting as the master of ceremonies. She seemed at home with the microphone, loud and clear, unburdened by nerves, but her loose hair and wide red-lipped smile took the edge off any officiousness.

'Please find your tables. Quick as you like, ladies and gentlemen. Grab a drink and take a seat please. We have a very few speeches. I'm told that they're super short.'

'We lied!' Luke heckled his friend.

'Well, long or short, you're getting them and then you'll get fed.'

People shuffled around the tables till most were seated. Linda looked at Connor.

'Speeches first? Jesus, it has been years since I've been at a wedding.'

A flash of memory passed between them. The wedding that never was from all those years before. Ignoring it, Connor said, 'I think they were scared people would get too drunk.'

Luke's mother spoke first. She was so nervous that all Connor could focus on was the shaking of the long green feather protruding from her hat. She spoke briefly but sincerely, and her speech ended in tears. Luke stood to comfort her, and she sat down to sympathetic applause.

'Sweet,' was Linda's review.

Patricia was on her feet again.

‘Now it’s time to hear from the grandfather of the groom: please welcome Dan Hayes!’

A clatter of applause and whoops, and Dan, with a little stiffness, got to his feet. He pulled his glasses from his inside jacket pocket. Connor wondered when his eyes had got bad enough for glasses. He looked over at Ellen on the top table; she was gazing up at her daddy, willing him to be good. Finbarr had originally asked her to speak but, worried about any excuse for awkwardness with Martin, this had been the compromise she had come up with. She could tell that her father had been thrilled and touched to be asked.

Dan cleared his throat, and putting his hand on Chrissie’s shoulder, made it clear that he was speaking for both of them. He began with thanks. The venue, people for coming, the flowers, the food, each got a polite smattering of applause. Then Dan looked down and smoothed out the paper on the table before him. Raising his head, he looked at the happy couple.

‘There was a time,’ he began brightly, ‘when we might have said our grandson Finbarr was not the marrying kind.’ A little ripple of uncertain laughter went around the room. Connor felt tears filling his eyes as his father found his face across the crowd. Dan continued.

‘And that was wrong.’ He stretched his lips tight and looked to the ceiling, trying to avoid tears. Chrissie raised a hand and stroked the sleeve of his jacket. Finbarr turned to see where his grandfather had been looking and saw his uncle Connor with a napkin covering his face as his shoulders shook. Dan tried to speak again. 'That was wrong. We lost a son . . . ' His head dropped and he put both his hands on the table to steady himself. Chrissie half stood to put an arm on his back.

'Go on, Dan!' an old man's voice called from the crowd, breaking the tension. Dan raised his head and laughed, letting the tears drop from his eyes. 'We lost a son because of that old-fashioned way of thinking.'

Chrissie was dabbing at her eyes with her napkin. 'So, on behalf of the Hayes family I want to say how delighted we are that we have now found a new grandson. Luke, we are very happy to welcome you to this family.' The whole crowd roared its approval, and also its relief that the moment when emotion had threatened to overwhelm proceedings seemed to have passed. Only Connor continued to weep.

The meal was served. Drinks were dispatched. People passing by Rivendell would squeeze Connor's shoulder or crouch to say how lovely his father's speech had been. He smiled in agreement. Linda, after a few more glasses of wine, asked him how he felt seeing all this liberal acceptance. 'If I was you, I think I'd be so angry.'

Connor thought about it. 'No. No, I'm not angry. I'm glad. I have to be. Isn't it great how far these people have come? That was my father saying those words out loud in public and . . . ' His face crumpled once more with emotion.

Linda comforted him with a 'Shush. I didn't mean to upset you.'

He grinned at her, his eyes glittering with

tears. 'I can't be sorry. We're here now and that's all that matters.'

'I wonder how he feels.' Linda nodded her head in the direction of Martin.

'Fuck knows. Who cares?' But despite his words Connor found himself stealing glances at Martin's table. Aisling hadn't left his side all night. Was that why he had made no attempt to come over, or did he intend to ignore Connor and Linda? He knew they were going to be at the wedding so why come if he wasn't willing to acknowledge their existence?

A little after eleven, the meal was finished and the younger guests, mostly friends down from Dublin, filled the dance floor. Linda checked her phone.

'That's the taxi. Can you give me a hand out to the car?'

'Of course,' Connor said, putting his glass down as he stood.

He navigated his friend to the door and then down the narrow gravel slope to the car park. The driver met them and together Connor and the driver got Linda up the short ramp into the back of the taxi.

'Goodnight. Thanks for asking me, I enjoyed it. No, really, I didn't expect to, but I did.'

'That's good. Safe home.' They shared a smile.

'Don't dance with the prick!' Linda called as the door was closed.

'I won't,' he mouthed through the window as he waved.

He stood and watched the car pull away and then for a moment breathed in the cool stillness of the evening. He looked up. Stars. Dozens of them. Such an abundance of beauty, it seemed too much; more than any of them deserved. He rocked back on his heels, drunker than he'd thought he was.

He crunched slowly across the gravel, his hands in his pockets. On the gentle slope up to the door there was a figure silhouetted against the flashing lights of the interior. It was only when Connor was mere inches away that he realised who it was.

'Connor.'

'Hello, Martin.' He went to walk past but an arm stopped him.

'I was hoping to speak to you.'

'Really.' He had no intention of helping Martin with this, whatever this was.

'I feel I owe you an apology.'

'An apology?' Something that began as rage had ended in laughter. Connor let out a honk. An apology. It seemed like such a ludicrous thing for someone to offer in exchange for altering someone else's whole lifetime.

In the glow from the shifting lights of the disco inside, Martin looked taken aback, offended even.

'What's funny?'

Connor stepped back and ran his hand through his hair.

'Funny? All of it, Martin. All of it.'

'I really am sorry.'

'I'm sure you are.' Connor felt sober. 'It's just this is weird. You know, after everything, after Ellen.'

Martin looked at his feet and scuffed the gravel with his shoe.

'Such a fucking mess,' he said, perhaps more to himself than to Connor.

'Martin, why are you here? Why come to this wedding?'

He looked puzzled, as if the idea of not attending had never crossed his mind.

'Finbarr is my son. He wanted me to be here,' he said stiffly.

Connor looked away, not wanting his face to betray Finbarr's lie or Martin's delusion.

Even in this light, Martin looked old. So far from the tall, broad-shouldered youth that Connor had admired from afar. He had imagined this meeting so many times. All the things he would say, the violent damage he would do to his nemesis. But now here they were, face to face on a mild September night almost exactly thirty-two years after the day that had changed their lives entirely, and what did he want to say? He didn't know. Connor had lived his life believing that Martin had won and he had lost. It had always seemed that simple, but not tonight. This man did not seem like a winner. From where Connor stood, it looked as if the life that Martin had ruined was his own. This man, with shoulders stooped, a pariah at his own son's wedding, seemed more of an object of pity than someone to be envied or admired.

Martin raised his eyes for a moment, and they looked at each other.

'Goodnight, Martin.' Connor walked back to

the party. He wondered if he would be followed, but no. Footsteps on gravel receded into the distance. Martin must have decided to leave. At the door he bumped into Ellen, her face flushed and glistening from the dance floor.

'Was that Martin you were talking to?'

'It was.'

'I wanted a word with him. Is he gone, do you think?'

'He is.'

'Right.' Ellen half turned to go back inside but then thought better of it. She steadied herself on her brother's arm.

'Did you know about Martin?'

Connor didn't want to assume he knew what his sister was talking about.

'Know what?'

'About . . . ' She threw her head back. 'About the men. Gilles, and I'm sure there were more.'

He wondered how much to say.

'I didn't know any of them. I didn't really know anything for sure, but I guessed.'

'I met Gilles.' She swayed slightly from the wine. 'A nice fella. Too nice for him anyway.' She prodded a finger into the darkness.

'I wasn't sure you knew. That's why I didn't say anything.'

Ellen nodded deeply to indicate she understood.

'And tell me this, and sorry to be asking you this, but — and it's the last thing I'll ask you — did you and Martin ever . . . ?' She braced her other arm against the door frame. Connor peered into her face. What could he tell her?

What should he say?

'No. No, we were never lovers.' And that was the truth.

Ellen considered his answer and then shrugged the moment off.

'Right.'

'Come back in; you'll be frozen and Shane will be looking for you.'

His sister let her head fall back against his chest.

'Isn't he lovely?'

'He is. He is.' Connor assured her as he steered her through the door.

Making his way to the bar, he bumped into his parents. Chrissie was wearing her coat.

'You're off?'

'We are,' his father replied and then whispered in his ear, 'Your mother has had a bit too much.'

Connor bent to kiss his mother's cheek.

'Goodnight, Mammy.'

'Your father is drunk,' she confided as quietly as she could.

'Right.' Smiling, he watched them go, their arms around each other, unclear who was being supported.

At the bar, he found a dry patch of countertop and leaned against it. The party was in full swing. Ellen had re-joined Shane and the young people on the dance floor. It was lovely to see his sister so happy, being twirled around the floor, holding her high heels in one hand. Luke and Finbarr, jackets and ties long gone, were dancing with their friends. It was just another scene from a happy family wedding, but it was his family. He should go. A walk back to Ellen's would do him good. There was no reason to have a hangover the next day.

'Another?'

It was a young barman, smiling at him.

'No thanks. I'm grand.'

'Are you sure now? The night is still young.'

'The problem is that I'm not.'

The barman raised his eyebrows. 'Oh, I'd say you're still young enough.' He gave Connor a wink. Flattered, he smiled, but declined. 'No. That's me done. Goodnight.' He buttoned his suit jacket and walked away back towards the door. He was about halfway across the room when he stopped and turned. The barman had his back to him, tall, with the tanned skin of his neck leading up to cropped blond hair.

'Excuse me!' Connor was back at the bar.

'You changed your mind.'

'I did. A vodka and soda please.'

The barman grinned. 'Why not?'

Why not indeed, thought Connor. The party was far from over.

Acknowledgements

It may take a village to raise a child, but it required something approaching an urban sprawl to bring this book into being. So many people have had a hand in the story, writing, production and sales of my novel, that it would be impossible to thank them all individually, but I am nonetheless eternally grateful to every single one of them.

This is my third novel and I'm thrilled to still be in the capable, steady hands of my editor Hannah Black. Working with her makes the writing process challenging and inspiring but never daunting. My thanks also to Erika Koljonen for all her assistance in getting the book across the finish line. No one would have heard of this book, and certainly wouldn't have purchased a copy without the supreme efforts of Catherine Worsley and Richard Peters. Stepping into the world with a new novel can be a tad panic-inducing so I'm indebted to my cheerleaders Emma Knight and Alice Morley for holding my hand while pushing me firmly forward. Alasdair Oliver and Kate Brunt are responsible for how beautiful this book looks and without Claudette Morris it wouldn't exist as a physical object. Thank you. Producing an audio book during a pandemic had a few extra challenges so hats off to Dominic Gribben, along with David Roper at Heavy Entertainment in London and

Conor Barron at Half-Light Studios in Cork. If you are reading this book anywhere apart from the UK or Ireland, then please join me in thanking Grace McCrum and Melis Dagoglu.

Huge thanks are also owed to the Hachette Australian and New Zealand teams and everyone at Hachette Books Ireland.

My good friend Elaine O'Driscoll helped with some questions I had about the law in Ireland in the late eighties, while John Martin, volunteer archivist for YHA (England and Wales) provided details for Connor's arrival in London. Thank you both.

I am also very grateful as always to Melanie, Dylan, Rebecca and Jono.

Finally, I would like to thank all the people who stayed in Ireland to fight for the modern, tolerant country it has become. I took the easy way out and left to find places where I could be myself. The dedicated, passionate, tireless campaigners who remained, mean that I am proud and privileged to return. Your extraordinary achievements make writing a novel seem like a very small task indeed.